The Lost Tale of Socratis

Ethan Clerck

Grosvenor House
Publishing Limited

This book is published by
Grosvenor House Publishing Ltd
Link House
140 The Broadway, Tolworth, Surrey, KT6 7HT.
www.grosvenorhousepublishing.co.uk

This book is a work of fiction and, except in the case
of historical fact, any resemblance to actual persons,
living or dead, is purely coincidental.

A CIP record for this book
is available from the British Library

ISBN 978-1-83615-128-9

For my Mum who, through everything, has inspired me to be better but most importantly, encouraged me to be myself no matter what.

And for my Grandad, whose help was very much needed in making this dream of mine, a reality.
Thank you.

Contents

PROLOGUE

There was complete and total silence. No sound plagued the air until the deafening creaking of the huge metal gates. The gates swung open, creating an opening for the esteemed carriage. Accompanied by numerous guards in crimson armour, the carriage rolled forward into the quiet town of Socratis, with a deep, black, blanket of stars covering their entrance.

The guards moved alongside the carriage, before turning and lining up against the looming, stone brick walls that surrounded the town. Before long, the rusted gates closed once again to stop any intruders, though it was unlikely that anyone else would arrive that late at night.

Up in the closest of the four towers, placed at the corners of the town, was a man and two children. The man was broad and tall, and he had a thick brown beard and beady eyes. His hair was straight and slick, and the same colour as his beard. He wore a red tunic lined with small gold dots indented every few inches along the sleeves. He also sported a black belt that wrapped itself around his waist until reaching the metal buckle at the front.

The older of the two children was equally tall although he was skinny and pale. His face was gaunt and he looked as if he would faint at any second. His eyes were drooped and distant as if he were staring into another universe. He wore a similar tunic to the first man, except it wasn't as polished or pampered as the other. This child sat in an olive-green armchair, with his hand scratching his clean-shaven chin.

The younger child, on the other hand, was small and scrawny. His hair was a mess and his face dirty and unclean. This child oughtn't have been more than seven if you saw him, but Atti acted like a three-year-old. He was in a tight brown tunic and on his feet were argent silver boots that he had got as a present on his last birthday. However, at this moment he felt frightened and scared about what was to come, the time for playfulness was over.

The shutters were open, and a cool draught of air sifted into the conical room. Atti shivered and looked back and forth between his father and the trapdoor they had entered from. Numitor gave a stern look to his youngest son and then looked away swiftly. Atti moved to an open chair and sat down carefully.

"Up!"

His father's word was sharp and strong like a stab wound. A bolt of lightning struck the side of the tower, momentarily illuminating the night sky. Atti leapt out of the chair instantly, nearly falling over in surprise.

"That chair is for our *guests*," Numitor scowled.

"Sorry, father," Atti said guiltily.

"Humph!"

Suddenly, there was a thud on the trapdoor, followed by two more in quick succession.

"Enter!" Numitor's voice boomed, echoing throughout the tower.

Then, Adrian, the eldest son of the quaestor to the governor, whispered, "Are they here?"

Numitor turned to his youngest child, nodding ever so gently.

"Atticus, you have to leave now."

Disappointment gripped his insides, but reluctantly Atti opened the trapdoor and let the people in, before climbing down himself. As he was going down, he took a glance at the men who had entered and then at his brother who had a look of horror written across his face.

"See you later," Atti whispered, before shutting the trapdoor above him. He climbed down onto the next floor and sat on a wooden bench. Two minutes passed, then three, then four. Thunder boomed in the far distance, frightening Atti even more. In the fifth minute, a terrifying scream rang out through the tower, followed by another, and another.

All the while Atti was cringing in pain, not daring to even think about what was going on up there. He just hoped that his brother would be okay.

After what seemed like an excruciating amount of screaming, the noises soon stopped, and the trapdoor opened above him. The two men who had entered the room before were now climbing down, and Atti seized his chance to ask, "Is he alright?"

The older of the two men turned towards him. Atti silently gasped. The man's face was charred and blackened, his broken mouth growling with intensity. Atti recoiled, shrinking back inside himself.

After the unusual pair were gone, he got up from the bench and called up to his father, but received no reply. Worried, he started climbing up the ladder as his sense of dread ascended alongside him. When he reached the trapdoor, he opened it slightly and peered into the room. His brother was in his chair but obscured from view. His father's golden boots were standing where Numitor would be, and it seemed as if he was looking at something on the wall in front of him.

Atti opened the trapdoor ever so slightly, but a haunting creak rang in the silence. With inhuman speed, Numitor closed the trapdoor with his boot, almost trapping Atti's fingers, quickly pulling them out of the way.

"Do not come in here!" his father shouted, his voice echoing throughout the tower.

"Why?" Atti whimpered, "I want to see my brother."

There was silence for a while, and then the lock on the trapdoor clicked and it opened slowly. Atti stared into his father's face, and he saw the look of sadness and anger written upon it.

Numitor didn't move, he just stayed kneeling by the open trapdoor. Atti climbed into the room and scanned it for his brother. And sure enough, there Adrian was, paler than before, his eyes open but unmoving, his whole body, lifeless.

"What happened to him?" Atti whispered, before repeating it loudly in anger.

"It was a last resort," Numitor said, "He was going to go, either way, the procedure was an attempt to prevent his... passing."

"You didn't tell me! Don't you think it would have been right to tell me that my brother was *dying*!"

Numitor looked at his son through blurred, teary eyes, "I didn't want to worry you, and I'm truly sorry son."

Atti felt an immense rise in his rage, and he flung himself at his father, his hands balled into threatening fists. He pummelled Numitor, making sure he landed every single blow. Several seconds later, Atti stopped and sat on the hard wooden floor, accepting his loss.

"Why?" he cried out, and this time it was his voice that filled the eerie silence of the town.

CHAPTER 1 – The Red Azalea

8 YEARS LATER ...

It was a bright morning, and the yellow sun shone through the various plants and flowers decorated in the town square. It was early; hence the square was empty of civilians, and the birds' calls were the only sound in the peaceful environment. Leaves flew in the air, spinning and floating in strange ways, and in the centre of the square was a quartered fountain, topped with a smooth stone statue of Governor Cicero. Cicero was the appointed governor of Socratis and its province which spanned hundreds of square miles. Surrounding the centrepiece were stone benches, parallel to the edges of the fountain. Each of the benches had large amounts of ivy curling around the legs, poking its way out of the top.

On one of these benches sat a young man with dark brown hair and a thin face. He had bright blue eyes and light freckles upon his nose. He looked up towards the tall towers in the corners of the small town. They were made of grey stone bricks with red tiles forming a cone on top, and each one sported a SPQR flag, with the gold leaves creating a ring around the letters. He soon became lost inside his mind with confusing thoughts. Unaware of his surroundings, he jumped at a voice speaking behind him.

"Atticus Caeso! You're up early! What are you doing out here?"

1

Atti shook his head and looked at who was speaking. It was an old woman with long, grey hair braided into a ponytail. She had a kind and caring smile, and an energy that seemed positive and inviting. She wore a white toga and a green robe which she had supposedly knitted herself. She also carried a small purple bag printed with an image of a grapevine.

"Domina Delphi, what a surprise! I guess I'm out here because I like the environment and nature. In my eyes, it's beautiful, sacred, something that shouldn't be disturbed."

Delphi's smile widened a little, "I think I agree with you Atticus, you are definitely more intelligent than I was at your age," she laughed.

Atti chuckled as well, and a small smile came to his lips, a rare sight in his life. He stood up and bowed shortly before hugging the woman and bidding her farewell. Sitting back down on the bench, Atti looked across at a building, a very old building, in fact, the oldest in the town. Nowadays it was off-limits but a couple of hundred years ago it was a bustling inn, known as The Red Azalea, full of fun and laughter. A luxury for Atti and for Romans in their time.

The antique inn was branded with a faded reddish-pink flower that was usually found populating the mountains in the north. Most of the red paint had been scratched off, and if it wasn't for the sunlight, Atti doubted that he would even recognise the flower. It sprouted outwards like a cabbage, and the middle stem had been integrated into the framework of the building. It was beautiful, in an old-fashioned sort of way.

The inn, as far as Atti could remember, hadn't ever opened in his lifetime, nor his father's. And yet, it still stood there in the early sunlight, a relic of a past age. There was something mystical about the building, and it intoxicated Atti and dragged him in while overly piquing his curiosity.

Minutes went by, and then by the ninth hour the town square was busy and crowded, all the residents setting up shop or browsing the newest wares, and suddenly the quietness of the morning was lost. As Atti sat there, lingering in the middle of the controlled chaos, he noticed that not one person had stopped and looked or even glanced at the small, faded building in front of him. It was slightly strange, but then again the citizens seemed busy and they didn't seem to recognize any part of the world around them.

After some time, something remarkable happened. There was a white flash in minuscule time and the world was not changed in the process. The townsfolk were dazed slightly but after a moment everything went back to the way it was. Except, Atti suddenly felt a strange impulse to look back at the ruined building in front of him, and he noticed something odd about the old inn. He didn't know what just yet, but it was unusual enough to intrigue Atti even more. With a strange feeling in his chest, he slowly walked towards the building, entranced in its spell, as the rest of the world disappeared into darkness.

And then he was at the foot of the mysterious place, and all Atti could hear was the thumping of his heart.

He extended his arm outwards towards the door, and then stopped abruptly, as he heard a familiar voice call out his name.

He was back in reality now and his father stood behind him, looking down upon him with a scowl.

"What do you think you're doing?" Atti stuttered in response, eventually managing a skewered, "Nothing."

Numitor's gaze tightened even more than before. Then, after a moment his expression softened ever so slightly as he visibly relaxed his gargantuan muscles.

"Come boy, we must not be late for the event. As you know I have an important role within the spectacle and you are supposed to be up there with me."

Jokingly nodding, Atti followed his father through the busy crowd who parted to let the quaestor through before entering a house down the side of a murky alleyway. The building was empty except for a table with refreshments, an armchair in the corner, and the grand staircase on the opposite wall which seemed heavily out of place compared to the rest of the murky house. Slowly, the pair ascended the stairs like gladiators before a fight in the great amphitheatre. Then through blinding light, Atti heard immense cheering from the many citizens in the stands.

Looking to his right Atti saw the cause of all the ruckus. The grand governor himself, Cicero, was standing proudly on the centre stage with his arms raised in a winged shape, addressing the crowd of the amphitheatre. The crowd was delivering a raucous applause. The governor stood tall in his long, deep purple robe with gold lining and was flanked by four servants each wearing a green tunic with purple accents making them look like jesters. Cicero had long sleeves down to his hands and a grey tunic underneath his garments. On his feet were beige sandals with rounded fronts and gold straps. Even if he had not been standing there you could tell he was a man of significance.

A few steps in front of them was an unusual man with foreign clothes.

I wonder who that is? Atti thought, as the governor's voice boomed and called to the excitable crowd, "Good morning Socratis!"

The raucousness increased and many Romans clapped. Atti scanned the endless faces in the amphitheatre for some time and realised that they were all in obtuse bliss and none in despair.

Doesn't anyone find this boring? It's like they're hypnotised.

"Stand up straight Atticus," Numitor remarked with a slight tone and sneer, "you would do well to respect our governor. After all it was him that granted me this position. I expect you to be more presentable when we meet the New Guard who have come from overseas. We *don't* want to give the wrong impression."

Atti frowned at his father and reluctantly obliged. Cicero continued his grand speech and to his delight, cheers and shouts came in his direction. The boastful governor then sat down and beckoned the man on his left over to him.

The soldier was tall and thin with slightly darker skin, and he had deep blue eyes under his black hair. He wore a predominantly blue set of armour and held a shield with a strange pattern on the front of it. On his feet were heavy black boots with blue buckles and he wore a brown belt which wrapped around his waist.

Discreetly, the governor whispered something to the sergeant who then stepped back and turned towards the crowd. First, he waved and when he opened his mouth, he spoke with authority.

"Greetings. I am Sergeant Decimus Titus of the New Guard. I have come from overseas with my army to the town of Socratis to help you and aid you in battle!"

If Titus expected an uproar, he would have been mistaken for most of the crowd were confused and shaking their heads in dismay. Then a few shouts could be heard and shortly there was indeed an uproar, but it wasn't the good kind. Many shouts included:

"Go back to your country!"

"We don't need your help!"

Others were less mild.

Worried for the first time in a while, Cicero stood up and addressed the angry and uncontrollable crowd. He waved his hands frantically but to no avail. While this was going on, Atti looked to his father who had a determined expression sprawled upon his face. He took a few steps forward and walked past the sergeant, standing next to the governor. Taking a deep breath, he boomed:

"SILENCE!"

Immediately a few Romans sat down feeling ashamed. After two or three seconds everyone was calm and seated.

Flustered, Governor Cicero mumbled to him, "My gratitude, Numitor."

Numitor stood up proudly and stepped back to where he stood before. He took a deep breath and smiled. Looking down he went to speak to Atti, only to realise the boy had shockingly disappeared.

CHAPTER 2 – Hidden

As the shouting of the crowd slowly faded, the exit to the outside of the amphitheatre came into sight. Atti ran as fast as possible to get out of there. He was nervous concerning what his father would say about his disappearance, but thought that he could deal with that later. He reached a large hall with a tall ceiling like a cathedral. There were three large archways decorated with detailed statues of the governor.

He departed outside into the calm, tranquil air. He looked around to see that no people were about, to his favour. The town centre was empty and desolate. If it wasn't for the running fountain it would be as if time itself had stopped.

"ATTICUS!"

The deafening voice of Numitor brought Atti back to himself. Rapidly he ran to the nearest building and hid inside behind a counter. Seconds later his father came into view by the fountain, and shortly after two of the New Guard soldiers could be seen also.

"Spread out and find him," he said to the soldiers sternly. They parted with him while Numitor worriedly sat by the fountain. Someone then walked over to the spot and spoke in a demanding voice, "This is very worrying Caeso, you do understand that the Rangers threat *is* a very serious matter, do you not?"

Rangers? Who are they?

Atti peaked over the counter to see who was addressing his father. It was Titus.

"Of course I understand the threat Decimus, but I also don't believe that my son is a traitor! He has been through too much, and I feel you are overestimating Atticus."

"I have watched your child, Numitor. He is not as loyal as you may suggest."

They continued to stare at each other intently until the sergeant backed away slowly. Once he was gone from sight Numitor sighed heavily. Soon the sound of heavy footsteps could be heard. The soldiers from before both returned from different areas and started exclaiming how they had not found the child.

After scouring most buildings in the area, the soldiers started searching the shops by the fountain. Slowly but surely, they searched every one until they reached Atti's hiding spot.

The larger of the two barged in with impatience and started wrecking everything in there like a bull in a China shop. He knocked over a lantern which crashed onto the floor next to Atti. The boy stifled a gasp but unfortunately it was enough to give him away.

Grinning, the brute leapt over the counter and shouted gleefully. But to his dismay there was no one there.

Disappointed, he walked out of the shop and signalled to his friend. The two ransacked the rest of the shops in frustration but were unlucky in their findings. Shortly they returned to Numitor who was pacing up and down in the town centre.

"We searched everywhere Caeso, your son is not in this town. Maybe he is still in the amphitheatre, and you are wasting our time. I wonder if you are the traitor that has been leaking information?"

"Do not ridicule me!" Numitor commanded, and that's all Atti heard as he descended into the secret caverns beneath the town. He made sure the trapdoor was fully shut before climbing down the rickety, wooden ladder to the stone floor underneath. The walls were cliff-like and caving inwards toward the ceiling, making a triangular passageway. There were torches on poles throughout the area which illuminated strange markings on the walls.

Atti became stationary for a few moments to let his eyes adjust to the sudden change in light. Pacing forward he used his hands to guide himself through the passage. In slow succession he reached a wooden bridge which extended over a deep ravine beneath him. As he stepped onto a crooked plank, it fell into the darkness below. Atti rapidly recovered and shuddered at the thought of falling into the abyss.

Across the bridge was a small area with many doors. Some were bigger and wider than others but all of them were made of the same reddish-brown material. After some hesitation, Atti turned to the door on his left. As he pulled on the handle, he heard indistinct voices in the distance. He hesitated for a moment before turning it towards himself.

The door was heavy and stiff, as if it had not been used in some time, and there were cobwebs in the corners of the corridor inside accompanied by two large spiders dwelling there. The passage was similar to the previous one, however it was significantly larger in width and height. Jagged and sharp to touch were the cave walls, steering Atti into the middle of the passage.

After what seemed like hours, he reached another door of the same kind. Through the door was a more homely living area, with an ancient looking shelf stocked with undusted codices on one side and a seating area in the corner. The walls were decorated with drawings and paintings of great battles. In another corner was an old-looking armchair, and sitting in it was an equally old person, with rags for clothes and a black hood obscuring their face.

Atti stood still for minutes until he was certain that the figure was either dead or asleep. He crept to the ladder on the other side of the room quietly and started on the first rung. The trapdoor above was jammed shut at first, and Atti had to use all his strength to lift it open. When there was enough room to get through, he climbed through and assessed his surroundings.

Atti was in the middle of a wine cellar, where multiple bottles were lined on the walls between heavy wooden frames. Opposite to him was a door that was open, leading to a stone staircase. He started ascending through the narrow stairway and reached the building on surface level.

After shielding his eyes, taking a second to adjust to the outside light, he looked around at the new surroundings. Unsurprisingly, it was a wine shop and it was decorated with images of wine and grapes with vines seeping throughout the paintings on the walls. The drawings depicted grape farms and bathhouses with crowds of Romans, each one dressed in similar tunics and shorts. They all seemed jolly and content, too full of themselves, Atti thought.

Atti dashed behind the wall and peered sneakily through the window. He had ended up by the outer wall, which rose fifty feet into the air. The wall was made up of mainly stone and wood and was decorated with some red and golden banners. On the top were stone blocks and sharp spikes to prevent people from climbing into or out of the town.

He snuck next to the wall and behind a cart with a barrel on top. It was silent at that moment but Atti remained apprehensive. Time passed until he was sure that it was safe, and then was the time to relax and reflect.

Atti stared at the blank wall in front of him and imagined the world outside. His father never let him out and used to say he was too young to leave, and that the outside world was too dangerous. Numitor had hinted at evil soldiers and devils in the ocean, all of which were legends based on *some* truth.

Atti closed his eyes and recalled a story. In particular, the one about a sailor named Marco and his crew.

'Marco was admired within his group, and they went on many fishing trips in the seas bordering the country.

However, on one occasion Marco had had a dream in which a young-looking, beautiful mermaid visited him on his ship and told him a prophecy. This prophecy was brief and short, but most importantly to Marco, it entailed the death of his crew.

Marco was sceptical about the dream, and cast it off during the day's fishing trip. Instead of warning them, Marco started boasting to his crew about how he had 'the life' and that no one could replace him as captain. To prove his point, he started bossing around the crew in harsh ways and they were slowly getting angrier towards Marco, understandably.

To retaliate against Marco's hostility, the ship's first-mate, Carinus, gathered all the crew and decided to throw Marco off the ship and teach him a lesson. In fact, they never meant to kill him, but when the time came, Marco was hauled off the ship and sent splashing into the sea. Shortly after, Carinus tossed down a rope, but then he remembered something. Marco could not swim.

After minutes of searching, they concluded that their captain had drowned or been eaten. Once he was gone, the crew started to realise how much their captain had helped them, and that everyone makes mistakes at times. Marco, while seeming insufferable to his crewmates ever since that dream, had his actions interpreted in a way of protecting his crew, cautioning them not to step in the wrong direction.

Ironically, as soon as the crew had thrown Marco off the ship, each one was punished harshly by the gods, and the ship was struck by lightning that very night, leaving only Carinus alive so he could be forced to live with his actions for the rest of his life, educating others on the folly acts in life...'

Atti opened his eyes and stared straight into the eyes of a mouse who was staring right back at him. He picked it up and held it in his hands, letting it go after a while. It was early evening when the sun began to set, and the dimming light cast shadows into the alleyway where he was hiding.

Atti inevitably began to feel hungry and tired, and so decided that he had to act now. Swiftly, he dashed through the buildings and swerved left and right until he got near the entrance to the town.

Nearby, Atti happened to find a dusty cloak on a bench. Donning the disguise, Atti approached the two guards by the big, rusted, metal gate. The first one turned and inspected the strange figure approaching the gate. His eyes thinned and he gripped his sword tighter.

"Halt! State your name and business at once or fear being prosecuted!"

Atti stood still and masked his voice, saying:

"My name is Augustus Gorek, I have come from Rome and I have important information about the Rangers threat that has to be received by midnight tonight, so I think it would be wise if you let me pass."

The guard listened intently and then looked to the other, and they exchanged a few whispers. Then the first guard spoke again, "You speak of Rangers, what business do they have with our town of Socratis?"

Atti shook his head and replied, "I cannot tell you classified information, guard, but I assure you the name Gorek will be familiar with my fath... Numitor the Powerful. If you were to contact him, he would see to my safe passage."

"Even so, your name does not register as a citizen of Socratis and therefore you must stay until you can get Caeso himself to come down and speak for you. I am truly sorry."

Disappointed, Atti retreated a few steps and turned around. A thought flashed across his mind, but he dismissed it immediately. He was about to leave when a familiar voice filled the silence.

"What seems to be the problem, guards?"

Atti swivelled to see his father standing there proudly with his silver sword buckled to his black belt and his armour rattling in the breeze. His hair was combed and smooth, his hands soft but strong by his sides.

The guards were surprised and shocked, the first one stammering:

"Quaestor Caeso, what a surprise to see you down here at this time. We were just questioning this traveller who says he is from Rome and is under *your* jurisdiction. Is this true?"

"I'm afraid I do not know this traveller who hides his face, who I demand must reveal himself; BOY."

The game was up, and as quick as he could Atti ran to the streets, but he was cornered by the two New Guard soldiers from earlier.

"Come here!" Numitor shouted, hauling the cloak off Atti.

"Do you not have any sense in you boy! Running off like a chicken will only get you so far! You have no idea of the danger outside; do you really think you can defend yourself out there?"

Atti's eyes burned and he didn't back down from his father. His feet were locked into the ground and his cloak blew in the breeze, the evening light shining upon his eyes as if they were on fire.

"How am I supposed to know if you don't show me what's out there? I must resort to sneaking out because you think I'm weak, like, like Adrian!"

Numitor's fiery gaze lingered for a couple of seconds before growling and walking over to Atti, firmly grabbing him by the shoulder, pulling him with large amounts of force. Atti struggled as much as he could but soon gave in to his father's inhuman strength.

The two went across to the other side of town as the citizens looked on in curiosity. Atti's legs scraped against the cobbled stone floor and he cut them several times. He grappled at his father's hands but to no avail, and Numitor just stared ahead and strode with immense force, dragging Atti as if he were a sack of potatoes.

After an excruciating while, the two arrived at their living quarters, where Numitor bashed the door open with his leg. The room inside was homely and comfortable, it had two beds in each compartment and was filled with a bright light reflected through the large square windows indented in the roof. The trees outside cast shadows depicting strange shapes into the room which fell onto the two heated figures.

Atti finally shook off his father's grip after they had entered and stormed into his room where he leapt onto his bed and lay for the remainder of the day. As the sun lowered below the horizon, darkness dominating the room, the various lights in the town dimmed and extinguished, sleep overcoming all the inhabitants, save for a few.

In the far distance, a few miles away from the town, Decimus Titus and three of his most loyal guards met up with a mysterious figure with a dark, black cloak, showing only its strange red eyes peering through the black space where its face should appear. It cawed and screeched like a demented bird and had strange claws instead of hands poking out of the sleeves.

The exchange lasted for only a few minutes, but its secrecy was key, and the knowledge of the Warlock was also key, in ways important but unknown to Atti at that time...

CHAPTER 3 – The First Move

The morning was bright and the sky was filled with golden sunshine that radiated through all the small windows of each homely building standing in a neat formation, lined throughout the quaint town of Socratis. On the border of the town was a huge stone wall that stood about fifty feet tall and had large spikes on top of it with sharp metal in between them. On one side of the town, a large, black, metal gate protected the entrance and was always guarded by soldiers clad in bright red armour and iron shoulder-guards plastered with the town emblem. Their armour had been crafted from chainmail and clinked every time the soldiers moved.

Blinding was the early sun which reflected off the metal bars as it rose above the far horizon. Gradually the early morning turned to midday and the town was bustling with the Roman inhabitants. The multiple smells of baked goods and cured meat filled the air and nostrils of the customers in the streets. The sky was bright blue and as clear as glass, with no sign of white clouds anywhere. The surrounding area had steep hills and mountains covering the terrain, with snow-covered peaks at the highest altitudes.

Few had tried to climb the peaks, and the ones that had rarely returned. Most of the ones that survived had only travelled up half or even a quarter of the treacherous path.

This was partly because the path up there happened to be incomplete, due to the general fear of the mountains within the townsfolk. The few that returned sometimes wrote stories about their travels. One, in particular, became so popular he was known as a sophisticated author and was loved by the Romans in the early days of Socratis. That writer rose to fame because of his enticing mountain tales, due to his natural skill and way of writing; an individual who went by the name Armitage Ignavus.

In his teenage years, Armitage showed a passion towards the Empire and always aspired to be as great as Caesar one day. By writing about his aspirations and outlandish improvements for the Empire, nearly everyone came to like his work, and when the people found out about the murder of the current governor (of the time), they were surprised to find that his only heir was Armitage, and he soon became a great governor who cared for his people. As Armitage had always disliked his family name, and because he wanted to disassociate from his father's terrible legacy, he changed his name to Cicero out of admiration for his hero.

However, as he got older, and fatter, the sheer size of the power went to his head, and his heroic aspirations quickly dissipated as well as the support of the people, with only a few people, actually respecting this governor. To retaliate against the disrespect, he created rules commanding the citizens to support him or be severely punished accordingly.

The truth was that they thought Armitage was weak and that only a brave soldier would lead Socratis into battle, not a poet. One person who did respect the governor was Atti's father Numitor, who sucked up to Cicero and acted like his loyal pet. Because of this loyalty Numitor was escalated into the position of quaestor.

Cicero lived in the grandest building in Socratis, a twenty feet tall quartz palace that was so polished it reflected sun-rays onto everything around it. It was placed in the centre of town, and had a Roman flag perched upon the large dome. These flags were also hung on the extravagant, white pillars by the entrance, and above the enormous wooden doors for everyone to see.

Through the doors was a circular room with a high ceiling and hanging from it was an extravagant chandelier in the centre. Lots of doorways led to different sections, and many servants were inside, some cooking, some cleaning, some sleeping on the job. But nowhere to be seen, on this particular morning, was the governor himself. One servant had spotted him leaving the palace early at sunrise in a carriage, but he hadn't been seen since.

The absence of Cicero was not unnatural amongst most days, but after midday, Servius, his top advisor, began to become concerned for his master's safety, and later that day he sent out some of the New Guard to search for him.

Titus wasn't pleased about his army being used as a search and rescue team, but he remained silent throughout the proceedings to avoid any complications; he was already against the idea of being stationed in Italy. Hours passed, and soon the afternoon came, and the governor had not been found inside the town or in the surroundings around Socratis.

The next morning came and Sergeant Titus announced he would be travelling to Rome at noon, to the relief of the civilians. As the highest-ranking military combatant, Numitor became in charge of the town's requirements and complications, to his delight. Because of his temporary promotion he neglected Atti even more, and the boy was mostly left alone throughout the next week.

One evening, while Numitor was at home - albeit for a short time - a letter was delivered to the house which was branded by a red seal with a strange bird-like creature depicted on it. The letter, to Numitor's surprise, was directed to Atti, who read the letter out loud to his father and to Matteo, their servant,

'Dear Atticus Caeso,

How I've waited for the opportunity to speak to you for the first time. You see I've been trying to contact you for a while now, which is near impossible when your town is as protective as a turtle within its shell.

Do not be concerned, this is not a threat. In fact, I am asking you for a friendly favour, which Cicero, that old fool, must not get word of. You see, my position is one that the governor is afraid of, but he is too gullible and weak-minded to do anything about it. Unless you count that Titus fellow. We can change that, as I'm sure you will see soon. But enough of that.

All I ask is for you to meet me so that we can have a truthful and honest discussion, as you are a fascinating young man, or so I have heard. I request that we meet at the foot of Rakusa Peak. And you must know, if you do not attend this

meeting, I will find other ways of contacting you. Hopefully I should see you soon my dear Atticus.

Take care,
Octavius Karvajal

Numitor did not say a word, though his look spoke a thousand words. Matteo looked terrified and was shaking at the core, while looking side to side in rapid succession.

"What is the matter, Matteo?" Atti asked politely, to which Matteo replied shakily:

"Karvajal sent you that letter! Don't you see boy?"

"Matteo, Atticus does not know of Karvajal and his rebel group. Though it might be time for him to learn."

"This is about those Rangers, isn't it!"

At the mention of Rangers, Matteo rushed off in tears, and Numitor's eyes widened with shock, then changed to an understanding, and then finally to a stern stare.

Numitor turned to Atti, "So, you *do* know something. When did you learn of Rangers?"

"A couple of weeks ago, on the day of the New Guard's announcement. I overheard you and Titus speaking about them..."

"So, you do not know as much as I might have believed. However, I do think it is necessary that you hear their story, because, as you evidently are unaware of, Octavius Karvajal is the Warmonger, the Silver Tyrant, the arrogant Leader of the Rangers. Now hear his tale."

Numitor sat down in his chair and inclined for Atti to do the same. The chair beneath him felt overly soft and comfortable, and Atti virtually sunk into it as if he were being devoured by quicksand. Numitor took a minute to settle in his chair, asking the now returned Matteo to fetch him a bottle of wine with two glasses. Atti took this as a significant sign, considering his father never drank wine, or not as much as he would like to admit, and Atti had almost never been offered any.

Once the drinks had been served, Numitor began in a low, deep voice as if he were telling a deep secret, "Octavius Karvajal was a good ally of mine for many years, and I trusted him with my life, which was a mistake. You must know this story, Atticus, and I regret waiting until now to say it, as this story concerns your mother. And if it's any consolation, Adrian did not know of Octavius and his wrong-doings either.

Firstly, I should start when I was around your age. I lived in a small town known as Salerno, in the South of Italia. I was an only child, and my father was rarely around - as he was a Roman Officer - and sadly he died that way in battle, against a savage group of Britons in that cursed country. When I heard news of his death, I was upset, but mostly angry that my father hadn't spent more time with me in Salerno. You see, I don't want that for you Atticus, that's why I want you protected and safe, away from tyrants like Karvajal."

Atti wasn't deterred. He looked at his father intently, urging him to continue.

Numitor spoke once again, "After my father died, I felt lonely, even with my mother, so one day I left Salerno and travelled far and wide across Italia. I walked across expansive roads that led across wastelands and forests, through valleys and around mountains. Finally, I found it. A place where I could do right. Rome.

At this time, I was around nineteen and when I entered Rome I discovered the Trials. These were a set of challenges in a tournament that you had to complete to become a special Roman Soldier for the emperor, Alexius. As you already know, I completed the Trials successfully and earned myself a status recognised by the emperor himself. But as you also know, I didn't stay in Rome. There was one thing that held me back. A girl I had formed an attachment with, Cecilia - your mother. We loved each other dearly, and I knew I wouldn't be able to leave her in Rome while I went travelling again. I thought of everything to try and persuade her to come with me, and so I forged her a golden necklace with the help of a friend I had made in the Trials named Vulcan - he was a blacksmith, the best I've ever known. The necklace was perfect, it was beautiful and not too heavy. I planned that day to give the necklace to Cecilia in the hope that she would leave with me.

However, another, richer man, Octavius, who I had met in the Trials, also had feelings for Cecilia, and later that night I learned that Octavius had proposed to her, and they were getting married in a week. I became enraged towards Octavius, who was once my friend during the Trials. In fact, I had helped him during the water task. But most of all I was angry with Cecilia for agreeing with the marriage.

The next day I found Octavius and did something I do not regret to this day. I stabbed him with a silver dagger and left him bleeding in the river, after uttering these words to him: 'Stay away from Cecilia or next time I will not let you live.'

The threat worked, as in the morning I found out the wedding had been cancelled, so I sought out Cecilia. I found her at her home - or at least where she was now staying in Rome as she was from somewhere far, and there I told her about my true feelings for her, while also lying about my confrontation with Octavius. I admit that it was shameful, but I knew she would never agree to come with me if she knew what I did. That day I gave her the necklace, and she agreed to travel, but we had to sneak out in the middle of the night as her mother disagreed with her departure.

After a month we arrived in Socratis and we lived a happy life for 5 years until we had Adrian, and then 6 years after that, you. However, a lot happened in that 6-year period which I have not mentioned. Specifically, just before you were born. You see, at this time we were definitively settled in Socratis, and I was mainly staying at home and occasionally working as a servant for Cicero. He saw me as a good candidate for a bodyguard, so he kept me around and paid me highly. This is why it was a surprise when I was visited by Octavius.

It started as a knock on the door. When I looked into his eyes I knew that he still had that anger in him, very similar to that of mine all those years ago. I knew immediately that he had come to settle a score. Cecilia was out, so I was left with Adrian. I backed off him and made sure Adrian was safe before signalling Octavius to go outside. I remember his words perfectly. He said to me, 'You can't suppress your fate, and like a false promise, I have come back to bite you.'

We battled fiercely, our swords clashing repeatedly when Cecilia returned. I remember the look on her face, a look of shock but mostly disappointment. Octavius turned, and in his surprise, I attacked him, tackling him to the floor and pummelling him in the face. I could hear the cries of Cecilia but through my rage I continued. Eventually, Cecilia grasped my shoulder and pulled me back. I stared at Octavius, then at your mother, then at Octavius again.

Octavius smirked and said, 'This is not the first time your *husband* has done something like this Domina.'

She was horrified at his words and when I tried to explain Cecilia wouldn't listen. At that moment she left the garden and got a chariot out of town. I do not know where she went but I can guess it was Rome, back to her parents.

I was left standing there with Octavius bleeding everywhere, a broad, bloody grin painted across his bashed and bruised face. He shakily stood up and brought out his short sword which glinted in the naked sun. We stayed there for a while, Octavius's grimace taunting me while I slowly accepted my failure. I looked into his eyes and saw fire, anguish and pain.

'How could you do this to me, Octavius? We were friends once!' I shouted, so that everyone could see his wickedness.

He laughed in a manic and insane way, replying with, 'You can't blame me for this *Numi,* you may have forgotten by I haven't. You left me for dead in a river, all because you were *envious.* Pathetic!'

I swayed in the heavy wind and felt my heart beating out of my chest. He glared at me with bloodshot eyes. And then he left just as abruptly as he arrived.

A year later I got a letter from Cecilia's father which I have stored and it is now locked away in my room. The letter told me of Cecilia's death and that she had been pregnant with a boy she named Atticus. I said I would care for you and Adrian as repentance for the pain I had caused her and her family. And that is my history with Octavius. But it is far from the end of this story.

About three months ago I heard of a tyrant named Karvajal who was destroying small encampments and towns in the surrounding area with a concerning group of rebels, stealing and reaping the riches there. I do not know how he formed such a large threat like the Rangers, but I know first-hand how manipulative and strong Octavius is, and that's why I suggested bringing the New Guard to Socratis. I figured that he would come here for revenge, but so far that has not been the case. The letter he sent to you, Atticus, is the first time I have heard from Octavius in a long time, and to hear his words, I admit, is disconcerting. Now, you may speak."

Atti sat there, speechless, his mouth gaping, slightly in awe. A million thoughts and questions rushed through his mind, but he suppressed the urge to say them. Instead, it was Matteo who spoke.

"Dominus, what a story! Your bravery and strength aren't shown anywhere else as much as in this tale! We must tell the governor, when we find him of course."

"You are mistaken, you fool! This tale that you think of as valiant must never be told to a single soul, and especially not to Cicero. To think that you are the servant of mine. Matteo, go and clean yourself up and stay in your room until I call you."

"Yes Dominus!" came the reply as the young servant rushed out of the room.

Numitor stood up and paced to the window. He pulled the curtains together and then turned to face his silent son. Speaking slowly, he whispered, "My son, I have lost everyone I ever cared for except for you. I do not wish to lose another. But Octavius would hope for the opposite. Please, do not do as he says and ignore his words. Like I told you, he is a manipulative monster and he will stop at nothing to get revenge. I will need your help as long as you do as I say from now on. That means no running off Atticus. Just know, I love you immensely, and I will do anything to protect you...Now goodnight."

And with that, Numitor walked out of the room, Atti hearing the door shut in the distance. He stayed in his chair and tried to process all the information he had gathered. Hours went by, and the full moon shone through a slit in the golden curtains.

He yawned, and the sound echoed throughout the night. Standing up slowly, he walked to his room and clambered into his bed and lay there for hours, trying to get to sleep with a head full of thoughts. Soon the only sound in the air was the howl of wolves miles away in the snow-capped mountains.

CHAPTER 4 –
Provocation and Preparation

The search for Cicero continued over months, and soon the year was over. The original panic and distress subsided over this time, and Numitor felt more settled in his new position, which meant he didn't spend much time with Atti, contrary to his proposition. Instead, Atti spent most of his days in his room or the courtyard practicing his writing, arithmetic, and occasionally sword fighting.

As he was confined to the house, Atti didn't hear much word of the investigation and search into Cicero's disappearance, and for him, the days were arduous and lonely, Matteo being the only other person he could see, as well as the rare sighting of Numitor, who usually only returned to sign a document or two or to pick up a letter from other allies in Italy.

One dreary, dull morning, Atti was gazing from his window sill and out into the town now under his father's control, at which he saw a peculiar and large commotion by the west gate into Socratis. Smoke tinted with sparks of orange flames rose high above the crowd, followed by a deafening sound produced by a trumpet, which usually signified the arrival of a person of importance.

Could Cicero have been found?

Atti forcefully pushed open his door and hastily descended the stairs to the common room below, and to his assumption, it was vacant. Dashing out of the room and into the large entrance hall, Atti heaved the hefty, heavy wooden doors leading to the adamantine cobbled street in the centre of Socratis. The blazing sunlight dazzled Atti, causing him to recoil. The hot, humid air stuck to his tunic, and soon sweat started to pour down his face like a waterfall, under the gaze of the scorching sun. Clearing his eyes, Atti surveyed the square, noticing the two soldiers guarding the house. They turned to him, showing no emotion or incline to speak.

"What's happening at the west gate?" Atti panted, pointing in the direction of the smoke and clamour. The guard stared blankly as if he were in a simulation, frustrating the impatient teenager even more. Deciding that it was a waste of time, Atti shot down the west street towards the confusing commotion. He vaulted over a crate of apples, almost bumping into a bulky man hauling a similar crate of fruit, arriving at the end of the street and at the source of his inquiries.

A sea of people blocked the sight of everyone's attention, and Atti looked around frantically and desperately to look for a way in. Some men carried long torches and were shouting obscenities towards the centre of the circle. He was relieved when he noticed Domina Delphi at the edge of the crowd, trying to peer over their heads. She looked worried, which was strange for the woman as Atti was used to her being a warm and bubbly person. Disconcerted, he sidled up to the frail woman, whose face brightened at the sight of the young man.

"Atticus! Oh, thank goodness you're okay."

"What's happening?" Atti asked urgently.

"You don't know?" came the reply, "It's......"

An unintelligible shout came from within the ocean of heads, and unexpectedly the crowd dispersed, running as fast as they could away from whatever the tumult was about. A clear path opened for Atti, and he seized his chance, diving through the disturbed crowd. He pushed and shoved violently, determined to see what the fuss was about, which was shortly answered as Atti reached the scene.

The spectacle was mortifying. A pyre the size of a house was ablaze in front of him, and at the base was a pile of bodies, stacked up like crates of fruit. Each body wore the same distinguishable armour, that of the New Guard, and at the very top of the pile seemed to be the burnt corpse of Cicero himself, propped up like a ragdoll. On the ground in despair was Titus, motionless.

The courtyard had cleared slightly and Atti glanced around at all the shocked, distraught and terrified faces of the civilians of Socratis. The crackling flames of the pyre burned high into the smoky sky, where a small cloud of smog gathered above the area.

A stout, tall man brandishing a brass trumpet and an archaic blade hanging from his belt was ordering the onlookers to leave. He wore a maroon cape with a gold sigil on his back and a golden plate on his chest. His name was Lucien, the army general of Socratis, a trustworthy and dependable soldier who had risen through the ranks to gain his position. Numitor had been childhood friends with Lucien and had once told Atti that he trusted Lucien with his life.

In fact, Atti had taken a liking to Lucien, and when he and Adrian were young, the general would share his war stories and adventures. Atti had liked to imagine what it would be like to leave Socratis and fight for his town, for his empire.

How different everything is now, he wondered, before being thrown back into the present situation before him. Atti paced over to Lucien, who took a second to recognise the boy in front of him.

"What happened here?"

Lucien's calmed expression turned grave, and he tilted his head towards the ground. The glistening daylight shone across the dripping sweat cast across the general's brow.

"I think it is best if you wait, my boy. Have you seen your father anywhere?"

Atti shook his head and posed his question once more, but to his dismay Lucien said, "Atticus, it isn't wise to seek out answers. Especially with recent events, you would be inclined to stay out of this turmoil that has befallen us."

"I want to help, I'm not weak as father says I am, I could help you in the fight against the Rangers!"

Lucien recoiled at the usage of his enemy's name. Composing himself, he became stern and stared straight into Atti's shimmering, blue eyes.

"Trust me when I say this, Atticus, this fight is beyond your skill, no matter how much you may have trained. Now I don't know how much Numitor has told you about our 'situation,' but we are up against some *very* powerful enemies, and your father is striving to keep this town together as a result of Cicero's absence, though now we know how that has ended. So, I suggest you stay at home with your aide and keep out of this mess for your own good. I'm sorry Atticus, but that's an order."

Atti grunted frustratingly and stamped his foot like a toddler. He pleaded, "At least give me some interpretation as to what is going on!"

As Lucien was about to speak, a perturbed and tormented Titus appeared at his side. The disturbed sergeant whispered in a low, saddened voice, just loud enough for Atti to hear.

"Listen to me, General, this act of impertinence will *not* go unpunished, and therefore I require some of your finest men, because, *Lucien*, you do not win a war by sitting idly by."

He finished dramatically before storming off and shoving Atti out of his way. Lucien showed a visible disgust to Titus, but Atti was mindful not to question the general when he was angered. But, to his surprise Lucien turned to Atti and whispered, "Titus believes that war is the only path to peace, which is why he will fail in his endeavours, but that, unfortunately, is the side he has chosen."

"And what side are you on Lucien?"

"That of the winner."

An hour passed by and a perimeter barricade was set up by Lucien and his guards with metal barbs on poles. Soon, Numitor arrived with three decorated soldiers on his flank. At the sight of the pyre, Numitor was aghast and dismayed, although relieved at the sight of his friend, the general. Atti assumed that Lucien had recounted the events of the day, including his encounter with Titus, however the pair were just out of earshot of Atti, who was sitting on a bench nearby.

His father, who had neglected him for the past few months rushed over at once and embraced Atti, which stunned but overjoyed him. Numitor stood back and clasped his shoulders, a single tear running down his cheek.

"Are you alright?" he asked sincerely, no hint of anything but seriousness. Atti nodded, tears welling in his eyes.

"What happened?" he whimpered, darting his eyes over to the pyre.

Numitor shook his head and released Atti, saying, "There will be a time and place for explanation, but it's not now. For now, go home and get safe, I will join you I promise."

With that, he patted Atti on the shoulder and retreated to Lucien. The boy swayed in the air, the immense heat causing his clothes to stick to his wet, sweaty skin.

Atti spotted Matteo by one of the guards in the courtyard. Reuniting himself with his servant, the two returned to their estate, where Atti's thoughts raced in his mind like the great chariots of Rome. He felt as if there were more questions than answers, and that pile kept growing.

As Atti lay on his bed, throwing a leather ball up and down in his bedroom, the dignified sergeant lay similarly in his quarters while speaking to his loyal advisor.

Infernal rage had engulfed Titus, and his will for retaliation blinded his intelligence. He ordered immediate preparations to commence a direct attack on the Rangers, while also hoping for an assist from Numitor, Lucien and his army of Socratis. His plan was one of ambition and recklessness, one which his advisor noticed, but he was forced to silence himself to not feed the flame that was growing inside his sergeant.

Once the plan was finalised, a messenger was sent to the residence of Lucien and then Numitor, and that night the preparations began. Unbeknownst to Atti, dangerous catapults, war chariots and horses armed with lances were brought into the city and out to the gate. As the proud and courtly Decimus Titus stood in front of his commissioned army, the horn was sounded, and the attack had begun.

Atti woke in the dead of night, to the sound of silence and false tranquillity. An owl in the far distance could be heard hooting, the only noise in the populated town. He sat up and ripped off the covers, strolling to his window where he had been hours earlier. He looked out to where the pyre still stood, its once bright flame extinguished and darkened, no longer illuminating the courtyard. Resting his arms on the window sill, Atti listened to the owls hooting and the crickets chirping around him, but the lack of chattering and speech disturbed him.

The old oak frame of the door creaked as Atti tip-toed out into the hallway in his house. Creeping towards Matteo's room, he slightly pushed the door open and peered inside, but to his surprise it was empty. Next, he tried his father's room, also vacant. Perturbed, Atti descended the stairs and observed the living room for any sign of his father or his servant, but they could not be found.

However, at that moment, a slight breeze of air flew through the thin gap by the open back door. Investigating further, he saw that a vase had been knocked over, possibly in a hurry. Atti fled the house, escaping to the street outside.

First, he visited Lucien's house, but there was no answer when he called in. Worry started to set in, causing him to jump when he heard a clattering of boxes in a back alley behind him. He slowly moved over to the disturbance, before barely hearing a sort of whisper from somewhere above him. Atti had reached the boxes, where a fox lay curled up in one, to his relief.

Then, as quick as a flash, a black figure jumped down in front of him and suddenly hit Atti on the head with some sort of weapon. Dazed and stunned, he fell back into the grip of another figure, who forcefully tied up his limbs with impressive speed, as the first man whacked him for a second time before covering his head with a sack. Atti kicked and shouted, flailing his body around like a deranged fish on land. The boy could just about hear one of the men speaking with authority, but he was uncertain as to what was said. Atti was then hauled over one man's shoulder, and that was the last he could remember before passing out entirely.

The first thing Atti could remember was a searing headache, and then the thick darkness he was smothered in due to the sack upon his head. After a few minutes, some distorted voices could be heard. Atti thought he could make out a deep, male voice not dissimilar from his own father. A second voice was feminine and sounded younger, but unfortunately their words were too hard to distinguish, and Atti only felt himself losing consciousness and swaying slightly back and forth. An unknown time had passed until his mind felt clearer, and so naturally Atti called out, "Hey! Can anyone hear me?"

Silence followed, and Atti held out little hope, but nonetheless his fear pushed him to shout more at irregular intervals, until Atti guessed that his captors must have been somewhere else. He moved his hands around to find that he had been tied to a chair. Every minute that passed Atti was conscious of the limited air he had been breathing in, and as the time of no response lengthened, his concern increased.

Soon, he began to think of his father, and a wave of horror washed over the boy as he realised his father would have no way to find him, or worse, if he had been killed during the assault. Then Atti's thoughts led to Matteo, and he wondered what had happened to his trusted servant and friend. The hotness inside of the claustrophobic sack brought drowsiness, and Atti shortly fell into a much-needed sleep, however vulnerable it might have left him.

Atti awoke to lack of vision once again, woken by the sound of two men, presumably soldiers, conversing in front of where he sat. They were discussing whether it was the right time to move 'the hostage' which Atti assumed to be him. After what seemed like an age of discussion, one soldier untied Atti's bonds as the older of the two voices instructed him to stand up. Grabbing the sack, the soldier hesitated before yanking it off and revealing themselves to Atti whose eyes seared at the sudden influx of light.

"We are trusting you not to do anything stupid," one guard uttered, "Any funny business and we will gladly gut you like the animal you are."

Acknowledging the threat, Atti started to follow the older soldier, the other following close behind. Atti began to inspect his surroundings, finding himself in a cold, damp, sewer-like area with cells lining the walls, iron barbs separating him and whoever was inside them. The hallway was lit by a dim torch which flickered, looking as if on the verge of extinguishing.

The trio ascended the many jagged steps up the stairwell which led up to the rest of the base in the mountain. Observing his captors, he saw that they wore brown tunics and had silver belts which held a sword and dagger, as well as a flask of water. These soldiers also wore iron helmets which were in an unusual style that were quite different from the centurion design. Atti could only guess that these soldiers were Rangers and that this was what Octavius was referring to in the letter. He had been kidnapped by his father's nemesis.

Soon Atti and the Rangers arrived inside the main area of the fortress, which was when he realised the base was built into a mountain, presumably the one Karvajal had mentioned, Rakusa Peak. The rough, cave walls ascended upwards for many feet, signifying the true height of the mountain. The room that Atti found himself in held many more Rangers who stared at him intensely. As they began to depart from this area, a higher-up Ranger started to speak with the older soldier who had been leading Atti.

Atti soon spotted an open archway which looked like the exit and so, when the older guard was distracted and the other was not paying attention, he took his chance.

Atti swiftly ran through the archway and explored the fortress he was trapped inside, frantically searching for a sign of an exit as his escorts chased him all the while. At one point, he entered a room where the door shut behind him, and a guard who was sleeping inside awoke suddenly and reached for his blade. Atti, quick-thinkingly, grasped a dagger from the nearby table and held it up against the Ranger, his heart pumping faster than he thought possible. The half-dressed guard looked manic and infuriated, and Atti took a step back fearfully. The guard then lunged forward with his sword while Atti dodged out of the way, leaving the Ranger vulnerable. Taking his chance, Atti thrust his dagger into the chest of the guard, and his blood spilled down onto the ground, splattering in a pool of red on the cold, stone floor. The man collapsed suddenly onto the ground, blood soaking his body.

Atti recoiled, frightful and regretful instantly, sheathing the dagger and taking deep breaths while leaning against the cold, brick wall. Atti felt like he wanted to rest for eternity, but he heard the footsteps of many soldiers arriving outside the door. Collecting himself, he found another exit out of the room and dashed down the tunnel, seeing light at the end - a gateway to heaven.

As Atti neared the end, he felt his knees weaken and the gravity of the situation came crashing down upon him, much like himself onto the floor.

I just killed a man, what has happened to me? I'm alone, helpless, trying to escape a giant fortress filled with men that probably want to kill me. I need to get out of here!

Grunting, he heaved himself up and staggered to the light, realising he had been cut in the leg. Limping faster than before, he reached the mouth of the cave where he felt a rush of hope, which was quickly cut off as several Rangers came rushing out of the doors from his left and right.

Leading the charge was a stout, respectable gentleman with long dark hair braided with golden rings on the end. He wore a black gown with purple accents along with a brass bracelet around each arm with words across the side that were too small for Atti to read. On his feet were heavy, black boots with golden straps and across his chest was a sparkling cloth which Atti deemed very expensive and rare.

The distinguished man walked over to him calmly, chuckling to himself but in a friendly, non-threatening way. In a deep, stale tone fed through a smile he declared boastfully, "My dear Atticus Caeso, son of Numitor Caeso and Cecilia Longinus, brother to Adrian Caeso, what a pleasure it is to finally meet you."

CHAPTER 5 – The Siege

Many murmuring voices and sounds of clinking glasses and cutlery filled the large, open hall Atti found himself seated inside. The area was spacious and had scarce furniture save for a few supports and the extensive feasting table laid out in front of him with an enormous selection of food, some of which Atti had only dreamed about. As far as he could see, there were mountains of breads, cheeses, meats and exotic-looking fruits unknown to Atti. The table was set up in a T-shape, so that he was sitting at the end of the table in the middle row, sitting next to the well-dressed man he had seen earlier.

The man, who Atti had guessed to be Karvajal, was politely speaking to someone across the table from him, an elderly woman with wiry, grey hair braided into a bun behind her head. She had a frail face and many wrinkles, but her green eyes shone ever so faintly. She chuckled lightly before turning to the gentleman on her right, leaving Karvajal to turn his attention to Atti. He stared down into Atti's eyes with a piercing, stern but also comforting gaze.

"Am I supposed to trust you?" Atti asked vigilantly.

Karvajal smiled and said calmly, "Of course."

"Why should I believe that? I just murdered one of your men! I should be dead by now."

"Nonsense!" Karvajal said jubilantly, "That man, while in the infirmary, is very much alive. No harm is done. You are safe now."

Atti spoke again, not feeling as secure as Karvajal would suggest.

"While that might be true, I need to know. How did I get here?"

"Well, you see Atticus, after you tried a valiant but useless attempt to escape my home and I introduced myself to you, you passed out on the floor due to your injuries and I ordered my medical practitioners to heal your nasty leg wound. After that, we let you rest for a while before bringing you here for the great feast. Now come, eat and diminish your hunger, we have much to discuss."

Atti was sceptical of course, but he ate all the same as his hunger was immeasurable, so he grabbed a leg of turkey and a couple of bread rolls which he slipped into his satchel for later.

Glancing to his right, Atti inspected the gentleman next to him, a tall, broad, strong-looking man with short, brown hair grasping a silver helm that was sitting on the table. In his belt was a sheathed dagger with a golden engraving of a cyclical symbol unrecognisable to Atti. On his back sat a longbow crafted with a black wood and birch string. Along with this, a leather quiver with carefully-crafted arrows which had a roll of cloth just underneath the tip. Also on his belt was a small stick with more cloth over the top. Again, his eyes wandered back to the dagger and its intricacies.

"It means war." Atti looked up to see the soldier peering down at him, "It's Greek, so you might not recognise it. My family comes from those lands but I assure you, I am friendly. Most of the Rangers do not accept this, except Octavius of course, he has trusted me since the start. I am the tactical leader and commander of the Rangers if you will, Marcus Aurelius, at your service."

Atti nodded in return. He strived to appear polite to the Rangers in an attempt to gain their trust and leave the hell he had been trapped in. Sucking up to the commander, who seemed polite enough, he gestured to the strange arrows in Aurelius' quiver.

"Ah. Those are my 'véli pyros', or flaming arrows. I use a torch to set the cloth on the arrows alight before firing them at the enemy. Very useful if your enemy is cowering behind wooden structures."

"Flaming arrows, interesting. You said you come from 'Greece' right? What's it like?"

Aurelius chuckled, saying, "I'm glad you asked Atticus, because my homeland is beautiful. Imagine luscious fields and clear blue skies, marble temples and columns of stone, sculptures and statues populating the town, the Sun God Helios watching over you and protecting you at all times, though I have not and will not visit in a long time. I have no desire to, as I am an Italian now, through and through."

While Aurelius was describing his home-life, Atti looked around for some sort of escape, showing calmness on the outside while his internal panic built up over time, exponentially rising like the lava in a volcano. In the far corner was a stairwell that spiralled up to the ceiling and out of sight. Two armed Rangers stood guard at the bottom of the stairs, each wielding a bow.

Other exits Atti could see included a couple of doors spaced around the hall as well as a large tunnel indented on the east wall. On top of the arch was a phrase which said 'Ala Orientatum', or the Orientation Wing. The words were carved with a sense of delicacy and preciousness, and the curves of the letters twisted fantastically. Guarding the tunnel were three more Rangers, two on either side and one pacing up and down. The darkness inside it seemed to never end, and Atti's curiosity took over briefly. The only other possible escape he could see was a door to his left which he guessed was the kitchen as the door opened constantly for servants and butlers to enter and exit.

"I think Atticus has heard enough, my dear friend." Karvajal's voice struck like a hammer on steel, forcing Atti back to the table he was seated at, trapped between the two enemies of power.

"Oh, of course, my apologies," Aurelius exclaimed, his voice quivering with loyalty and fear.

Karvajal smiled in his unusually friendly manner, and signalled for Aurelius to leave in a polite tone. The broad warrior stood up impressively and moved over to a woman further down the table. Karvajal then turned his attention to the boy next to him, holding a slice of bread which he took a minimal bite out of without breaking eye contact with him.

Atti sat awkwardly in his chair, and he thought that his discomfort must be visible to Karvajal. Trying to contain and collect himself, he sat up straight and took a deep breath, not letting his concern show. Karvajal just continued to smile, his expression inviting and giving out kindness.

"You know, despite what others might say, you look so much like your father."

Atti felt a rush of anger evolve inside him at the mention of his father, and for a second he wished to grasp the knife on the table and slash the neck of Karvajal; being reminded of the story recounted by Numitor only a few weeks before. Karvajal held his chin quizzically, keeping eye contact all the while. Atti calmed himself, not wishing to create more problems for himself.

"Most say I resemble my mother more, though I think you know that already."

Karvajal's face was unreadable, and all Atti was given in return was a kindred smile.

"It is true that I knew your mother Atticus, and yes, she was a wonderful woman whose death pained me as much as anyone else close to her. Such a tragedy, and for you to grow up without her, it must be devastating."

Karvajal's statements were true of course, and Atti assumed that it was a ploy to gain his trust, therefore he stayed sceptical while showing a fake interest so as not to arouse suspicion from the Warmonger.

"Atticus, I want you to understand that you are safe here, and that honesty is valued high here in my fortress. In fact, I created this place so that I could protect and house those in need of assistance, a haven, if you will."

"If you care about peace so much, why kidnap me?"

For a brief moment, Karvajal's expression turned hostile before switching back to his friendly default as if nothing had been said.

"While I agree that some of my guards can be a bit... forceful, my true intention was to make sure you were safe. Now, I know you may distrust me for whatever reason, but I must tell you a story involving your mother which you should hear."

Losing his patience, Atti blurted out, "I've heard it already, and I heard about what you did!"

Karvajal's convivial facade really dropped this time, and he lashed back in anger.

"What *I* did? Your father is the one that left me for dead with a hole in my chest! You want to know the truth? I had no idea Numitor had feelings for her, as well as the fact that my father arranged the marriage with Cecilia's parents! I had no say in the matter, Atticus."

Atti stared at Karvajal's face, trying to see if he was telling the truth. Then he thought of his father and questioned whether he was in the right. But Atti thought better of his only relative and countered Karvajal, saying, "But if that was true, why find my father after all that time?"

Karvajal smiled maniacally, different to his previous, friendlier smiles.

"Because... your father was my friend, your mother too. I had heard that they had birthed a child, and so naturally I visited, to the apparent dislike of Numitor."

Atti shook his head in disbelief, replying, "Father said you threatened him when you arrived, you're lying!"

"You may disbelieve it, but it won't change the past. The truth is the truth, and your father is more ruthless than he lets on. After all, he did win the Trials."

Shock groped Atti and, staggering out of his chair, glanced around worriedly. In his usual, friendly manner Karvajal spoke, "If you are finished, my guards will escort you to your living quarters so you can rest, and reflect on the other lies your father must have told you."

He gestured to two guards who stepped forward and turned to Atti, who looked up with blurred eyes. Shaking his head, he followed the leading guard to his room.

The path was long and nearly every corridor looked identical, each one having a blazing torch every few feet and a rounded wooden door with numerals etched into the front. Atti passed CXVI, CXVII on his left until the guard stopped outside a room numbered CXVIII. He grabbed the stone door knob and pulled open the entrance to where Atti would be staying.

Atti was comforted as he inspected his room; a homely dormitory decorated with a red-sheeted bed and a tall wardrobe as well as candles in holders dotted around. On one side, a sink and a bath, both made out of stainless white marble. A single, circular pillar stood in the centre with depictions of warriors battling. There was also a wooden desk with empty drawers.

Shortly, the guards left the room leaving Atti alone and in peace.

First, he bathed to clear his mind and changed into provided fresh clothes. Atti ultimately wanted to escape, and so his logical thinking was to explore the labyrinth of a fortress and find an exit of sorts. Putting on his sandals, he crept out of his room and peered down the hallway. Atti spotted a guard down the far right, so naturally he departed in the opposite direction, hoping for any sign of escape.

Finding some stairs, Atti descended as fast as possible without making too much noise before reaching a floor marked VI. He would have continued down the stairs, but he thought he heard a few guards ascending in his direction. Frantically, Atti rushed down a corridor past identical doors before he reached a strange tunnel entrance. The tunnel was built out of mossy bricks and it had a stone floor which led to a staircase declining down into darkness.

Could that lead to a sewer?

Atti glanced back before diving down the deep stairs, the light slowly diminishing the deeper he went. Soon, the steps stopped and the ground became level. The thick darkness was so immense. Atti waited a moment for his eyes to adjust before continuing. The hallway seemed similar to the prison he had been kept in earlier; he hoped that it would have an exit he could use to escape. Advancing down the grimy, slime-filled hallway, he thought he saw a cage-like structure at the end, and hence he slowed his pace.

Atti shuddered as something small and hairy brushed past his leg and scurried away from whatever he was walking towards. The begrimed iron bars were all Atti could see, the inhabitant of the cell creeping behind the blackness. Just as he neared the locked door, the ground began to convulse and in only a few seconds the whole mountain was shaking like an oak tree in the wind. After an extreme quake, the iron lock on the cell door bounced and broke, clattering onto the floor.

Atti didn't dare to look back. Swiftly, he ran back up the stairs and into the warmer areas of accommodation as a hurried guard rushed past Atti without a moment's notice. Confused, he retreated to the stairs and climbed up them rapidly. Atti sped up the stairwell and just as his legs were about to give way, he reached the top floor marked I. Taking a moment to regain his breath, he started to hear the shouts and war cries of soldiers in the distance.

Hurriedly, Atti pushed open a wooden door and ran in the direction of the commotion, the mountain quivering violently every few intervals. Reaching the end of the hallway, Atti stepped out into the bright, blinding sunlight, seeing the chaos developing in front of him first-hand.

It was a battlefield. Roman soldiers were climbing up ropes onto the parapets, Rangers letting loose arrow after arrow, most getting caught up in the melee combat. Catapults flung indomitable, heavy boulders at the archer towers, creating catastrophic amounts of destruction. Ballistae were firing hundreds of small, armour-piercing arrows up at the outnumbered Rangers as fast as the Romans could load them. And right in the centre of all the action, with a blood-stained sword and stainless silver helmet was Numitor, slaying soldier after soldier, shouting as he did so. Following close behind, with flourishing attacks was Titus, not caring about the blows he was continuously taking.

Atti froze and gazed out at the havoc burgeoning before his eyes. A gust of wind pulled across his face as a steel-tipped arrow flew past him. He jumped back in surprise, ducking as another flew over his head. Atti turned to see his attacker and, seeing a Roman he shouted, "Hey! I'm one of you!"

Realising that he was wearing the clothes of the Rangers, he crouched behind the parapet and held his heart, taking heavy breaths every few seconds. Suddenly, a Roman soldier leapt onto the ground in front of Atti. He covered his face with his arms in fear, cowering up against the wall.

"Atticus! Are you alright?" a concerned voice asked and, removing his arms he saw Lucien standing in front of him, blood and sweat dripping from his face, his steel sword painted crimson. Blocking an arrow with his shield, the general crouched down next to the scared teenager.

"I... I'm fine Lucien, thank you."

He nodded in return before spotting a Ranger advancing towards them. Spearing him through the heart, Lucien picked up the dead man's sword and threw it to Atti.

"There, to defend yourself," he said before leaving to help in the fight against the Rangers. Flustered, Atti grabbed the blade and hurried after the general. Many arrows rained over Atti like a tidal wave, spurring him to run faster while searching the chaotic scene for his father.

Atti stopped to catch his breath just as a boulder crashed into the parapet, causing the ground underneath him to crumble. Atti's knees buckled and he started to slide down the rubble, scraping his legs and back. As he was about to fall, a strong, firm arm gripped onto his wrist and heaved him up, back onto the fortress wall. Looking up, Atti saw an agitated but worried Numitor, scarred and bloodied as he fell onto his knees.

"Atticus..." he breathed, raising himself back onto his feet.

"Father! Are you alright?"

"I'm fine, don't worry about me. I'm more concerned about you. Why are you here?"

Just as Atti was about to answer, a rogue arrow flew and sunk into Numitor's shoulder, activating excruciating pain.

"No!" Atti shouted as another boulder smashed into the wall, cracking the stone floor beneath them. The parapet crumbled, and Numitor, who was in agonising pain, was launched into a wall which broke apart, causing him to fall off the wall itself.

"Father!"

Atti rushed to the edge as the wall started to dismantle. Another stone boulder crashed into the wall and Atti became off balance. Just as he too was going to fall onto the ground thirty feet below, Lucien grabbed his arm and hoisted him back onto sturdy ground.

"But my father!" Atti pleaded, but Lucien just shook his head and told Atti to run to the forest and escape the battle. He protested to the idea, but as more arrows rained upon them, Atti understood and reluctantly traversed the destroyed stairs, escaping into the nearby forest where he raced as far as he could, the battle fading in the background before he collapsed onto the floor, passing out in an instant, all his surroundings turning to black.

CHAPTER 6 – Tree's Company

Atti stirred as he heard the repeated caw of a bird circling high above the trees around him. The luscious, wet grass was soft to his touch, and through half-open eyes he could see the base of a towering tree ahead of him, at the bottom of which sat a squirrel with a nut in its grip, watching him through curious, beady eyes. A strong, appealing smell wafted off the assortment of strange and wonderful flowers laid out in bunches around the forest while humid residue floated down from the leaves like little raindrops in slow motion.

Groaning obnoxiously, he slowly rose to his feet, spotting the sword he had retrieved laying on the grass next to him. Picking it up, Atti surveyed his surroundings, marvelling at the tranquillity of the forest and its beautiful preservation of nature. In addition to his awe, he felt another, fainter feeling which he could only explain as mystical.

Something was unusual about the forest, or at least it felt that way. The bird above stopped its crying as it swooped down to the ground, snapping up a worm in its beak before retreating up to a branch on a nearby tree. Behind him Atti could hear tiny feet scuffling through the detritus and broken bits of branches layered on the forest floor. Faint sounds of insects humming could be heard, the thin rays of light beaming down upon Atti like a spotlight on a stage, casting a warped shadow at his feet. As he moved forward the squirrel cowered and rushed up the ancient tree to its home in a small, spherical indentation in the aged wood.

The metal hilt of the blade felt weighty in his hand, and the weight of the broadsword felt unnaturally heavy compared to the short swords Atti was used to battling with. Carrying the blade was taxing, hence he sheathed it, to his relief. Free from the burden, Atti ventured into the vast forest he found himself in, lost in a labyrinth of flora.

The forest itself was virtually silent, only the rustle of animals rooting in the underbrush piercing the placid tranquillity. The long, wavering grass underneath his feet was substituted for exposed roots, clumps of twigs and fallen branches. Many various insects dwelt on the ground underneath the canopy of leaves like a sea of bugs. The smell of mint and herbs attracted Atti and drew him towards large bushes populated with colourful berries bearing a pleasant smell. Atti was no longer famished and yet he had a desire to taste the berries before getting distracted by a distressing call of a bird in the far distance.

At this moment the cordial feeling faltered as Atti's fear surfaced unanticipatedly. He spun around hurriedly, the once congenial forest seemed now to be a haven of darkness with unknown areas harbouring additionally unknown characters of danger. The light above seemed to fade and blacken as feelings of hopelessness enveloped him rapidly. The world around him seemed to shift and convulse, as if the very fabric of reality were to shatter; a hammer to glass.

Atti's dread built up momentously and he cowered down to the floor, covering his ears to block out the now deafening, screeching sound resonating throughout the forest. He bowed his head, tears flowing down his face as the world tilted into shadow.

And then, just as abruptly as it had started, the commotion ceased and the forest returned to its original state, the biodiversity unharmed and undeterred by the devastating event Atti had just experienced. Bewildered, he wiped his tears and stood up steadily, his heart beating repeatedly while accelerated.

Shock enveloped him as if he had seen a ghost, the empty silence disconcerting to Atti. The amiable forest relieved him slightly as he gazed at the unchanged forest with bafflement and apprehension. The squirrel sat content, gnawing on the nut in its claws, unaware of the previous happenings. Carefree, the jovial bird once again circled in the sky, searching eagerly for more prey to devour, while Atti clutched his chest, breathing heavily, watching the leaves overhead wave at him, in an assuring way.

Once he had recovered somewhat, Atti felt recomposed and determined, hence he once again chose to search the forest, wishing, hoping for any sign of his father, the Romans or even the Rangers. The toll of his fright felt too great to bear alone.

After a period of journeying, Atti felt as if he had been walking for miles and for nothing. The section of the forest he found himself in seemed almost identical to the location where he started. Accordingly, he felt desperate and forlorn for any sign of help.

As he begrudgingly continued further into the forest, Atti gradually attained the feeling that something or someone was watching him from behind the shadows of the trees, and the coming dusk loomed ever closer, the promise of night permeating Atti with fear once more. His uneasiness was hard to ignore and all he could think about was the potential danger of the forest. Spurred on by worry, Atti reluctantly moved at a quicker pace to the dismay of his already exhausted legs.

The indistinguishable trees and surroundings left no sign of variation and Atti felt at times that he was travelling in circles. The uneven ground covered in roots felt sore on his bare feet, his vision slowly blurred together into a green and brown hue as if he were underwater. Fatigued, Atti collapsed down by a tree, leaning on the uncomfortable, hard bark, only caring for a much-needed rest.

Atti slept through the night, awaking at the crack at dawn. A minute amount of light danced across his battered, dirty face, arousing him from sleep.

Alluvium and leaves filled Atti's once perfect brown 'Roman' hair, soil and mud caking his white and maroon clothes. Barely awake, he stretched his arms upward before glancing around at the forest. Due to his weariness, his alarm was obsolete as he gazed at the strange, tattered figure sitting across from him, staring with hankering blue eyes.

She sat silently, her black hair flowing down to her feet, wearing dilapidated clothes and a frayed tunic. Her sandals were decayed and broken also, but underneath her imperfections and degeneration lay hidden beauty, an innocent soul poorly mistreated.

As Atti's senses came back to him, he gasped and retreated up against the tree, clasping the hilt of his sword at the sight of the dagger held by the girl. He recognised it as the ones carried by the Rangers back at the fortress.

The stranger sat, unmoving, her eyes fixated upon the startled teenager backed up against the fragrant oak tree. Her stillness unnerved Atti but, gaining some courage, he relaxed himself without reducing his vigilance, slowly getting up onto two legs.

The unusual figure simply watched with intrigued pupils, showing no intention of harm, yet Atti was deterred nonetheless.

After a few moments, and the girl had made no sign of attack, Atti started to walk through the forest, when she rose to her feet and moved a few feet behind Atti. Curious, he briskly traipsed forward, wary of his silent stalker following him persistently. Then he stopped and, like a human mirror, the girl stopped also. Fed up with the silence, Atti turned and questioned the girl, "Who are you and why are you here?"

No response. Atti followed up with, "My name is Atticus. Atticus Caeso."

And then, "Can you understand me?"

She made no inclination that she could nor any gesture either. Confused, Atti signalled a speaking movement with his hand, to which the girl just stared. She seemed not sad or happy, scared or relaxed. She seemed lost but curious. Atti then continued to ask questions about her family, home and the reason she was in the forest in the first place. Atti thought of the dangers of the forest, especially come night. Worried, he exclaimed, "We must seek shelter before nightfall hits. If you want safety, you better come with me."

The girl nodded, to Atti's surprise.

"So, you *do* understand me," he whispered before continuing into the depths of the forest.

The pair walked non-stop for five hours until finally Atti found something of note. In a clearing similar to the rest of the forest, an old, abandoned camp lay, to his delight.

The fire had been extinguished, so he commanded the girl to search for firewood while he set up makeshift beds to sleep on. Soon after she returned with a bundle of sticks and kindling, Atti lit the fire and then noticed something unusual about the night sky above.

In the sky there seemed to be miniature, almost green stars blinking intermittently. Unlike stars, the lights moved around slowly, gliding in the thin breeze above the trees. Then, these stars descended, their luminescence shining upon the faces of the parallel figures seated by the fire in the dead of night. As they came closer, Atti realised that they were not stars but actually small bugs, their tails glowing like a radioactive substance.

He reached up to feel one and they dispersed, scattering in the air, creating a blanket of miniature lights. Across from him, the mysterious girl looked up in wonder as if she had never seen anything like it before, as if it were magic. Suddenly, Atti's tiredness disappeared and his hunger diminished. His surprise was echoed in the girl as well, meaning it wasn't just him feeling such sensations.

Soon the fireflies dispersed and the pair's exhaustion returned, hence they laid back and went to sleep, somewhat enchanted. In his sleep, Atti was reminded and haunted by the dark essence that had tortured him previously. Awakened in a dream, he stood in the clearing but during midday, the sky a shade of azure blue, and tranquillity prevailed. Then the same strangeness started again, the peacefulness ruined by a clouding dark force, the trees and the grass turned from a luscious green colour to a violent purple, the whole forest transformed into the chamber of hell.

From miniscule segments a malicious figure began to form in front of him, a slender shape built from the new surroundings. Its face was covered, its body translucent with a shade of dark purple. As the demon-like creature advanced towards him Atti froze, unable to move. Then, once more a deafening screech rang out across the clearing.

The last thing he saw being the landscape in a bright, hopeful green quickly turned to a violent purple. The malevolent figure advanced towards Atti, reaching a violet claw towards him, parts of its skin merging together as it did so. It screeched once again and as it reached Atti; the world faded to black.

Then he awoke for real, the morning light of the dawn bouncing off his sweating body, his breaths heavy and shaking.

The girl was roused from sleep seemingly undeterred from any nightmares she may have had.

She rubbed her eyes tentatively to beat the sun's glare. The forest was placative and still, the only sound coming from the early birds circling once again above the canopy.

Atti's fatigue remained and he felt too tired to walk any further; he stayed in the camp while the girl simply sat and waited as she had done before. The day grew on slowly, with Atti and the girl both sleeping at different times throughout, and the day itself remained uneventful until the late evening when Atti was lying awake, diving into his deepest thoughts. Not knowing if the girl was asleep or not, he voiced his thoughts out into the cool, open night.

"I miss home. I miss the bustling streets of shops and carts, the kind people who cared for me. And most of all, I miss my father. In fact, I bet he is as stressed as me or even more so at trying to find me and bring me back. See, I used to think he didn't care for me as much as Adrian – my brother – which is why he doesn't talk to me as much, but now, now I think it's because he cares for me more and protects me. I think it's only fair if I return the favour though, right?"

There was no response as usual and Atti continued to lie in his makeshift bed, staring up at the twinkling stars above. The hollow silence was calming and unnerving all at once, the pitch-black surroundings possibly harbouring dangerous threats lurking behind the curtains of darkness. He half expected to see small, glowing eyes peering out into the clearing, watching the two intently, waiting for the right chance to strike. Atti lay still nervously, wishing for sleep to overcome him when he heard what sounded like a conversation in the nearby forest.

Alarmed, he got up quietly and reached for his sword, slowly advancing to the direction of the voices, not realising that the girl was watching his moves silently from her bed across the fire. Moving the bushes and low-hanging branches out of his way, Atti began to close in on the speakers behind the bush.

As he got closer, he distinguished one of the men to be Decimus Titus, speaking in his classic, indignant, intelligent tone. The other figure was harder to identify and when Atti could now peer at the men, he could see the unknown person wore a heavy black cloak, casting his face in shadow. His voice was jarring to hear, croaking like an ill frog, his hiss similar to that of a vulture.

When the moonlight shone upon Titus it revealed his many injuries including gashes and scars, arrow wounds and many cuts. In fact, it was surprising that he was able to stand at all. Then he heard the sergeant say, "And my wounds, will you take care of them like you promised?"

The mystery figure cackled hoarsely and replied, "Of course, anything for a customer..."

To Atti's disgust, the cloaked man revealed his ugly, dishevelled claws for hands and started to whisper a saying in a peculiar language. As he said this, a bright green glow appeared, flowing out of his crooked fingers which seeped into Titus like verdant vines of purity. Shockingly, by this strange magic, Titus' wounds started to heal rapidly, his cuts and scars sealing up and repairing as if they had never been there.

In surprise, Atti gasped, stepping on a branch and snapping it in two. Alerted, Titus turned his head to where Atti was standing just as the boy started to run in the opposite direction. He ran swiftly, avoiding hanging branches and obstructing trees, hoping that he wasn't being chased.

Then, arriving at the camp he finally stopped, catching his breath. He looked back for a second to see if the coast was clear before falling back into his bed relaxedly. Once his breathing had become calmer and his head had stopped hurting, Atti glanced over to the bed across the fire. Suspiciously he couldn't see anyone inside, hence he got back up and strolled over to find it strangely vacant. Now alone and remarkably worried, Atti sat back down on his bed and gazed upward again at the shimmering sky, the stars illuminating the path ahead, the path to the end.

Atti's dreams were darkened that night as his thoughts wandered from his father to the missing, unusual girl to the extraordinary event he had just witnessed.

Could that have been... Magic? he wondered, and soon the night above turned to a bright, early dawn.

CHAPTER 7 – The Spectral Cave

The harsh morning sunlight once again woke Atti who groaned as he rolled out of the makeshift bed he had made for the camp. He shielded the blinding light with his bruised hand, wincing as he did so. His whole body was seared with general pain, but despite this Atti felt an urge to be active, to do something in the day.

Firstly, he was incredibly hungry. After standing up painfully and reaching for the sword he had acquired, he hauled a cloth sack that he had crafted over his shoulder and journeyed out into the open forest in search of some sort of food, whether it would be from an animal or plant of any kind. At this point Atti was too deprived of food to care about what he found as long as it was edible.

Fortunately, Matteo had taught him a few tricks about foraging in the wild, the first one being avoiding most berries as they were usually poisonous.

The forest itself was difficult to traverse, the uneven ground putting strain upon Atti's bare feet. He was searching for about an hour and had come across nothing except a squirrel and a few small birds. Atti's craving for food grew worse as the morning disappeared and was replaced by the afternoon.

Then, just as he was considering returning back to the camp, Atti spotted a deer lying on the floor, a couple of arrows in its side, crimson blood dripping down its underbelly. His arms weak and weighty, Atti struggled to lift the deer, so using his sword he skinned the deer and cast it aside, precisely cutting into the carcass and pulling it out, placing it on the skin that lay flat on the grass beside him. He then continued to wrap the meat up tidily with the skin before putting it into the sack he had conveniently carried.

Not wanting the meat to spoil, Atti hurried back to the camp as quickly as possible, while he thought about who must have killed the deer and why they had left it there.

The arrows seem similar to those of the Rangers, which would mean that some of them are in the forest with me. I better watch out.

By the time he had returned, the sun had started to lower and Atti's hunger was critical. He unwrapped the carcass and reached for a long stick which he stuck through it and laid it across some brushwood as a spit. Lighting the fire with a piece of flint and his blade, Atti twisted the deer repeatedly, the heat wafting up into his face making him sweat.

Soon the deer was cooked and, stabbing it with his sword, he bit into it enthusiastically, the taste enlightening and much-needed. After he had eaten almost the entire carcass, he stayed awake for a short while before taking an all-important rest.

When dawn came and Atti awoke, he decided that it was finally time that he searched for his father, hoping that he was still alive somewhere nearby.

Full up from the night before, Atti geared up and sheathed his sword, prepped to set off on his new quest of fulfilment. He started in a direction opposite to the one he arrived in and vowed to not stop until he found either signs of civilization or a place of interest.

Each section of the eternal forest seemed unnaturally identical, each tree and branch the same as before and sometimes Atti wondered if he was actually moving anywhere at all.

After a walk that spanned countless hours, Atti finally noticed light at the end of the forest, an exit to this seemingly never-ending hellscape. There seemed to be an opening ahead basking in pure sunlight. Motivated by the promise of an exit, Atti ran towards the light desperately, desiring an end to his forestral torment.

As he neared the edge of the forest, he lost his breath and collapsed onto the grass in front of him, the radiant sun shining upon him like a spotlight. Now eager to explore a new area that wasn't full of trees, he got back up and surveyed the surroundings he found himself in.

The land was open and flattened, the long grass waving in the slight breeze flowing freely, unobstructed by tall trees. A few hazardous ferns populated the mostly empty area, swarms of tiny bugs inhabiting the tight crevices in the ground.

Ahead of Atti, standing out from the rest of the green scenery was a large opening to an enormous stone cave, one misshapen and crooked, the tunnel too dark to see through. The cave entrance stood at least twenty feet tall and the gaping hole reminded Atti of gigantic monsters with gargantuan jaws which he had heard about in mythological stories. It was mostly made up of a greyish stone with diagonal patterns of granite dotted about and a darker, basaltic rock further into the cave. It was a mystery how the effulgent sun wasn't able to illuminate the entire insides of the secret cavern that just seemed to exist atop the luscious, natural landscape.

The whole structure felt ancient in some way but also magical, causing Atti to stare in wonder from his position in front of it. As he was doing so however, a fierce predator stalked the forest behind Atti, watching him with greedy intent. It came closer, and as he was entranced by the mystical cave, Atti was unaware of the animal preparing to strike. A few feet away from the unsuspecting target, the bear reared itself onto its hind legs and growled intimidatingly, taking a swipe at Atti with a sizable paw.

Just in time, Atti ducked out of the way, broken out of the trance. He stared up, horrified at the beast which was snarling at him ferociously. Drawing his sword, Atti slashed at the bear, slicing its front leg, though the creature seemed unharmed. Caught off guard, Atti was smacked to the ground by the bear, its sharp claws digging into his side. His sword was launched out of his grip, and Atti was left on the ground, defenceless. The boy scrambled backwards as the bear advanced vehemently, snapping its jaws wildly, getting awfully close to Atti's legs.

The bear was almost on top of him now and Atti felt hopeless. He was bathed in the shadow of the beast, blocking the promising sun. As it brought its jaws down, viciously growling, terrifyingly, Atti silently prayed, hoping he would be able to see his father for just one more time.

Suddenly, out of the corner of his eye, a blurred figure wielding a brass knife leapt across him and onto the indomitable bear. The figure yelled as it vigorously stabbed the creature in the eye causing it to yelp in pain. Frightened and injured, the bear released Atti, dropping him onto the hard ground before running off into the forest. Atti honed his senses and took deep breaths before looking across at his saviour.

There, standing still in front of him panting heavily, holding a bronze knife in one hand was the mystery girl who had accompanied him for no more than two nights. Her tattered, black hair swayed in the wind, a stream of sweat pouring down from her brows glistening in the refreshing sunlight. Bewildered, Atti spluttered, "You, *you* saved me. You *saved* me. Thank you."

And then to his prodigious surprise the girl answered, "No problem, Atti, was it?"

The girl's voice was soft and well-spoken but had a hint of joking sarcasm, revealing some of the reason why she had remained silent, or at least Atti guessed so. He nodded in response through habit while staying motionless, his mouth automatically gaping open. Atti attempted to speak but his words fell short and he made no inclination of movement or liveliness.

"I am sorry about how I acted earlier. I admit it was childish of me to ignore you but I needed to see if I could trust you, Atti. My name is Ennia, by the way," she said calmly and hospitably as she stuck out her hand in order to shake Atti's hand.

At first, he simply looked at her hand while his brain slowly turned trying to comprehend what had just happened. After a few seconds he shook his head and apologised before shaking Ennia's hand.

"Nice to meet you Ennia, I have a lot of questions..."

"Same here, so it would be nice to get acquainted. But first, let's find some shelter."

Atti nodded in agreement before gesturing toward the huge, abnormal cave that lurked ominously beside the grassy area. The two started on the path to the cave, silence replacing the lack of communication between them until they neared the cave entrance.

"This place is huge!" Ennia exclaimed, rushing up to the walls and examining its structure, feeling the texture of the different stones etched into the cave wall. The deeper they went the less light accompanied them which unnerved Atti considerably.

"I don't think we should go in too far," he stated, "I haven't got anything to light up the area."

"Maybe you're right, but I still want to explore. Why don't you grab some kindling from the forest? *If* you stop moaning about the dark," Ennia replied, before stopping and leaning on the side of the cave.

"I liked it better when you didn't speak," he mumbled to himself before heading back out into the midday sun.

After gathering the necessary items and setting up a temporary camp a few feet into the cave, Atti sat down by the fire and took delight in finally resting. Ennia sat across from him cradling what looked like a blanket made of leaves and straw.

"So..." Atti prompted, "What is your story? Why were you in the forest?"

"It's a long story, you do not want to hear it," she replied definitively.

"I do, trust me."

"Okay..., but I want to hear your story first..."

Atti agreed with content before recounting how he had been captured by the Rangers in his house before having dinner with Octavius Karvajal, up until the siege by the Romans, when he escaped. Of course, he left out some details – including his relation to the Romans – but the basics were all in his retelling.

After he was finished Ennia scoffed, "Quite a tale you have, but most would not believe it."

"It's true, I assure you. Now, your story?"

Ennia rolled her eyes and reluctantly began her tale.

"Well, my story begins quite similar to yours. I was also captured by the Rangers – funnily enough. The reason, I am still quite unsure of, but that's beside the point. This was before you were captured as it was a while before I escaped. Those wretched soldiers kept me in a gross, grimy cell so far underground there was no fresh air anywhere, I almost suffocated to death because of it. Considering I was a weak, defenceless girl this was overkill, and torture!

Every so often while I was down there some old man – the Warden I think they called him – would visit and pressure me with questions I knew nothing about. Every time I told him I knew nothing and every time, without fail, he would torture me, cutting me with his stupid bronze dagger. Scarred me so many times I lost count."

At that moment, Ennia pulled back her tattered sleeves to reveal to Atti the numerous scars on her arm, the sealed cuts plaguing her body.

She continued her story.

"Whenever I was alone, I kept trying to improve, to become stronger. So that one day I could kill that man and reap in his sorrow. It was what motivated me to keep going. Not the thought of escape, the thought of murder. After months had gone by I thought I wouldn't see the day, but then, on the day of the siege, the mountain shook and the lock on my cell broke and fell. I seem to remember hearing what sounded like someone rushing off and up the stairs. Once I was out of my cell I felt freer than ever before.

The first thing I did was look for that bastard, the Warden. I soon found the coward panicking at the thought of battle. I disarmed him easily and took his bronze knife; I was about to chop his snivelling head clean off when Rangers reinforcements arrived.

I knew I had a choice. Either risk my freedom to kill the man I hated most or live to kill him another day. I made my decision and ran, escaping through a secret tunnel I happened to find in one of the vacant prison cells. It led out the side of the mountain and into the forest where I ran into you, cold and afraid and terrified for my life. I didn't speak because you were wearing their clothes, but after I had left you I realised you cared for me, so I came looking for you. That's my story."

She smiled briefly before returning to her neutral tone.

Atti sat silently throughout, intrigued and hurt by the girl's story. The pair continued to chat about their recent experiences before both turning to sleep after a short while.

During the night, the cave drastically decreased in temperature, the interior becoming frozen to the touch. Shivering awake, Atti got up and looked around the cave and into the darkness. Perplexed, he could have sworn he heard a voice calling him from further in the cave.

Apprehensively, he began to explore without awaking Ennia, his intrigue pushing him to search for the cause of the mysterious, distressed voice. Deeper inside, the cave shrunk; its walls carving upwards to a low ceiling.

Unexpectedly, the voice cried out again, sounding like a baby bird crying out for its mother. Atti kept at his constant pace staying vigilant, the darkness concealing the way ahead.

"Save me!" it called, and Atti flinched at the sound. He reached a junction leading to two different entrances inside the cave. After waiting for a minute, he managed to deduce that the voice was coming from the left passageway. Not wanting to waste more time Atti dashed down the hall, slowing once he came to a particularly thin, low section of the cavern, forcing him to crawl on his hands and knees over hard jutting rocks and many bugs which dwelled inside the restricted cavity.

Carbon residue dropped frequently from the small stalactites dotted throughout the cave. Atti reached the end of the cramped spaces, bumping his head on the rocks before heaving himself up with grazed hands and knees.

He found the chamber to be substantially spacious, the height of which was impossible to estimate. It was shaped circularly, with the lowest point being in the centre, a crystal-clear lake settling there. Sharper, more pointed stalagmites and stalactites populated the area. Copious amounts left hanging from the ceiling and rising from the ground as if the whole chamber would chomp together like the jaw of a dragon. It was virtually silent, the only sound being the drip of acid from the tips of the spikes upon the lake.

Atti gingerly made his way down to the lake, stepping attentively on the slippery rocks of varying shapes and sizes. He gasped as he stumbled, nearly falling onto an exposed spike protruding out from the ground. Atti clasped onto a nearby stalagmite for balance, swaying back and forth before he felt secure. Continuing, he gradually descended to the lake where the voice called out once again, louder than previous times.

I must be getting closer.

Then, arriving at the pool of water, he stared out into its murky depths. Looking down, he saw his own tainted reflection staring back at him, the water unmoving. Leaning over to grab a pebble, Atti skimmed it across the lake, watching it bounce once, twice, before it sank depressingly to the bed. Just as he started wondering how to get across, an emphatic scream made him jump in shock.

Unequivocally it came from the other side of the lake, prompting Atti to start clambering across the edges of the lake, gripping onto jutting rocks so as not to fall in to a depth of which he had no idea. His bare feet seared as he crossed the rock wall that bent round the border of the lake. The climb was brief but for Atti it felt like hours, holding overwhelming fear of falling into the peculiar pool of water inches beneath his feet. Triumphantly and hurriedly, he jumped down onto the safe ground on the opposite side of the lake just as another cry for help rang out.

Around him stalactites blocked all the paths except for one which led into an even darker hallway leading to a smaller chamber. After once again crawling through the passageway, Atti surfaced into the new section which seemed to have no more entrances or exits. It was misshapen with a low roof, its walls illuminated from the light in the centre of the den. In the middle was a flickering lantern sitting upon a bluish grey pedestal made of a sort of marble. He came to the lantern and lifted it by its handle, watching the light spin and bounce off the ridged cave walls.

"Where are you?" he whispered, searching around the chamber for the source of the voice.

"Help!" it cried causing Atti to rush up to the wall where the sound was coming from. With his one free hand, he slammed his fist against it, wincing after hitting the impenetrable stone. Then, unexpectedly, the shouting stopped and changed to a burst of hurtful laughter; the scared, hopeless voice distorting to what sounded like a cackling hyena, ringing aloud throughout the cave. Staring straight forward Atti could see what seemed like a broad, thumping, monstrous creature advancing towards him at a steady pace.

He took a step back slowly, panic gradually overtaking his mind. The monster came dangerously closer until it was nearly fully visible. It then crashed through the stone as if it were paper, roaring magnificently. Because of the lack of light, the creature remained in shadow, making it difficult for Atti to see where it was. It then hit its head on the low ceiling comically before reaching a hand out to grab Atti.

Just as its ugly, bulbous palm lowered to get him, Atti was yanked by his shirt and pulled out of harm's way. It veered its rounded head, its bellowing permeating throughout the entire cave to the point of the ceiling starting to shake. Atti turned to see that Ennia had grabbed him, bruised from her own adventures in the night.

With mutual understanding, they both ran back through a different passage to the one Atti had entered, one he had not seen before. The path was much wider, allowing the cave monster to enter with only a slight difficulty.

Enraged, it lunged at the sides, clumps of rock crumbling and falling to the ground. The pair continued to dash through the cave, searching for the area they had entered whilst the creature roared ferociously behind them. With as much speed as humanly possible, the two navigated the cavern, its many paths and chambers acting like a never-ending labyrinth.

"That's twice I've saved you!" Ennia shouted from in front of him.

As he started to tire, Atti cried out in pain, slowing down to walking speed and leaning on the rigid cave wall beside him.

"We can't stop now, Atti! Do you really want to be monster food?"

Looking back, he sighed before hauling himself back onto his feet as they continued through the last passageway, the dim daylight seeping through the cracks in the cramped path up ahead.

Relieved and exceedingly exhausted, the pair collapsed onto the soft, luscious grass just outside the cave.

From deep inside the cavity of mysticism and wonder, a final roar echoed from the beast of the dungeon, unsatiated and in turn, hungry for its prey.

Atti stared back at the cave which began to crack, the monster's attacks having weakened the support of the cave walls. The roof of the Spectral Cave crumbled inwards and the creature was buried inside, doomed to never see the light of day ever again.

CHAPTER 8 – Unlikely Allies

Late evening had arrived in the quaint town of Socratis, the villagers had started to close their shops and head back home ready to enjoy the night's sleep or go to the local bathhouses to relax. These options were nothing but luxurious dreams for Numitor who paced around agitatedly in his new briefing room in the great palace after his inevitable promotion to governor – Cicero had no known heir to relieve his title to.

Though he had had his success in the siege against the Rangers, they had gained few prisoners. Octavius Karvajal had escaped and worst of all his own son was now missing. Most days he was in a furious state, snapping at nearly everyone that spoke to him, some days where he would virtually pull his own hair out.

Countless patrols had been sent out to find Atti, spanning a wide perimeter around Socratis, all of them returning with little to no information or results.

Sighing heavily, he sat down in his commodious leather seat and leaned back comfortably, looking out of his window at the peaceful, prospering town. He reached forward for his glass of wine and finished its contents steadily. Breathing rhythmically, Numitor calmed himself and watched the bustling streets from his window. He slumped back, his angered thoughts surfacing to the front of his mind.

He thought of Atti and every location he might be. After the siege when they had reunited, Lucien had told him what had occurred after he had fallen off the parapet. Lucien had ordered Atti to escape into the forest and afterwards had regrouped with some soldiers to capture a few of the Rangers who were still alive and hadn't fled the fortress or perished. Then the general had searched for Numitor, finding him collapsed on the ground beside the crumbled wall, clutching his leg in agony.

Reliving the memory he rubbed his leg, flinching as it flared up in pain. Though many had suggested him unfit to rule, Numitor had insisted on leading both a search for his son and an eventual final confrontation against his old nemesis Octavius Karvajal. Just as he started thinking of ways to destroy him, Numitor's good friend and second-in-command Lucien entered through the side door, his broadsword strapped to his back, reflecting the light from the candle sitting on the oak desk.

He spoke just as the door behind him lightly shut, "Numitor, I mean, *Governor* Numitor. I bring news."

"By all means speak Lucien, and please you are my oldest ally and dearest friend, it's Numitor to you."

"Thank you, our friendship is everything to me. Especially now that you are governor after all."

Numitor nodded in return, gesturing for Lucien to continue.

"Oh right, of course. One of the scout teams reported back last night. They had no luck finding Atticus but they did stumble across one of the Rangers' temporary camps. They must be hiding there after the fall of their fortress. What should be our plan of action Numitor?"

There was a small pause while he pondered his options before replying, "Unfortunately, as we do not know of Atticus' fate, we must refrain from battle for the time being, especially as we have lost contact with Sergeant Titus. In the meantime, before he returns, send all of our remaining soldiers back out into the forest. I want my son back here in Socratis as soon as possible, or at the very least any news about his outcome or whereabouts. It is unbearable not being able to contact him."

Lucien nodded in approval, and just as he turned to leave Numitor declared, "I promise you Lucien, Octavius will pay for his despicable actions. The nerve he has to kidnap my own son! Evil like him must be eradicated, I just hope you will join me in this."

"Numitor, if you are so adamant about this, let me personally take over the search for Atticus while you plan and prepare for a final push against Octavius with Titus."

"You would do that for me?" Numitor said gratefully, standing up jauntily and grasping Lucien's hand.

"Of course, anything for a friend."

"Thank you Lucien, truly."

With that interaction, Lucien returned to his own quarters to sleep the night off whilst Numitor sat back in his chair and stared off into the horizon, wondering where in all of Italy his son could be.

The golden sun was shone high in the morning and Atti's feet felt sore and numb after walking all through the night. Leaning on a pine tree, he collapsed by its trunk. He and Ennia had been walking nonstop for almost eight hours at this point, and he felt like he couldn't move a muscle further. In their search they had come across nothing as they probed the border of the forest, not daring to stray away from its side.

The sky was bright and hopeful, but it did not reflect the pair's sense of failure. With no camp the two lay uncovered and exposed at the bases of trees for the duration of the night, waking in the early morning as the parched sun had just started to rise.

"We'll have to leave now if we want to get anywhere by nightfall," Ennia asserted, searching for her bronze dagger which she had placed underneath a specifically spiky plant.

"I can barely walk and you want to spend *another* day searching for nothing! It's a useless caper," Atti replied agitatedly, gesturing towards his legs and throwing a small clump of dirt at his neighbouring tree.

Ennia sighed and grabbed Atti by his legs, dragging him away from the forest.

"I guarantee we will find something out in the plains. All we need to do is leave this stupid forest and we *will* find civilization or accommodation of some kind! Mark my words."

"If we leave the safety of the forest, the Romans won't be able to find me!"

"What?!" Ennia shouted, puzzled and annoyed, grabbing Atti's shirt and demanding him to explain.

"Okay, okay! I didn't want to bring it up because of what you said, but my father is Numitor Caeso."

"Who?" Ennia replied in even more bafflement, taking a step back from Atti.

"Numitor Caeso, former quaestor of Governor Cicero, now newly appointed governor of Socratis and its province, servant of the Roman Empire."

Ennia breathed heavily before screaming, "Your father... is a *governor*?!"

"Yes, Ennia. I am sorry I didn't mention it sooner. I hope this doesn't change your opinion of me."

"You're fine, Atti. Even though you waited till the 'opportune moment' to mention it," she scoffed, gesturing for Atti to follow her out of the forest before mumbling, "Besides, everyone's got a secret."

For the next four hours the pair walked over the hills in silence, Ennia still mad at Atti's withholding of startling information.

They journeyed for almost half the day, desperate for a sign of anything unnatural, until they started to suffer from a lack of water.

"We'll die of dehydration for sure!" Atti called out from behind exasperatedly, but to no response.

Atti was used to this treatment by now, but then he realised Ennia was refraining from speaking for a different reason. Looking ahead he could see the girl had stopped abruptly at the edge of the hill they were upon.

"What is it?" he questioned, limping over to her, glancing over to see what she was staring at. A stream, filled with gushing, pristine clear water. Nothing had seemed so pleasant to Atti as he rushed down with eager enthusiasm and leapt into the stream, soaking himself and the surrounding river bank.

Ennia soon accompanied him, bathing and drinking the heavenly liquid that they now had in abundance. Atti felt as if he were floating on the clouds of heaven.

For a short period of time, the two teenagers laughed and felt alive in the water before exiting and drying off promptly. Soon after, with heightened spirits, they both decided to follow the river west in the hope of finding some source of food and shelter.

They had not walked for long when Atti spotted a place of interest. It looked to be a camp of some sort, temporarily set up by the river. An active one by the look of the smoke billowing up from a campfire. They crept up to it stealthily, peering at the people going to and from the tents. The inhabitants were Rangers, each one mostly armed with swords or bows, the largest tent marked with a unique symbol, possibly for their leader, Atti guessed.

Crouching behind a rounded bush, Atti stuck his head through the sticks, spines and leaves, familiarising himself with the camp. In the camp he saw multiple temporary tents and a tall, wooden watchtower which inhabited a particularly stern Ranger. He carried a bow and more of the fire arrows Atti had been shown earlier. He pulled back quickly once he thought the guard had seen him.

"Well, what do we do?" Ennia asked, peering through the bush once Atti had moved out of the way.

"I don't know but…"

His words were cut off as a tall, broad Ranger stepped behind their bush, viewing them from above and chuckling in a deep voice.

"Well, what do we have here?"

Atti unsheathed his sword subtly, hiding his rising fear. He moved next to Ennia, glaring at the Ranger staring down at them. Ennia also drew her weapon, breathing heavily and slowly lifting to her feet.

"Easy, easy. It's alright. We are quite friendly. You seem lost and starved, it would be our pleasure to house you for however long you need, honestly."

The pair remained sceptical but nevertheless they followed the man to the humble camp.

"Luckily we have two spare tents where you may stay."

Atti hospitably nodded in gratitude before checking out his quarters. Later, they were given fresh clothes and a hot dinner in the evening. Atti had guessed that they had been so welcoming because he wore the clothes of the Rangers and in addition the fact that this specific subset of Rangers did not know who he was and his relationship to the Romans.

The two of them gladly enjoyed the food and comfort especially after having barely survived the previous week. During their dinner of wild deer and chicken along with some vegetation found bordering the river, the outsiders were introduced to the temporary leader of the survivor camp, a man Atti recognised, a man who could be problematic to their situation.

The voluminous warrior greeted them both from across the table, introducing himself as Aurelius, someone Atti remembered from his dinner with Karvajal.

Aurelius knows who I am! He'll probably rat me out and dispose of me knowing the attention I will bring from the Romans. I have to get out of here, but how?

"Hello," Ennia said with a hint of hatred and taciturn manner, staring him down with a stern, unbroken gaze. Atti didn't speak but inclined his head towards Aurelius, him doing the same.

"Nice to meet your acquaintance once again dear Atticus. And please, do not think that we have any preference to kill you or cast you away. Us Rangers are a very welcoming group and we would gladly bring you in as one of ours for the time being. If it is okay with you of course."

Atti felt as if he were being led into a trap, despite him reluctantly going along with Aurelius' plans.

That night he slept alone, on a comfortable bed staring up at the tent roof overhead. He pondered over whether he should trust Aurelius and the Rangers and weighed up both the pros and cons. So far, he had gained nothing but warm hospitality, food and no hostility and he also felt safe when accompanied with the Rangers, but he knew his father was out there somewhere searching for him, and though Numitor had never cared much for Atti in recent years, the boy had a feeling his father was doing everything in his power to find him.

Getting up and out of his quarters he searched for a piece of paper and something to write with before returning to his tent. Then, under the light of a lantern he began to write a letter to Socratis for his father, for which he spent the whole night working on, correcting himself over and over until he was happy with what he had written.

Numitor was back in his new office, a painting of himself now cast upon the east wall. He had endured a terrible night's sleep, his eyes droopy and baggy. Slumping in his chair, he clasped another wine glass and slurped its contents, repeating the day before. His cycle was broken however when a stern Decimus Titus entered clutching his safely sheathed sword's hilt while his other hand remained secretly behind his back.

"Ah, Decimus, you have returned. To what do I owe the pleasure?"

"There are no pleasures in a war, Governor, but for victories there are plenty, and a victory we may have soon."

"How do you mean Sergeant?" Numitor questioned, placing his glass of wine on the table beside him and standing up while wincing to greet his guest.

"I have decided that now is the time to reveal my weapon, my secret which I had hidden from the prying eyes of Cicero, you and the entire Roman Empire."

"Tell me at once what you refer to Decimus!"

"Not a what, but a who. And all in due time. In fact, I shall show you."

And with his comment, Titus opened the door to an odd figure, a stooped, hunched, cloaked creature which only revealed its claw-like hands.

"This is the Warlock," stated Titus, "A creature capable of harnessing the peculiar phenomenon we have come to know as Dark Magic. His manipulation of the elements allows us to make the impossible possible, giving us a huge advantage towards any of our adversaries. He truly is our secret weapon to win this fight!"

The governor stepped back, aghast, examining the cloaked figure that stood in front of him. Stuttering he exclaimed, "Of course, I believe you but by all means, give me a demonstration!"

Titus nodded accordingly and on his signal the Warlock planted his feet and started to speak in a strange language. As it did so astonishing energy started projecting from his claws, rings of green light circling his hands. Then with a singular word, he flung the beams at Numitor's chair, striking it and alighting it immediately, the chair emitting a threatening green flame.

"Astounding," Numitor whispered. He was flabbergasted at the sight he had just witnessed.

"Absolutely astounding."

Titus signalled for the Warlock to leave. Just as he was about to depart, he turned to Numitor and spoke with a snarl, "I am leaving my friend here in Socratis for the time being, I hope you enjoy his company."

"And what of you, Decimus?" Numitor questioned, sitting back in his chair.

"I am going to kill the Rangers," the sergeant stated, smirking as he did so, exiting the office with an obnoxious grandiose.

Just outside the office, through the open window the clouds above congregated as lightning formed high up, linking together the malevolent weather forming overhead the quiet town, as if something had caused the weather to change. As if it were a warning of the very dark days to come.

CHAPTER 9 – The Night Terror

Dear Father,

If you are alive and well somewhere, I am writing to inform you that I am well after the attack on the Rangers' fortress. My capture was harsh and rough, although I was greeted with unexpectedly welcome arms. I had a meeting with your old enemy Octavius Karvajal. I was sceptical of his antics and adamant that I did not let slip anything that he could have been listening for.

After this meeting, I was given a room and fresh clothes. I do not think they were expecting a siege, or at least so soon. When the siege took place, I was deep underground in the mountain when I felt it shake, prompting me to return to the surface. I met up with Lucien and you know most of what happened next.

When you fell, Lucien instructed me to flee into the forest which I did. After waking up I wandered the forest for many days. I became lost.

At the minute I camp alone in an abandoned mine in a cave. I think I am east of where I started but I am truly unsure. In the morning I will leave and get this to you. I miss you every day, father. We will reunite.

From your son, Atticus

A tti took the makeshift pen off of the page and placed it on the side table in the middle of his tent. He got up out of his bed, letter in hand before laying it beside the pen. He sealed it in some parchment before leaving it on the table.

Undressing, he slid back into his bed and hauled over the cover. Atti yawned loudly before blowing out the candle inside the lamp hanging above him. Then, consumed in darkness, he fell into a much needed, comfortable sleep.

The next morning Atti awoke early to the sound of birds cawing, who were circling overhead. The shimmering sun beamed through the small cracks in the tent, somewhat illuminating the interior of Atti's accommodation. He got dressed hastily into fresh clothes that had been prepared for him the night before.

Leaving his tent, he was introduced to the few Rangers that were awake and ready by Aurelius who complimented the morning and greeted Atti.

"Good morning, Aurelius," Atti said with a monotonous tone, staring blankly up at the strong, fearsome warrior who had a surprising sense of friendliness about him.

"Now Atticus, I must tell you that if you are to live here with us or even back in Socratis, you need to know how to survive a war, and to do that...You need to know how to fight. Do not worry, you are in safe hands!"

Chuckling, he strolled over to a crate not too far away and grabbed a sword, gesturing for Atti to grab his. Once they were both ready, Aurelius planted his feet and assumed his stance, peering over at Atti to see his moves. Atti gripped his stolen Ranger blade and wielded it carefully, holding it at his hip height.

"Spar much Atticus?"

"You're about to find out, Ranger," he exclaimed calmly, remembering his sessions with Matteo, the advice and lessons he had been told.

With his feet a healthy length apart, Atti lifted the blade up in front of him so that it sat across his face. Sweat started to drip from his face as the relentless heat of the sun shone down upon him.

Across from him, Aurelius smiled, not moving an inch. He stood unmoving, not breaking eye contact with Atti as if he were waiting for something, for Atti to strike first.

He's not gonna get the chance!

Atti breathed in heavily, feeling the weight of the blade in his now sweaty hands.

The sky above was clear and as blue as the sea, few clouds crowding the beauty of the smooth view. Distracted, Atti turned his attention to his temporary foe, still waiting coolly a few feet from him.

Enraged, Atti leapt forward speedily, lifting his sword over his head and bringing it down upon the Ranger who raised his broadsword at that same exact moment, blocking the attack with ease. The two blades locked, Atti's force weakening as Aurelius gained the theoretical high ground in the battle.

Stepping back Atti readied himself, slowing his breathing and not breaking eye contact with Aurelius. This time the Ranger struck, dashing forward with quick feet, raising his own blade. Confused why Aurelius would copy his move, Atti went to block the attack. To his surprise, the Ranger changed his trajectory, bringing his blade back and striking Atti in the chest with its hilt. He keeled over in pain as Aurelius hung the blade just over Atti's neck.

"It looks like you have much to learn, Atticus, but I would be glad to teach you, and your friend if she wishes."

Atti glared up at Aurelius with frustration but also newfound respect, a bond of trust starting to form between the two. He stood back up and sheathed his sword, leaving the camp to get away from the Rangers for a moment.

Atti wandered and found a nearby hill. Striding up the side, he sat at the peak and gazed out across the valley, the morning sun casting its light out onto the plains. The towering mountains stood tall as silhouettes in the far distance. The cawing birds flew over his head, swooping down to catch their prey.

As the day wore on and the sun traversed the sky, both Atti and Ennia trained with the Rangers, improving their combat skills. Atti learned how to properly wield a sword without losing energy, mastering the ways of the blade by training with a dummy made of hay and sticks which the Rangers had set up by the camp.

Ennia on the other hand opted to train with a sleek, wooden bow carved out meticulously by the Rangers. She practised firing arrows at coloured targets, honing her aim.

However, she wasn't allowed to use the flaming arrows just yet, to her disappointment. Atti spoke to Ennia less and less, and he became unaware of whether she felt inclined to escape the Rangers and return to wherever she came from.

The week passed swiftly and Atti became more safe and secure. He found that he began to trust the Rangers evermore, especially Aurelius who always checked up on him every day as if he was ordered to.

Another Ranger which he had become fond of was a young warrior named Tatius Marcellus. He was a similar height to Atti, though he was around five years older, and had golden brown hair which reflected the sunlight as well as his bright blue eyes that were the same shade as the crystal-clear sea along the coast of Italy. His face was dotted with spots and he had a slit through his left eyebrow.

One noon Atti awoke to find Marcellus sharpening his sword on the grindstone outside his tent. Grabbing his own sword, Atti greeted him and sat on the log beside him.

"Afternoon Tatius."

"Good afternoon to you too. Did you hear about tonight?"

"Tonight? What's happening tonight?" Atti questioned inquisitively.

Marcellus smiled and looked to the sky as if expecting something to happen.

"So, Aurelius hasn't told you yet? Interesting. You see tonight a scout team is being sent out to search for the rest of our group, and if you want, you can come too, if you aren't too scared that is."

He smirked and continued to grind his sword against the hard steel, watching as sparks flew off and into the surroundings, creating a horrible screeching noise.

"I'll go, I'm not afraid. I'll show you Tatius, you'll see."

"I'm sure I will, friend. Now go and get prepared, we leave at sundown."

Atti nodded and returned to his tent, gathering his provisions and other things he would need for the hike. Then he visited the communal kitchen for a bite to eat and continued to train throughout the rest of the afternoon.

Atti entered Ennia's tent briefly while passing to ask if she was coming along. She shook her head solemnly, saying that she would prefer to spend the night alone. Understandingly, Atti left her to her own devices and went in search of Aurelius.

Soon the sun lowered and nightfall was incoming. Meeting up with the crew which consisted of himself, Aurelius, Marcellus and four others, they left as darkness came and paced hastily in search of any sign from their fellow Rangers. Atti carried his sword in hand at all times, a dagger in his belt along with a torch. The limited group of seven moved for an hour before stopping at the edge of a forest which appeared vastly different to the one Atti had spent his time in.

The trees were thinner and bore yellow leaves, a few sparrows nesting in the higher branches. They mostly moved silently, save for the odd branch a soldier would step on. Owls hooted, crickets chirped in their familiar voice and woodpeckers tapped against the extensive trees.

The forest felt dangerously alive, and Atti felt as if they were being watched by a hundred beady eyes.

"Where are we?" Atti whispered to Marcellus who shook his head.

Ahead of them, Aurelius stopped abruptly and raised his fist. Looking back at the group he whispered, "We are being stalked. Follow me and try not to alert their attention."

"Who is it?" one Ranger asked, unsheathing his blade and brandishing it skilfully.

But before anyone could answer a daunting howl pierced the silence. The group all twisted their necks worriedly, peering into the darkness with hope of spotting the source of the noise. Atti held up his sword protectively, stepping back and pressing his back against Marcellus. Further down the line, a Ranger shouted out in pain, leaving Aurelius to charge after him. Around Atti, white, hungry eyes stared them down, growling softly.

"Be ready," Atti heard Marcellus stay as the eyes started to come closer.

Hidden mouths snarled as the threat advanced, Atti not knowing what to expect. Suddenly, a grey, furry blur leapt out of the bushes and onto the Ranger beside him. It sunk its large, pointed fangs into the man's shoulder, causing him to exclaim out desperately. Thinking quick, Atti jabbed his sword into the side of the monstrous beast feeding upon the soldier on the ground. It stopped for a moment and whimpered, turning its attention to Atti, the previous victim now dead on the ground.

"Wolves!" a Ranger yelled as Atti swung his blade at the rabid wolf, crimson blood spilling from its terrifying jaws.

The animal flinched before retaliating by snapping its mouth shut onto the sword. Fearful, he froze and struggled to move just as Marcellus surged forward and brought down his sword upon the wolf's neck, slicing all the way through. The decapitated head of the beast slid to the floor, Atti's blade still in the clutches of its jaws. Tugging it free, he turned and saw the massacre ensuing on the group of Rangers.

Close by, Atti could see Aurelius struggling with an egregious, black wolf which had delirious red eyes. It was unleashing relentless attacks upon the Rangers commander who parried and blocked as best he could. Rushing to help, Marcellus ran past Atti, lunging at the wolf with his blade. To his surprise, the sword penetrated its hide and stuck there, the attack seemingly having no effect on the creature.

It turned its head furiously, growling at Marcellus. Biting frantically the wolf chomped down upon his finger, pulling it clean off. Calling out in pain, Marcellus retreated while Aurelius recuperated and attacked once more. He stabbed the wolf repeatedly, as it growled intensely. Atti slowly advanced from behind the wolf, lifting his sword steadily, spotting Marcellus' blade sticking out of the body of the creature.

Aurelius grunted as he defended himself from the beast, planting his feet in the ground and pushing the blade forward and into the throat of his enemy.

Meanwhile, Atti sprang into action, grasping the other blade and heaving it out. "Here!" he called to Aurelius as he threw the sword to him. With the new weapon, he continued to slice the inside of the wolf's mouth while jabbing its eye with the sword now in his other hand.

It howled in pain, veering its head while doing so. Atti rushed to the warrior's side, supporting him as he fell exhaustedly. The wolf collapsed as the sounds of battle clamoured around them.

"Commander, we need to retreat. Our group is no match for those beasts!" a Ranger exclaimed, meeting up with the two of them. Aurelius nodded and, standing back up he called out:

"Men! Rally with me and form defensive positions. We must retreat to survive!"

The remaining soldiers gathered round quickly before departing swiftly back into the forest, hearing the howls of the wolves chasing behind them. Atti hopped over fallen logs and dashed daringly, hearing the screams of the Rangers getting caught by the rabid beasts. Close behind, Atti recognised a voice crying out for help. Turning round for a moment, he saw Marcellus flailing about, his foot trapped under a log.

Hurriedly, Atti retraced his steps and shoved his hands under the log. Together, Atti and Marcellus tried desperately to lift the log as the looming threat gradually progressed.

The two shouted in anguish as they just managed to lift the heavy log, dashing in the direction of the camp as the wolves behind them snapped at their heels. Running into hanging leaves and forestry on the ground, Atti paced through the yellow forest with urgency, relieved to see the clearing in the distance which housed the Rangers campsite.

As the first Ranger arrived and alerted the rest, a fresh battalion armed with bows and flaming arrows prepared themselves by the edge of the forest.

Once Atti and Marcellus had escaped the forest, the Rangers fired upon the pursuing wolves, burning a couple and scaring the rest off. Devastated, Aurelius regrouped with his team and counted the remaining soldiers, remorseful of his many friends that had fallen.

Afterwards, Atti returned to his tent, out of breath and in shock. He sat down on his bed, reliving that night over and over again.

CHAPTER 10 – Exposed

Atti was motionless, staring up at the roof of his tent, laying on his back in the dark hours of the night. His thoughts plagued his mind, the fear instilled in him by the terror of the night lingering like deep regret. The night's events had flashed by as a blur for the boy; hence he took more than a minute to analyse what had happened.

Luckily, he had survived mainly unscathed, unlike some of the other Rangers in the group. When they had returned, he overheard Aurelius mention they had lost three of the seven soldiers who had ventured out that night. Atti felt guilty about departing immediately to his tent, but he needed a moment to recuperate and rest in silence. As he thought this, there came a knock on the post outside his tent. Shortly after, the entrance flap to the tent was opened and a silhouetted, slender figure entered. Atti sat up so that he could get a closer look at the visitor.

"Atti, I hope you don't mind me being in here."

Ennia spoke softly, sitting down upon the stool opposite the bed where Atti now sat.

"I heard the news about the attack and I wondered if you were okay."

Atti blushed, his ideas of being solitary slipping away, as he was grateful for his new company. He replied, "I'm fine, thank you."

"That's good to hear. And, I wanted to tell you something, something about me, a secret if you will."

He nodded his head in approval, inquisitive about Ennia's secret.

"I haven't been truly honest about who I am and why I was captured in the first place. It seems now that these Rangers do not know of my origin and I debated on whether to tell you or not, but as you can see, I trust you and care for you enough to give you light on my situation. You see, my full name is Ennia Domitia."

"WHAT?" Atti exclaimed, leaping out of his bed and backing up against the back wall.

"But, but that means your mother is Di..."

"Diana Domitia, yes."

"Your mother is a warmonger! *The* pirate queen of the seas! A warrior of the highest calibre, and you're her daughter, and you're here, with me! No wonder you were captured, this is so much to take in! I, I..."

"Atti, I have more to say if you would indulge me," Ennia said calmly, standing up and moving closer to Atti.

"Oh yes, sorry."

They sat down, a million questions rushing through Atti's head, only a few of them with plausible answers.

"This is probably a shock as most Romans and people in general do not know that Diana had a daughter, which works in my favour. See, after I was born, my mother only cared for me for a little while before sending me away to live with my father. However, he was disgusted at the thought of having a child, as I later found out, and therefore I spent most of my time being cared for by his servants. One day, quite recently, I decided to escape my home, to live free and find my mother. I left my town without my father noticing, and I fled to the nearby forest.

At first, I searched for another civilization but I found nothing of note. It felt as if the forest was endless. I tried for a few days to survive on my own, creating a small shelter, foraging for food consisting of berries and any meat I could find, which was mainly scarce. Then it got to the point where I started to struggle and I decided to try and find an exit once more. I ran straight in one direction and soon I found an opening.

After I escaped the forest, I searched for signs of life and saw a camp in the distance. As I was going there I was caught by some soldiers, similar to these Rangers but not as friendly. They brought me back to their fortress before their leader, whose name I cannot remember. I was immediately detained. At the time I didn't know why, but later I found out that my father had placed a nationwide alert to search for me.

Later, I was questioned repeatedly about the whereabouts of my mother and her plans, even though I had not seen her in over a decade.

Then I overheard the Warden saying that I was to be held as ransom to lure my mother to the base and kill her. However, I assume the siege on the fortress delayed those plans. It is fortunate that these Rangers know not of my heritage and 'importance,' but I fear the event of us returning to their leader and the rest of the army.

So, in truth, this is my story, and I regret not telling you sooner Atti. You truly are becoming a great and honest man, and a truly compassionate friend, if you also think that way."

Atti sat throughout the story in silence, marvelling at the girl's tales of excitement not unlike his own. The night was late and tiredness overcame him, though he was uncertain and unconcerned about the time. His respect and care for Ennia had been raised, and he felt obliged to aid her in many ways, as having an ally like her would be a useful profit, especially as she was the daughter of the pirate queen herself.

"Of course I do Ennia, and I am immensely grateful for hearing your tale in full. I am glad to see we can trust each other."

The girl smiled at his words, sidling up on the bed next to Atti. For a few moments they sat in quietness, enjoying each other's company. The moon outside shone brightly like a spotlight in the sky, beaming down upon the camp as if watching over them protectively. The cold breeze sifted into the tent, and the pair huddled closer together in embrace. Atti felt sleep arriving, his eyelids closing shut, just as an urgent shout was yelled across the camp.

"AMBUSH!"

Atti and Ennia jumped up from the bed as sounds of screams and shouts filled their ears.

Running out into the open air, Atti assessed the chaos developing around him. It was a legion of soldiers evidently from the New Guard, identified by their specifically

101

coloured armaments and weaponry. At the forefront of the army, proudly riding a black stallion was Sergeant Titus, ordering his soldiers to release arrows down upon the Rangers and demolish the camp in its entirety.

The Rangers, tired, frazzled and unready, stumbled out into the battle without armour, some armed with just a shortsword. The New Guard advanced swiftly on horses, riding by Rangers and slicing them efficiently. Atti looked around for Aurelius whom he spotted engaged with a particularly bulky soldier. He then turned his attention to Titus who had now dismounted and was pacing towards him.

"Caeso! You traitorous menace! I told your father you would betray us all. My suspicions were correct!"

"I'm no traitor Titus!"

Atti revealed his blade which he had nabbed from his tent before exiting it, "I just have respect and trust for those who give it back the same. And so far, these Rangers have done so, unlike you and my father and most of the other Romans back home. Besides, how did you find us?" Atti exclaimed, his chest expanding and retracting repeatedly in the torrential rain now unexpectedly falling.

"You think we won't notice streaks of fire in the air? Who do you think set off those wolves, fool?"

Grimacing, Atti gripped his sword tightly as Titus opposed him, mania in his eyes.

"You may believe I will spare you for the sake of your father, boy, but be mistaken. Whoever you side with, you'll die just the same. Now prepare to perish!"

The dark-skinned warrior unsheathed his silver broadsword and grabbed his shield from the side of his steed before pulling the metal visor down on his stylised helmet.

"I will take great pride in this," the sergeant stated before charging at the boy.

Atti, suddenly afraid and not knowing what to do, dodged to the side, rolling onto the ground before standing back up in a hurry. In the corner of his eye, he saw Ennia engaged with a soldier, holding up her own pretty well.

"You are delaying the inevitable, worm!"

He lunged once more, bringing down his heavy weapon. This time he caught the boy, a spray of blood spurting onto the ground beside him despite Atti rolling out of the way. Atti felt his fatigue increase as he suffered a severe headache.

Taking a slow breath, Titus attacked once more with more rage to which Atti blocked with his lesser blade. Laughing, the sergeant retracted his blade and used the hilt to hit Atti in the stomach, causing him to fall back onto the hard ground.

"Not so strong now traitor!"

Standing straight, he raised his sword above his head, winding up to strike on the exposed Atti in front of him.

"What would your father think, hmm?"

"He would be proud to know I would never join a man like you, Titus!" Atti shouted back, spitting in the sergeant's face.

"My father will realise you are evil incarnate soon enough. Besides, I never liked you from the start!"

He smirked, just as the blurry sight of an arrow flew over Atti's head and struck the chest of Titus. He yelled in pain before yanking the arrow out of his skin, dropping it on the grass beside him.

Looking behind him, Atti saw Ennia equipped with a longbow, smiling at him.

"You think you, a weak girl, can stop *me*?" Titus questioned.

"Maybe she can't, but I can," a bold voice announced from behind the sergeant.

Wielding a bloody sword and a battered set of armour, Marcus Aurelius stepped towards Titus who grinned at the challenge. Seeing his chance, Atti tried to stand back up, though to his despair he lacked the energy to rejoin the fight.

"Let the Ranger handle it," Ennia pleaded, rushing to Atti's side, "We've done all we can."

"I can't walk Ennia. Help me to that log."

The pair limped over to a nearby log bench, Ennia assisting the injured Atti to sit down and rest while the strained battle continued around.

In the centre of the scene, Aurelius stared down the deranged sergeant with a fiery hatred, gripping his blade tightly. He gritted his teeth together and held eye contact with his opponent, waiting patiently for him to make the first move.

Titus cried out as he ran toward Aurelius, his sword pointed forward. The aciculate edge reflected the orange flames surrounding the camp. Shouts and screams of anguish and anger could be heard resulting from the devastating battle. It seemed that the New Guard were triumphing over the smaller force of Rangers, aided by the advantage of surprise.

Enraged, Aurelius blocked the oncoming blow with ease, pushing forward his sword and kicking Titus in the shin, causing him to fall on one knee. However, before the Ranger could attack, Titus swung his sword at his feet, creating a wide, open cut on Aurelius' leg. The inky red blood flowed out of the gash, dripping onto the lime grass underneath.

Titus returned to his feet first, picking up his fallen shield. As he was doing so, the commander struck him unprecedentedly, using the hilt to strike the sergeant in the chest. Winded, he stepped back, holding his blue shield encrusted with the New Guard emblem in front of him. With a mighty force, Aurelius then grasped onto the shield before yanking it out of Titus' hands and casting it aside and onto the ground before swinging his blade with immense strength, Titus barely parrying the critical attack with his own sword.

Aurelius continued his flurry, narrowly missing the sergeant until he had him backed up against a tent, where the Ranger let go of his sword with one hand and balled it into a fist which he used to punch Titus on the right cheek, stunning him. While his enemy was dazed, Aurelius took his chance to clasp onto Titus' shoulder and plunge his sword into his stomach, the tip resurfacing on the other side of the sergeant's chest, the sanguine fluid spurting onto the roof of the tent behind him.

Once the commander had pulled the broadsword out of him, Titus slid to the floor taking strained, raspy breaths. He started to chuckle painfully, managing to produce a few words as Atti and Ennia had arrived by Aurelius' side.

"You made a mistake, killing me. Your day of reckoning will come, and your army shall fall along with you. Take this as a warning to not mess with me and my people."

Coughing loudly, he gripped onto Atti's arm and stared right into his eyes while saying:

"Say hello to your father for me."

Then, the dim light faded from his eyes and his body slumped over, his sword falling onto the stained grass.

Once he had slightly recovered, Aurelius turned and faced the remaining battle before bellowing:

"Sergeant Decimus Titus is dead under my blade, and all of you shall die a similar death if you do not choose to surrender and flee at once!"

Nearly all of the New Guard stopped fighting and turned towards Aurelius who lifted Titus' shield for all of them to see. The emblem had a red X painted across it with the blood of the dead sergeant.

Some of the soldiers started to run while some were captured and brought before Aurelius who was soon accompanied with the surviving Rangers.

"Listen men, this attack has left us more vulnerable than ever but tonight we must rebuild what we can and gather what supplies we have. A few of you shall interrogate these soldiers for information whilst the uninjured do their jobs.

Those unfit to do so shall rest for the foreseeable future until fully or partially healed. Does everyone understand?"

There were multiple answers of "Yes Commander" as the soldiers departed in separate ways and immediately got on with their tasks. After he had finished speaking, Aurelius found Atti who was huddled with Ennia, suffering from his gash in his chest.

"Atticus, my boy, are you alright."

"I'm just a bit hurt, that's all Commander."

Frustrated, Ennia spoke, "*A bit hurt?* You need medical attention! Or at least a few days' rest."

Atti reluctantly agreed. and so Aurelius led them both to a surviving tent where they stayed for the time being. After most of the repairs had been made to the camp, Aurelius, Marcellus and a few other Rangers finally started to revel in their triumphant victory, leading to many drinks being downed and songs being hollered throughout the long night.

In the slightly smaller tent, Atti hauled himself into the bed while Ennia crafted a dressing for his wound, treating him with her limited medical knowledge.

Soon, Atti began to drift into a deep sleep where his thoughts, burdens and troubles sifted away and all he felt was contentment.

CHAPTER 11 – The Search

Opening his eyes after what seemed like an age of sleep, Atti glanced around his sparse tent. It was dimly lit with thin strips of light slipping through the narrow gap in the entrance to the tent. Above him, the extinguished lantern hung plainly, spinning around ever so slowly. To his side, a table on top of which was his blood-stained blade and his clothes. Across from him was the chair Ennia had been sitting in, which was crooked and now empty. Atti sniffed his clothes and winced at the stench.

I smell terrible. I wish I had time for a dip in the river.

Despite his previous injury, Atti felt mostly healed as he could freely move and get out of his bed. Putting on his clothes and belt while leaving his sword in the tent, he opened the flap to the camp that for Atti had been destroyed moments earlier, though it seemed as if a long time had passed. Atti could see that most of the tents had been resurrected and that the watchtower had been repaired, but there was a lack of people about. Seeing a Ranger by the edge of the river, he called out to him but to no response. Puzzled, he walked over to the man and spoke once again.

"Hey! Where is everyone?"

The Ranger, who was elderly and had a particular arch in his back turned to face Atti, before speaking in an unexpected, deep, commanding voice.

"The camp was raided, just last night. Provisions, weapons, essential items all stolen, as well as a body."

"A body? Whose body?" Atti enquired confusedly.

"The sergeant who had attacked us, I think his name was Titus if I remember correctly. I believe his followers are the ones responsible for raiding our camp, though what plans they have for the body I do not know."

"I see no need to recover a corpse, but whatever the New Guard are planning must not go unnoticed. Besides, where are Aurelius and the others?"

"They departed early this morning to track down the thieves and supposedly kill them, however I feel that is a difficult task. Your female friend also went along with them, mentioning something about avenging what they did to you and the murdered soldiers. Made a whole speech and everything. Quite amusing actually."

"So Ennia's gone with them. Doesn't she know she could get captured or worse, killed!"

"Those who perish in war are those unfit for the job. Do you think your friend is unable to handle the danger she is heading towards?"

"No, but I am still worried nonetheless. Thank you, Dominus?"

"You can call me Florian, and I am sure your friend will fare well, I can sense it," Florian said with a smile, turning back to face the river.

Atti lingered by the river for a minute or two, calming himself down and going over the battle from just a few nights ago.

Titus is dead! I wonder if father knows. His death could prompt him to attack, and if the Rangers here keep suffering we will break eventually. This has turned into something of an unwanted war for both sides.

Afterwards, Atti bathed in the cool, clear river, feeling much more refreshed than before. The feel of the chilled, flowing water relaxed him, easing him of his worry. Later in the starting embers of the evening, Aurelius, Ennia, Marcellus and the rest returned looking tired, exhausted and without results. Ennia was glad to see Atti recovered and in better condition and on seeing him she ran over and flung herself onto him in an embrace. Flustered, he hugged her back before stepping back.

"What were you thinking going after the New Guard? You could have been killed!"

"Yeah, but I wasn't. So, what's your point?"

"You frustrate me," Atti said annoyedly.

Aurelius spotted him and came over, standing beside Ennia, who walked off to leave the men by themselves.

"A tough one, that girl is," the commander chuckled, clasping his hand on Atti's shoulder.

"I thought you should know that before the raid, we interrogated one of the soldiers who told us a story of a very peculiar man, or creature as he referred. Turns out the 'creature' which they refer to as 'The Warlock' was a gift, a weapon of immense power to your father from Titus before he died. Descriptions of the creature involve a dark cloak and hood and bird-like features, and it is said that this creature wields magical powers. Hard to believe, isn't it?"

"I wish," Atti replied "But I have seen something which backs up that claim, to our despair."

"What was it, and when?"

"A while ago in the forest, before I had found you. It was a late evening and I couldn't sleep when I heard voices in the distance. I went to investigate and I saw Titus with a cloaked figure, the one you may be referring to. It was soon after the siege of the fortress and Titus was badly wounded. The cloaked creature muttered a language which I had not heard before and it held out his hands, procuring this greenish light which was projected out of his claws. Then, miraculously, Titus was healed in an instant and all his scars from the siege were gone. It was bewildering."

"This is useful but disconcerting information. Thank you for sharing this with me. Now excuse me while I think of our next logical move."

Aurelius went in search of his closest advisor back at the camp. On reaching the largest tent, his own, he entered to find his appointed temporary second-in-command Ranger whose name was Lupus Martialis, a decorated soldier who was younger and faster than Aurelius, but lacking the commander's strength.

He was tall and dark-skinned, with unusual amber eyes and a lack of hair on top of his head and across his face. He was mostly stern, though loyal and followed every order issued to him. Originally Martialis had lived in Greece where he had trained heavily both physically and mentally. Anyone who knew him would say his intelligence matched that of some of the greatest philosophers, hence why he was Aurelius' advisor during this time.

Martialis had been seated comfortably inside the tent, his stainless steel blade – engraved with a Latin proverb - propped up against his leg. He sat with his strong hands clasped together, deep in thought and unfazed as Aurelius entered the quarters.

"Marcus, how was your plight against those despicable raiders?"

"It fared unwell Lupus. We failed to achieve any retribution or any further information aside from the news of the magic user, the truth of which was just confirmed to me by the boy we have taken in."

"Is that so? It seems that the son of the new governor is becoming even more useful to us by the second. So, my friend, what do you require counsel on if anything?"

"Lupus, I struggle deeply. Our men have been cut down and our provisions are running low, we are more vulnerable now than ever. Without help from an external source our fight would have been for nothing!"

Martialis smiled and stood, laying his customised blade on the wooden table in front of him.

"Then it is obvious what we must do, Marcus. We must find Karvajal."

"Of course, you are correct as always, friend. I shall send out a few scouts to find where he resides. Hopefully we may find him before Governor Caeso can. Thank you for your insight once again, Lupus."

After their conversation, Aurelius started to organise search teams at once, putting anyone fit enough to leave into his groups. By the end of the day many of the Rangers had left, leaving only a few back at the camp including Aurelius, Ennia, Atti, Florian and a few others.

Before that as early evening came, the teams gathered their things and prepared for long hikes, taking with a bird which would circle overhead and alert them of anything significant. Before he left, Marcellus was approached by Atti by the edge of the forest.

"Good luck out there, I hope you find him."

"Thank you, Atticus. I'm sure I'll need your luck," Marcellus replied while gearing up.

"Oh, and try not to die."

"Will do, brother," chuckled Marcellus, "See you around," he remarked before joining the rest of his group and setting off back into the endless wild.

Aurelius had chosen to stay behind as he felt overworked and stressed, as well as suffering from his injuries inflicted by Titus just a few nights before. He mostly rested in his tent for the remainder of the night, while Atti and Ennia laid on their backs by the river as the sun descended and the twinkling stars appeared above them in the thick blanket of the night sky.

Surrounding them, cries from animals rang out along with the chirps of crickets that were stealthily hidden in the longer blades of grass. The slow flow of the river accompanied the near silence as the pair rested together, staring up at the wonders in the sky.

Brightly, the circular full moon was illuminated like the end of a torchlight.

Later that night, when he awoke from his slumber, Atti couldn't remember the rest of the events that happened that night, but when he woke up to the sound of the footsteps of multiple soldiers he was a little surprised.

Getting out of his bed, he greeted Ennia who was sitting at the end of the bed. After dressing quickly, they both departed outside to see what the commotion was.

Aurelius was talking to Martialis about the two out of the three teams that had returned. Atti managed to overhear part of their conversation.

"...nothing, and it is the same with Antonius. Dead ends."

"And what of Quintilianus?"

"We have not heard back from him or any of his group."

"Then we must assume the worst, my friend."

Atti was shocked at Aurelius' words. He blurted out, "But that's Tatius Marcellus' group! You cannot just give up on them!"

"Child, I am afraid there is nothing we can do," Martialis said sympathetically before departing to speak to Antonius, the appointed leader of the second group. Aurelius watched him go before turning back towards Atti, away from the glistening sunlight that beamed down onto them all.

In a sudden movement, shapes of white clouds drifted in front of the golden light, casting a wide shadow down onto the distraught, desperate delegation. Promptly, Atti felt a gust of cold air breeze through him, causing him to shiver.

"Dark days are indeed ahead, closer than we may anticipate," Aurelius stated gloomily, peering up at the daunting atmosphere.

As he spoke, a sleek, black raven cawed above them as it circled and then landed on the top of the largest tent, a rolled-up piece of parchment held gently between its silver beak. It cocked its head to the side and stared down Atti as he, Ennia and Aurelius approached the bird. Reaching forward, the commander retrieved the paper and unfolded it, revealing words written inside in fresh ink. He went on to read the message written inside aloud:

"To Marcus Aurelius, or any other person who may receive this message.

We have successfully found Karvajal and the remainder of the Rangers. A new stronghold has been erected by a colossal waterfall in a mountain, the fortress of which we have named the Castellum Lapideum. Karvajal requires your information and requests that Aurelius tell him the story of his endeavours. All habitants of the camp are invited to the fort, and we request you leave with haste.

Food, drinks and provisions will all be prepared and a feast will be held when you return. We expect your arrival soon. The location maps have been sketched below this message. See you in just a moment, commander. - Quintilianus."

The crowd of Rangers that had gathered round were silent until the last word, after which they cheered and chanted in hopeful celebration.

Martialis had joined the group outside but stayed mostly reserved and content before quietly stating, "This is a promising development. Now, Marcus, we must leave now."

In a matter of hours, all of the tents were dismantled and most significant items were packed up into cloth bags. Atti and Ennia gathered their limited belongings – Atti his blade and Ennia her bow – before joining the rest of the group and waiting for Martialis to figure out the direction and location of Castellum Lapideum by using a makeshift sundial he had fashioned years before. Aurelius then checked to see if everyone was ready to depart.

By the time the battered, exhausted group of Rangers left their camp which had become a home to them, it was late afternoon and the sun had begun to set.

As they walked, they passed forests filled with heightened trees and a deep valley surrounded by mountainous peaks that seemed as if they were touching the very sky above them. While halfway through the rocky terrain of the u-shaped valley, Atti looked upwards and marvelled at the immense scale presented by the snow-capped mountains on either side of them. He looked across at Ennia who was similarly gawking at the palisades looming over them.

"I've never seen anything like this," Ennia exclaimed, tearing her gaze away from the cliff sides.

"Me too," Atti replied hesitantly as he spotted something strange in the distance. From afar there appeared to be a black line ahead of them which seemed to be advancing towards them quite quickly. He strained his eyes to see what the force could be before running up to Aurelius who had stopped in his tracks.

"By Zeus' beard," he muttered under his breath as the stampede came into view. No more than a hundred bandits were charging towards them on fierce steeds, racing with increasing speed. Each one was dressed in black overlapping cloth with head scarves covering their faces, their horses broad and strong. They carried a variety of weapons ranging from whips to swords to flaming pitchforks. Their speed kicked up the dust behind them from the sandy ground in the valley, the pounding of the horses' hooves upon it getting louder and louder.

At the front, leading the force was a tall, determined man wearing a similar outfit but white, brandishing a leather lasso which he swung around over his head and a menacing scimitar hanging by his side. He wore gold jewellery displayed all over him, flashy, golden rings on each of his fingers. As the bandits neared, they started chanting, ominous shouts echoing throughout the valley.

"What do we do?" Atti asked, backing away slowly, his eyes fixed on the advancing madmen.

When they had mostly closed the distance on the vulnerable Rangers the bandits began to throw balls of fire and numerous weaponry at them, striking the ground and a few soldiers. Martialis, who seemed composed and unfazed, spoke out loud in his commanding, authoritative voice.

"It is not what we will do, but what we can do. And all we can do is run to our deaths."

"No, there must be a way!" Aurelius exclaimed, pacing around agitatedly and hurling his sword on the ground just as an arrow landed a few feet from him.

"We are too far into the valley to turn back, and if we continue forwards we will be struck down in an instant. We do not have the strength nor the numbers to defeat a group of that size and any help we may call upon will never get here in time. We are indeed helpless."

Shaking his head at Martialis, the commander looked back at the now deafening stampede of horses that were closer than ever.

Afraid, Ennia clutched onto Atti's hand and squeezed it tightly while he unsheathed his blade from his belt, discarding his fear and replacing it with determination and anticipation.

"We must fight, even if it is to our deaths," he stated, planting his feet in the sand and dust.

Composing himself, Aurelius brandished his own weapon and turned to face the swarm of bandits who had started to slow. The leader signalled for his group to stop while he rode up to a few feet away from the Rangers. He dismounted his creamy-white steed and paced over to Aurelius; his leather lasso curled around a clip on his belt as his bandits surrounded the Rangers. He pulled down his reddish brown head covering, gripped the hilt of his scimitar and spoke in a gravelly, snarling, demeaning voice.

"Listen, my name is Felix Vesta, and I'm the leader of the most dangerous bandit group in the southern lands, you hear me? We are the Crimson Raiders. Now you and your little group here have two choices. Either you give us all of your riches and weaponry and the like, or..., we'll rip it from your corpses. And we would really like to do the second option."

Aurelius' expression remained cold and stern, never breaking eye contact with Vesta, wary of the bandits encircling the group of Rangers and staring at them with delight.

In a serious tone he said, "We have no riches upon our bodies to rip from us, bandit. Your time here is being wasted."

"So, you refuse?" He laughed, gesturing his hand toward the group, "Then that means we get to do the second option!"

No sooner had the words been said, the entire circle of bandits had their weapons directed at each and every Ranger in the group. Atti and Ennia backed into the middle of the circle, Ennia shaking frightfully.

"It will be okay," he whispered, keeping her close.

"How do you know?"

"I have a feeling."

Ennia scoffed as Aurelius raised his hand, telling the group not to panic before getting down on his knees before Vesta.

"If my sacrifice means the sanctity of my people, let it be so."

"I'm afraid I shall decline, O' great and noble one!" He cackled wildly, "Though I shall start with you!"

He untied his lasso and wrapped it round the commander's neck, gripping it tightly with his hand as he began to pull backward forcefully. Aurelius groaned as the lasso tightened ever more around his neck.

"STOP!" Atti shouted, as Aurelius endured the strangling, his face turning an unnatural shade of purple. He ran toward the bandit leader, being pushed back and threatened by a particularly brutish bandit who was much taller than himself.

"You can't do this!" the boy yelled, fighting against the grip of the brute.

"Who will stop me?" Vesta replied mockingly, tying the lasso tighter and pulling with even more force to the immense despair of the commander who was on his last breath, just as an almost magical, hopeful noise sounded out into the valley, a noise that could have alerted the whole of Italy.

CHAPTER 12 – Reunion

"Enter," Numitor mumbled, slamming down an empty wine glass onto his desk beside many others while slumped in his grand chair. His beard was messy, his eyes now fully adjusted to darkness having not been out in the public eye for weeks. He squinted as the door to his office opened, with his appointed General Lucien stepping out from behind it holding a lit torch which he hung on the wall.

"Governor, I'm afraid I bring troubling news."

The governor did not stir, but instead clumsily reached out to another mostly empty glass, downing the last slither of its contents. Then slowly, as if a great dragon had been awoken from its slumber, he sat up and strained to lean forward, gesturing for Lucien to continue his message.

"We had a report from Sergeant Titus' group. In the letter they have described his death, to a rogue group of Rangers they had found by the outskirts of Birnam Forest, along the River Tabori. It seems that the group has fled since, however, there was something strange with the group."

"Titus is dead? Good riddance I say. What, what is the other thing, Lucien?" Numitor croaked, clearing his throat and standing up, struggling to balance himself as he did so."

"Your son, Atticus was seen fighting alongside this group of Rangers."

For a moment, Numitor remained still, staring across at the far wall. "What?" the governor mumbled in disbelief.

Lucien waited a moment before answering.

"I said..."

"I HEARD WHAT YOU SAID!" Numitor bellowed, hurling a glass at the wall and shattering it into little shards. He stood still, his hand shaking slightly as a red stream of blood trickled down his creased skin, dripping onto the wooden floor, the spot of blood staining the clean boards.

Numitor looked down at his bloody hand, taking in deep breaths, pressing his fingers against the cut. Wincing slightly, he reached for a cloth and wiped his hand clean, soaking up the red liquid. For a moment the blood remained on his shaking hand, disappearing in a blink.

"Find...find the Warlock. I need power now more than ever. Find him, and find him quickly!"

Lucien bowed his head and hurried out of the room, signalling to a servant to clean up the broken shards of the glass that had clattered onto the ground. Limping over to his window, Numitor surveyed his city through infuriated but teary eyes, clutching the bandage around his hand, the blood seeping through the cloth.

"What has happened to me?" he whispered, his voice hollow and distraught.

Across at the eastern gate, a commotion was afoot, and on closer inspection the governor could see that the crowd was in fact the New Guard, seemingly departing from the city of Socratis. Angered, he clenched his scarred fist and pressed on the bandage, enduring the infliction of pain, banging his hand against the glass.

"I have everything I need and everything I have wanted and now, I am still defeated. I am in a prison of my own mind, a paradox in which I cannot escape. My son, my remaining kin and my only worthy prize has aligned himself with the enemy and in return I drink and I sit and I drink some more. The Empire, *my* Empire has turned to ruin, and what do I do? I lay in my chair; I wallow in my incompetence. This cannot be surpassed. I will do everything in my power to regain respect, and I *will* find you Atticus, wherever you may be."

Deafeningly beautiful was the noise that resounded into the valley, echoing back and forth off the palisades as if the call of a great beast. The sound distracted the bandits and their leader Felix Vesta, causing him to cease strangling Aurelius whose face had gone a purplish colour. Both the bandits and the Rangers looked towards the top of the valley, Atti included, when at last they saw the source of the horn. The cliff tops of the valley were suddenly populated by a battalion of soldiers, Rangers who had come to save their brothers.

Rapidly the army of armed Rangers upon beastly steeds, descended the sides of the valley, yelling joyously as they did so. Atti chuckled and as the bandits were distracted, he took the chance to strike at the bandit holding him, hitting him in the chest and kneeing him in his unshaven head, knocking out one of his many golden teeth.

Taking action, Ennia loaded her bow and started releasing arrows with newfound speed while Aurelius regained his breath, tackling Felix while the Bandit's back was turned. The rest of the Rangers began to fight as the reinforcements closed in on the group in the centre of the steep valley. Knocking out his foe, Atti turned to see the rest of the Rangers battling the bandit group. He joined in to assist Ennia by lunging at the brutish man from before who was charging towards the girl, plunging his blade deep into the chest of the bandit.

Vesta stood up hastily, his head spinning wildly. He clutched the side of his horse until his dizziness had stopped before shouting out to his bandits.

"Men, we are outnumbered! We would be wise to flee before we inevitably lose this battle, and our heads! Quickly now!"

He mounted his horse hurriedly, kicking its side desperately just as the Rangers reinforcements arrived at the battle. Many bandits began to run back to their steeds, with one taking a last stern look at Atti before darting back to his mount.

Once all of the bandits had cleared off, he reunited with Ennia as the Rangers stopped and dismounted their horses. Leading the charge was Quintilianus who smiled at the sight of his commander. Aurelius greeted him pleasedly, grasping his hand and helping him off his horse.

"You know, for a second there I was worried."

"The great Marcus Aurelius worried? Never in my lifetime," he chuckled, "Karvajal sent us back to escort you in case you got into any trouble, which you did it seems."

"And if it weren't for you we would have been slaughtered like fresh sheep. I truly thank you for your group's assistance."

"Well, I accept your gratitude, although we didn't do much for physicality as opposed to intimidation. It was your little group here that did most of the fighting and I must say, the boy there is quite the warrior."

"Too much like his father, which is the path he is heading I fear," the commander replied.

"Wasn't that the plan though, Commander?"

Aurelius paused and stared into Quintilianus' eyes, "We must not speak about the plan, not now at least. Consult Octavius in your own time if you have any concerns, I am sure he will oblige. Now, let us return to our home."

"Of course, Commander."

Just as they had finished speaking, Atti ran up to the two, looking between them before asking, "Quintilianus, where is Marcellus? I cannot seem to find him and yet he was with you in your group."

"My boy, Marcellus decided to stay in our new base; he had suffered a minor injury in the forest on our scout trip. However, he should be fine in a few days if it is any comfort."

"Oh, thank you."

After a few minutes, the now stronger group of Rangers departed and began to trek the rest of the way towards the Castellum Lapideum, crossing through the extensive valley following behind Quintilianus and Aurelius who were leading the group.

As the company left the site of the ambush, they trailed along a glistening, crystalline river for a few hours before the sight of the new, developed fortress could be seen, the behemoth of a mountain towering into the sky like the fist of a god rising from the ground.

At the forefront was an enormous, gushing waterfall which cascaded into the river below, its source stemming from the mountain.

Jutting out from the cliff face, Atti could faintly see bits of scaffolding and construction put in place by the Rangers after the siege at the original fortress. The cliff was jagged and steep, the top having a near vertical incline.

Soon the group of Rangers neared the foot of the colossal mountain, where there seemed to be a gathering of people awaiting them.

Standing in front of them with a more significant apparel was Octavius Karvajal, dressed in a long purple robe and golden garments. As the company arrived, Aurelius dismounted from his horse and greeted Karvajal relievedly, to which he insisted that everyone rest while he heard of their endeavours, with Karvajal being very interested in Atti's experiences.

"Our adventure has been one of pain and torment, but fortunately we are here and standing! Let me recall our tale and then I must hear of yours."

"Yes, please continue Aurelius," Karvajal replied, tearing his gaze away from Atti who had just dismounted.

"If you remember the siege of the fortress, we were outmanned and unprepared. Once I had realised we were fighting a losing battle, I gathered as many men as I could find and we fled to the river, hoping to use its natural resources to rebuild and prepare for attack.

After a week or so we had built a camp big enough for all of us with materials from the forest, and I allocated groups to search and hunt for food. For a while we were safe, and it was only once Atticus and the girl turned up that the situation became dire.

One malicious night, I decided to take my men and Atticus to scout out for any sign of another civilization. At one moment, we had reached a dense part of the forest when we were attacked by wolves. I lost almost half my troops that night, and I would have lost more if we had not fled from the site. When we returned, our spirits had indeed been dampened and all hope seemed lost.

And then, we were attacked."

Karvajal was taken aback, "Attacked? By whom, the Romans?"

"Thus indeed, their 'New Guard' and Titus as well. He had ambushed us shortly after the night terror which they had supposedly set loose upon us. Our men were vulnerable and critically outnumbered, our weaponry severely unmatched."

"Then how on this green earth did you survive my dear friend?"

"It was a struggle, however with the help of Atticus and the girl Ennia, I was able to overpower the sergeant and now he lies with a hole in his chest."

"You defeated Sergeant Decimus Titus, with the help of Atticus Caeso of all people? I am sure that the new governor would not be very happy about that."

Yes, and it gets worse. After we had somewhat recovered, I was desperate to find evidence of any other surviving Rangers, so I went out on many scout trips but to no avail. However, we managed to track down one of the New Guard soldiers who had attacked us. It was from him when we learned about the Empire's secret weapon..."

"Speak, Commander."

"According to the hostage, and Atticus who claims to have seen this creature, Titus had recruited a malevolent creature known as the Warlock, who seemingly has the ability to use and wield dark magic."

"How... Interesting. Tell me more."

"I do not know much, I was hoping you could shine some light on the situation, however something peculiar did happen."

"And that would be?"

"During the night, shortly after our battle, Titus' body was stolen along with just a few provisions. It was like the corpse was the only thing they were after."

"That is peculiar. Is there any more to your tale?"

"Not much. After that I sent out more scout groups and by luck, we managed to find you. Apart from some trouble with bandits we made it here all well and healthy, though in dire need of a rest."

"Then rest my friend. We shall hold a council meeting tonight to discuss our plan of action. But for now, clean up."

Aurelius passed Karvajal and ascended the stairs carved into the mountain, which were outlined with strange runes and symbols. Karvajal watched him go before turning his attention to Atti and Ennia who had just arrived at the fortress.

"My boy, good to see you again! And I see you brought an old friend."

"I am not your friend!" Ennia snapped, snarling at Karvajal. He smiled and held out his hand, to be faced with the girl's glare.

"Note taken, but you are a prisoner anyhow, so please go with Cassius and Hadrianus to your new cell."

Shocked, Atti blurted out, "You can't just put her back in a cell after all she has done for *your* soldiers!"

"Why not?" he asked with a smirk, "She is a wanted war criminal after all?"

"What?"

Atti looked over at Ennia who lowered her head as the two soldiers apprehended her. Turning back to Karvajal he questioned, "What do you mean war criminal?"

"Well, that girl is the only daughter of the terrorist and pirate queen Diana Domitia. It is only sensible that we lock her up. We do not know what danger she carries."

Cassius (who seemed vaguely familiar to Atti) and Hadrianus – two Rangers close to Karvajal – had now cuffed Ennia's hands, beginning to take her into the stone fortress. Atti watched in despair, pleading to Karvajal who contained the same, content expression throughout the proceedings.

"How can you just stand there? That girl saved my life and many of your soldier's lives. If she had any ties to her mother don't you think she would have at least ran away? You can't do this."

Karvajal paused and stared at Atti, his expression now grave, which was unusual for Atti to see.

"Atticus, my boy. You truly trust this girl?"

"Yes of course, with my life!"

He felt his chin, and on seeing the last of the Rangers arrive at the mountain, he passed the boy and greeted them politely, his expression back to its standard, friendly tone.

Before Atti had a chance to act, Quintilianus spoke behind him, saying, "Atticus, Marcellus is upstairs in the infirmary room. If you would like to see him, he is eager to see you."

"Oh, okay. Thank you."

He stood on the spot for a moment, worried for Ennia, however he knew that starting a fight here would not be the wisest course of action. He decided it would be best to follow the Rangers' instructions and to not cause trouble, even though it pained him. Out of the corner of his eye, Atti could see a gentleman watching him from beside his steed, who he believed to be Aurelius' advisor Lupus Martialis.

Maybe he could persuade Aurelius to talk to Octavius Karvajal about freeing Ennia. I guess it is worth a shot.

"I know what you are thinking, Governor's son. But it cannot be done. The only possible way to liberate your friend would be to plead yourself. You might find it to be more persuasive than you realise."

Atti turned, stunned to silence and too scared to talk in the strange man's presence.

"But, I tried."

Martialis chuckled and took a heavy breath, clutching his longsword in his hand and began:

"You can't see it, but you know when it's there.
It lingers in the glances, suspended in the air.
It believes all things, and all things it bears,
And there are those who are its object, who entertain it unaware.
What am I?"

Atti pondered the riddle for a moment. "A ghost?" Atti asked curiously.

"Not quite, but I will leave you to figure it out, boy."

With that, Lupus Martialis departed and entered the fortress, where Atti followed after a brief moment of bafflement.

Through the carved entrance was a stone staircase ascending into the fortress, a burning torch positioned every few steps. The stairs themself were shoddily carved with uneven notches and scratches in the stone, Atti only a few inches from hitting the ceiling. He watched his shadow dance on the stone walls, reflecting from the flickering flames of the fiery torches.

After the steep incline, Atti found himself in a circular hub of sorts, with multiple doors leading to different corridors stemming off the room he was standing in. Some entrances were blocked, with the word 'Unfinished' written across the door.

A few Rangers were standing around, the men all in armour. The roof was higher in this room, with a candelabra precariously hanging in the centre by a single chain. Looking around, Atti saw a collection of stools near the far corner where he sat and waited for Karvajal to return inside the fortress. As he sat, he watched many people of all kinds pass through the room he was in, which seemed to be the central hub of the fortress.

Some seemed the obvious, warrior type; tall, broad and stern in the face. But he saw families also, hurried mothers with their worried children, wondering if they would be alright. A wave of sympathy overcame Atti as he realised the Rangers were helping those in need and providing them food, shelter and security. They were protecting them, seemingly from the oppression of the Empire, something Atti had known subconsciously but ignored as the people in power were among the ones he looked up to, even now.

As a younger child, when his brother was alive, their father would recount stories of great Roman warriors like Africanus the Elder who would traverse miles of land to go and slay an entire army single-handedly with confounding strength. The particular legend of Scipio Africanus was now a near ancient tale depicting the defeat of the Carthaginian leader Hannibal, in a legendary fight dubbed:

'The great battle of Zama." Numitor had said that it was believed that Scipio returned to Rome after the war overseas and lived the rest of his life in peace and comfort.

Africanus was just one of many generals that had fought for Rome and had inspired Atti as a young boy. With those stories he liked to believe that his father, when he was out on missions, was fighting evil and winning wars like the legends. Now his father was the governor of Socratis which should have been a fantastic moment of celebration, but to Atti it didn't matter. Atti had felt in the past that the Empire did nothing to help other people in need, and that with his father in charge their mantra would scarcely change. On the other hand, the Rangers seemed trustworthy and actually wanted to help others, taking in refugees and giving them a place to stay. Although he couldn't shake the feeling that something was... not right.

"Ah, Atticus. Glad to see you have waited for my presence," Karvajal spoke from in front of him.

"Let her go!" he shouted, leaping from his seat, stopping a few inches from the leader of the Rangers. Breathing heavily and not breaking a sweat, Atti inhaled the sweet scent that emanated off the Warmonger, creating an illusion of safe security. Karvajal kept his enchanting smile wide despite the outburst of the teenager in front of him.

After he simply waved a hand in dismissal, with Atti taking a step back while maintaining strict eye contact with his opponent, Karvajal said, "I can see by your hostile and rash emotions that I am not going to reach a suitable compromise with you that does not involve me

133

releasing the girl, and I acknowledge your strong feelings towards this."

He then gestured to a soldier and pointed in the direction of the holding cells and after a short but infuriating couple of minutes, the man returned with Ennia struggling in his firm grip.

"Get off me, you creep!"

She shook off the guard and rushed over to Atti, standing next to him, her breathing heavy and enraged.

The prison guard smirked at Ennia, only angering her further. She took a step forward but to her surprise Atti held out his arm to stop her, giving her a cautionary glance. Atti was wary of Karvajal's sudden change of heart but truthfully, he was relieved to see Ennia again, though he remained vigilant. He looked back towards Karvajal and nodded gratefully.

The Warmonger smiled once again and spoke, "In return for such a generous act, I request that you both attend the council meeting this evening. I am sure the council would love to hear your account as well as dear Aurelius' here. Can I count on your appearance?"

Atti observed the room of stern-faced, grimacing guards and took a minute to think before replying, "You may, Ennia too."

She nodded reluctantly.

"Wonderful, now rest and clean yourselves up. Cassius, find the pair some spare rooms and take them."

The guard bowed his head and left the room, entering the corridor on the far left, with Atti and Ennia following hastily. Once in his room after moving past the under-construction hallways, Atti fell back on the thatched bed and slept for a few hours due to the exhaustion he had accumulated from the journey to the fortress.

When he awoke, he bathed and dressed himself in new, clean clothes gifted to him by Karvajal, or so he assumed. Leaving his room to find Ennia, Atti stood in the corridor, buffeted by the many doors and rooms in that section of the Castellum Lapideum. As he was about to move in one direction, a door opened behind him, and out stepped Ennia in a long white gown, her dark hair flowing down past her shoulders, complementing her beige sandals. Noticing a shimmer of silver on the sandals, Atti laughed, "You could not stay unprotected, could you?"

"You will thank me when we get stuck in a fight!"

"Sure..." he replied, "I knew this wasn't your style. Shall we?" Atti asked, and together they searched for the council room where they were set to join the evening's council meeting.

The pair arrived at a set of weighted, spruce doors with two armed guards wielding broadswords who guarded the entrance. Before they had a chance to speak, the guards lowered their swords and pulled open the heavy doors, revealing a circular room with raised seats, a bit more than half filled with various people ranging from elders to soldiers.

Clearly the time of the other Rangers had been spent building this room as a priority, or so Atti thought.

Straight ahead was Aurelius standing beside the largest, grandest seat where Karvajal sat, who cheerfully greeted the two youths.

"Council, meet Atticus Caeso, son of Governor Numitor Caeso, and Ennia Domitia, daughter of pirate queen Diana Domitia. Take a seat near the front if you please."

As the pair went to sit down there were a few gasps and whispers from the members of the council. They became seated in sturdy wooden seats and awaited the rest of the members. Once everyone was present, the wooden doors were slammed shut and Karvajal stood up in his seat, addressing the entire room.

"Soldiers, Elders, Subjects, Friends, and... newcomers, we have urgent matters to discuss! I request that for this lone meeting, I start the discussion with a pressing matter concerning the future of everyone in this room, and quite frankly the fate of the country.

From the information provided to me from the prevalent Commander Marcus Aurelius, we have discovered that Sergeant Decimus Titus, our now deceased enemy, had employed the help of a mystical, iniquitous creature known as the Warlock, with eye-witness accounts of its witchcraft, dark magic and pure villainy. This magic-user has since been gifted to the governor of Socratis, and his plans for the creature are unknown to us at this time. Therefore, it is imperative that we find some possible way to defeat Caeso and this Warlock as soon as possible.

After some thorough research held by the elders of this council, they have deduced that this Warlock holds a weakness which we can exploit. Out there, somewhere in the country is a stone able to bypass this creature's power and weaken it definitively. It is known as the Gemstone of Moria.

Now, of course, the only problem we have is that we lack the knowledge of the whereabouts of such stone, and are therefore inferior until we gain such a source of power. So, in conclusion..."

"I might have some information on that."

All heads in the room turned to the well-dressed girl who had stood up from her chair at the bottom of the circular set-up of seats. She faltered as she felt the sudden gaze of these strangers she distrusted, although she stood tall and did not back down.

"Is that so, young Domitia?"

Atti looked up at Ennia who was oblivious to her surroundings as she took a deep breath before saying, "My mother, Diana, once embarked on her own quest to find the Gemstone of Moria, and despite her later abandoning this quest for more important business, I remember overhearing parts of what she was saying to her companion, something about a flower. A tulip or something. I know it's not much, I understand that, but I hope it helps somehow..."

"Thank you, child. Every little nugget of evidence regarding the gemstone's location could be significant in our capture of it. Please, take a seat."

The girl sat back down in her seat, flustered, as Atti pondered the clue mentioned by her. Ennia gazed back up at Karvajal who started to speak to the room once more, instructing certain researchers and soldiers to work on finding the stone he desired so dearly.

For hours after, the Warmonger addressed various, smaller issues presented by the elders of the council, problems like water distribution in the new base of operations and the construction of aqueducts leading from the fortress to the River Tabori, the sources of food available for the civilians in the Castellum Lapideum and the erection of disparate farms in the fields behind the cliff face; all projects which would take weeks to come to fruition without the proper equipment, tools and numbers to do so.

After the core meeting had been suspended for another time, the elders continued to mutter away in the hall while Karvajal sought out Atti, confronting him on the centre floor of the council room.

"I know, I know. These meetings can be a bore sometimes. I hope I didn't dampen your spirits too much Atticus!" he chuckled, with Atti giving a curt smile to respond.

The leader of the Rangers clasped Atti's shoulder, gesturing for him to walk with him. As they moved down the corridor, they passed many doors escalating in wealth until they reached the end where a surprising, less impressive door stood with multiple cracks looking like it would fall at the slightest touch. Two guards stood in front, nodding towards Karvajal who pushed open the frail door gently, it creaking as he did so.

Inside was a dimly lit living space with a strange tranquillity about it, a musty, comforting aroma dancing around the room. To the right were a few cabinets with bottles of pristine wine being held in each one. The room itself was lit by a single fading lantern which hung on a hook in the ceiling precariously above them. Karvajal retrieved a chair from the corner and told Atti to sit before beginning to speak.

"You know Atticus, I think we are overdue a conversation. One that has been delayed due to the shenanigans and disruptions that you and I have experienced in these past few months. I mean, for you, it must have been so hard. Not being able to see your father, to have absolutely no idea where he is or what he is doing. Though, you might already be used to that, correct?"

Atti stared at Karvajal's jovial yet mysterious expression, trying to gain an insight into what the man was suggesting. He nodded slightly and the Warmonger continued, "That's what I had thought. Your father's constant coming and going, combined with the lack of a mother and sibling must have been difficult. You would have had sparsely any social interaction with the one you needed most. Your surviving family member, responsible for your well-being is nowhere to be seen, seemingly making no effort to come and retrieve his only son. Perhaps he does not care, perhaps he wishes for your brother to be resurrected, or for you to replace him in the sarco..."

"Stop! My father would never say anything like that, he cares. He probably has hundreds of soldiers out there searching for me!"

"If that were true, do you not think you would have seen evidence of this? Besides, when has your father ever shown that level of compassion to anyone, let alone you? Cecilia? Perhaps, but he even let her die too. In my opinion, Atticus, I believe your father does not miss you in the slightest, and that you are clinging onto a false hope that he might be out there, the big Governor he is now, worrying about where a poor, curious boy like you has run off this time. That is what you have to accept, Atticus."

The boy gazed into Karvajal's seemingly sincere eyes, acting completely austere and never faltering. The underwhelming room had fallen silent, minutes passing effortlessly before Atti breathed in heavily, before saying, "Your words are logical, and I admit I had been letting my emotions cloud my judgement, and for that, I apologise."

"Apology accepted, my dear boy. And do not let my title of the 'Warmonger' deter you, it is just a name which has been exaggerated since its origin. My intentions have been true since the start, that is the honest truth. Now, how about a drink of some Posca? No one has to know," he smirked, grabbing a lime green bottle and pouring out two glasses of a reddish-purple liquid which watered Atti's mouth at the pure sound of its contact with the glass. He gladly took hold of the glass, lifting it to his lips.

"Wait!" he exclaimed, spilling a few drops of the precious liquid onto the hard planks underneath him.

"What is it, my boy?"

"It wasn't a tulip that Ennia mentioned. It must have been a Red Azalea. As in the inn!"

Karvajal's eyes opened in surprise, with him replying, "And where might this inn be situated, Atticus?"

The boy looked at him, half-jokingly, saying, "Well, in Socratis of course!"

The wind howled as it whipped through his long black hair, the sound of feet continuously pounding the rough ground filling the empty silence along the desolate plains, as trails of dust were kicked up behind him up into the air like smoke. Strong and tenacious was the beast he rode, its blonde mane flowing in his face, blocking his view of the quaint town in front of him. Small were the buildings in his eye-line along the horizon, getting ever closer as the scorching sun set gloriously across the evening sky, the darkness overcoming the colour above him, pink and red streaks beaming across the atmosphere creating a spectacular spectrum. Despite the rider's drowsiness, he continued on his mission, wishing for the town to meet him sooner rather than later.

After many minutes the horse slowed and the man slumped backward, unclipping the satchel from the animal's side, letting it fall to the sandy floor beneath him. The creaking, metal gates creeped open revealing the set of dimmed lights. Standing behind the tall blockade were a few men, the one in the centre broad and serious.

A singular roman soldier rushed to the horse, looking back toward the general who stood sternly with his arms folded, his sword sheathed to his hip. The rider in Rangers attire slipped off his stallion and turned to face the general as the Roman soldier dealt with the horse. The spy unbuttoned his disguise to expose the Roman tunic he wore underneath.

"What news do you bring, Kaecilius?" Lucien asked, holding out a large, muscular hand.

"All in due time General. First I require rest, but take me to the Governor, this news is of the utmost importance."

"As you wish," Lucien replied, commanding the soldier to take the horse to the stables while beckoning the spy to follow him towards the palace.

They entered through a side entrance and after scaling a towering staircase, the pair arrived at a bold, maroon door which the general knocked on four times before patiently waiting a moment for Numitor to signal their permittance.

An agitated "Enter" was heard. Kaecilius opened the door, the first thing he saw was the governor himself, restless and jittery, standing over a table with a map on top and several markers placed around it. Numitor turned his head slightly showing his raw, red eyes and scruffy hair.

"What news could you possibly bring, spy?"

Lucien gestured for Kaecilius to speak at last.

"Governor, I bring news of something urgent. I believe an invasion is imminent on Socratis."

The general audibly gasped before replying, "If the Rangers plan to retaliate against us in our own home we need to be ready. If it is okay with you, Governor, I will..."

An uncanny, croaky laugh emanated from the governor who stood with his back to the two confused visitors.

"The Rangers are coming *here?*" Numitor asked deliriously, cackling.

"Yes, Governor, it is most urgent."

The governor continued to laugh, "If they are coming to Socratis, my son will desire to come with them. Octavius Karvajal will be sending my boy back into my arms. All of this effort and for nothing!"

He gleefully chuckled, throwing his papers and maps into the air with them floating back to the ground elegantly.

"Prepare the defences," he said, now in a serious tone, "I want every soldier on the lookout for my son. Bring him back to me, alive. I will not fail to keep him here for a second time."

CHAPTER 13 –
The Return to Socratis

Clear, blinding white light streamed into the makeshift stables as the wooden shutters were opened, leading out to the flat land beyond the Castellum Lapideum.

Aurelius and Quintilianus both entered the cave, a musty smell hitting them. The latter quickly found his steed, caressing its mane. Aurelius turned to face the seven strong-looking soldiers that were following behind them.

"Each one of you has been chosen for this mission specifically as it will be an incredibly difficult manoeuvre and requires absolute precision. We leave at sundown tonight, so pick out your mount now and make any preparations you need to before that time. I will be waiting here for you."

The commander stopped abruptly as he saw an unusual shape crouching behind the edge of one of the stables.

"Atticus, explain your presence."

Sighing, the boy stood back up and moved over to where Aurelius was standing, the watchful gaze of the soldiers upon him.

"You are travelling to Socratis to retrieve the gemstone, are you not? I would think a guide would be necessary."

Aurelius looked down at him with stern eyes, seeming to take a few moments to fully process Atti's proposal.

"How do I know you will not betray us to your father, Atticus?"

"Because look where I have aligned myself! Would it really make sense to stay here all this time if only to take you down later? And besides, if that were the case why risk being killed in the process?"

"There are many reasons for why a man may betray his company, although they are valid points. However, I must speak to Karvajal. He will decide your course of action. Meet here at sundown and you will find the answer."

As the sun began to set, Atti made his way to the stable area, his silver sword strapped to his back, dagger sheathed on his belt, dressed in a brown tunic with silver armour plates and gauntlets. He traversed the many corridors until he found himself alone in a darkened hallway that didn't seem to end. For a moment the lanterns flickered off and the corridor was submerged into complete darkness.

Then, in the abyss, a pair of blood-red eyes became apparent, boring into Atti's eyes, causing him to spasm, falling to the floor in agony as a screeching sound rang out inside his head, an inescapable feeling. He shouted out for help despite the fact that he would not hear a response. The eyes grew larger, now peering down upon the cowering boy underneath it on the cold, hard floor. Atti screamed at the immense pain and writhed around in anguish as the red eyes physically scorched his skin, searing pain into the boy. It seemed that Atti could not escape and that this spasm would never end, until he saw a glimpse of golden light out of the corner of his eye.

Soothingly, a warm hand placed itself on Atti's neck, causing the overwhelming darkness to cease. He shook violently before managing to look up at his saviour, Ennia, who peered at him with worried eyes. She clasped his hand to help him up, bringing him into a comfortable embrace.

"Ennia," Atti gasped, panting heavily.

"What happened?" she questioned worriedly, stepping back and shaking him raucously.

"To be honest, I don't know. There was just this excruciating pain and this dark force that consumed everything. The only thing remotely close to this would be... no it couldn't, surely."

"What? What is it?" the girl questioned.

"My brother. Before he died, he slept in my room and sometimes, sometimes he would spasm and cry out in suffering. My father would fetch the doctors and Adrian would be hurried out of there on a stretcher, with me none the wiser. His condition only worsened and although my father tried everything he could, ultimately Adrian could not survive."

Ennia listened intently before replying, "That's horrible! And, you think you have the same condition?"

"I'm not sure, but for now I'm riding with Aurelius back to Socratis this evening, so I better go."

He turned to leave but Ennia grabbed his arm and pulled him back.

"Are you sure that's a wise idea after what just happened?"

"I'll be fine Ennia, you don't need to worry."

She scoffed and rolled her eyes as Atti continued down the corridor towards the stables.

Ennia watched him leave longingly, a tear sliding down her cheek as a faint memory flashed to the front of her mind. It was the silhouette of her mother, tall, strong and proud walking away from her, surrounded by soldiers and pirates. Ennia had pleaded and begged, but she was powerless to her father's firm, tenacious grip and her mother's fierce determination. Diana climbed on top of her white steed, taking one last look of her only daughter before embarking on her ship into the night with her crew of warriors. She blinked and the vision disappeared, her mind back in the empty stone corridor.

On the other side of the fortress, Atti had arrived at the stables, joining Aurelius, Quintilianus and the other Rangers chosen for the mission. He became a part of the circle of soldiers surrounding Aurelius who stood in his cavalier manner.

"Ah. Atticus. You have arrived."

"I had a bit of trouble on my way but I'm ready now," he replied eagerly, putting his hands behind him while straightening his back.

"My final decision on the matter on whether or not you will join us on this mission is, no, by order of Karvajal himself."

"What!" Atti exclaimed, breaking his posture and rushing up to Aurelius, "You have to take me. You'll need me!"

"I have stated the decision. I am sorry Atticus, you may not return to Socratis, despite whatever intentions you may have."

After a moment, Atti turned and left the stable, hanging by the door to listen in on the group. He overheard Aurelius mention they were leaving within three hours from the back entrance, and so Atti returned to his room and began to make preparations of his own.

As the golden sun began to lower beyond the horizon and the fortress became quiet, Atti changed into his battle gear disguised with a Ranger cloak over him.

He swiftly navigated the hallways until he came upon the stables which, at this time, were deserted. Desperately, he scoured the room and to his favour, he found a lone, brown horse at the end stall. Mounting the steed he urged it to move, but to his frustration the horse refused to budge. Atti kicked his heels against its body, causing it to squeal ferociously, lifting its front legs into the air. Surprised, Atti clasped onto its mane, yanking onto its reins finally causing the horse to move quite quickly.

Rapidly, Atti and his steed raced down the narrow corridors towards the back exit of the Castellum Lapideum, fortunate enough not to encounter any Rangers on patrol. Soon he reached the archway leading out to the plains beyond the fortress, where there seemed to be no sign of Aurelius or his group. Then, off in the far distance, Atti spotted a faint speck of dust retreating from view.

"Come on!" he yelled, flicking the reins causing the horse to sprint expeditiously across the open plains.

The night wind whipped through his hair as the luminous moon loomed above them, surrounded by bright clusters of dazzling stars. Together the pair raced towards the group of horses in front of them, speeding across the great landscape, the repeated sound of hooves drumming against the hard ground the only noise in the tranquil, undisturbed environment.

Pushing the horse to its limits, Atti gained on the advancing group ahead of him, racing towards them with breakneck speed until they began to slow. The group had now stopped by a collection of trees a short distance from the now visible entrance to Socratis, lit by its flaming torches at the metal entrance gate. Atti waited a moment before building the courage to reveal his presence. He dismounted and crawled through the bushes.

"Hello, Atticus," said Aurelius who was standing right in front of him, peering down disappointedly. The rest of the group turned to look at him through the thick darkness, "How did you..."

"Do you really think you would be able to sneak up on us? This mission is incredibly important and dangerous and therefore I had been checking every flank at all times. Besides, it's quite difficult to hide on flat land."

Atti bowed his head in embarrassment.

"I guess I must allow you to join us for our mission now that we are so far from the fortress. So, let us continue with the plan. Quintilianus, if you will."

The soldier took a deep breath before reiterating the plan, all the while side-eyeing Atti. When he had finished, each Ranger donned their respective gear and prepared to ride the last leg of the journey.

On each horse was a coiled rope with a grappling hook attached on one end as well as a backup sword and quiver of arrows. As Atti had come unprepared he was told to share with a Ranger called Cassius tasked with keeping an eye on him. This man still seemed awfully familiar to Atti.

One by one they mounted their horses and stealthily moved towards the town wall.

When they had all arrived at the wall, the Rangers began to haul the grappling hooks over it, using them to climb up efficiently. Once over, Atti gazed upon the town for the first time in what felt like forever.

I'm home...

He quickly descended the steps, following Aurelius who turned round and whispered to the group, "Split up into pairs, look for any sign of the gemstone, report back to me here. Go now!"

Atti and Cassius advanced round the edges of the town, trying to avoid any Romans on patrol. Atti peered up at the palace, imagining his father inside fast asleep, unaware of his son being right under his nose. Then, unexpectedly, a familiar whiteness flashed in front of him, dazing him, although seemingly not affecting Cassius beside him.

The inn. It's calling to me. Just like it did all that time ago. It must have been the gemstone. It has to be!

He ran swiftly now, caring less for any noise he made, Cassius following hastily behind. As they passed an alleyway a quiet grunt could just be heard. Cassius stopped for a second, curious about the sound, allowing Atti to get to the Red Azalea alone. Atti manoeuvred through the streets he grew up in until he reached the old, derelict building in the centre of the town.

It stood shakily, the shattered windows looking as if they belonged to a haunted house, seeming even more ancient since the last time Atti had set eyes upon the building. Slightly ajar was the cracked wooden door up the stone steps in front of him. A pale orange light seeped slowly out of the slim opening, as if afraid of exiting the building. Atti cautiously tip-toed towards the Red Azalea, keeping a firm hand on his dagger, kept at his side. As he neared the door it peculiarly moved outward to him, the handle turning upwards toward his hand. Pulling it open, he set his eyes upon the interior of the ancient building.

The main room inside was mostly bare, although the lack of light hindered his eyesight, save for the unusual orange glow emanating from beneath a rectangular area in the floor. A broken chair lay on top which Atti cast aside, looking around the edge of the floorboards for a sign of an opening. Seeing a carved notch, he yanked the boards upward revealing a chiselled stone staircase leading down to what could have been a wine cellar.

A few unlit torches hung on either side of the ruined staircase, redundant when compared to the overpowering imitation of sunlight being projected throughout the dilapidated, descending corridor. When Atti reached the bottom, the altar was revealed to him.

A perfectly cut slab of stone placed upon carved arches depicting men lifting up the stone which bore the beautiful gemstone laying atop an intricate, faded red cushion laced with gold.

The Gemstone of Moria sparkled with phosphorescence, its golden luminosity bouncing across the cracked stone walls illuminating the crypt-like room. On the far wall was an ancient inscription written in an unfamiliar language. The letters were curved and twisting, conjoined and difficult to read. Atti dismissed the text and cautiously moved toward the altar, shielding his eyes from the scintillating gemstone. It seemed to pulse frequently as he got nearer.

The gemstone was flashing intermittently now, a high-pitched humming sound originating from it. Piercing was the noise that droned on as Atti edged toward the altar, outstretching his arm to it. Opening his hand, he motioned to pick up the gem, hesitating at first. Then, with little care Atti snatched the gemstone.

His hand began to sear in pain, as if it were burning in fire. He recoiled, stepping back and staring at the orange stone flashing effervescently. Peering at his hand he saw scorch marks which hurt as he rubbed his finger over them. Looking back at the altar and then down at his tunic he gained an idea. Atti ripped off a piece of fabric from his tunic, wrapping it around his hand tightly. He edged back over to the altar, his breath heavy and shaking. Atti opened his hand around the gem reluctantly, hesitating.

A crash occurred at the top of the staircase, causing dust to fall from the ceiling. Atti could hear shouting and sounds of anger and anguish above him, prompting him to take the risk and grab the stone once again. Closing his eyes in fear, he then opened one to see his hand completely fine, clutching the Gemstone of Moria, which had dulled in brightness and was just pulsing dimly. Atti turned around toward the stairs as another crash shook the crypt.

He dashed up to the next floor, getting in cover behind a column in the inn. He could hear the commotion more clearly now as Roman soldiers ran past the windows shouting loudly and aggressively. On the other side of the door in the centre of Socratis Atti could see each of the Rangers from the scout group sat tied up bereft of weapons. Surrounded by Romans, Aurelius bided his time by acting calm and signalling to the rest to do the same. Prancing about next to them was seemingly a Roman general, known to Atti as Lucien. He stared intriguingly at each one of the Rangers, walking past them until he reached Aurelius.

"I assume you are the commander of this particular group, or am I incorrect?"

"You are correct, *caenum*."

"Ironic, the only filth here is you. Gladius, pass me your blade. I shall execute this *caenum* myself."

From inside the Red Azalea, Atti tried to listen in on what was being said. Lucien had grasped the silver sword and he began to raise it above Aurelius' head. Desperately Atti struggled to think.

Do I help the man who I have known all my life and is a friend to my father by not disrupting his plans, or do I help the man who has aided me the past year and taught me to be my better self, but risk being captured by my father? Choices, choices, choices...

Aurelius looked up toward the blade and then at the numerous Roman soldiers preparing to execute his creed, his brotherhood, his family. He turned his attention back to the Roman general just as there was a thud behind him. He spun around silently praying, not caring about the sword above his head to see the slumped body of a headless Ranger, the crimson blood spilling and seeping across the brick pathway. The heartless Roman stood above the corpse, his silver blade tarnished with red streaks which dripped to the floor, each patter a beat of Aurelius' heart as he stared upon the lifeless body of his friend, Quintilianus.

Aurelius roared, ripping apart the ropes to charge at Lucien's legs, the Roman's blade falling to the ground. As he did this, Atti jumped from the roof of the Red Azalea, gemstone in hand, onto a Roman soldier, knocking him out cold. He got up quickly, catching the eye of Lucien briefly who was soon tackled once again by Aurelius causing them both to thump to the floor. Now all the Rangers had started to retaliate, fighting against their captors.

Atti had retrieved the sword of his unconscious enemy, engaging in combat with another soldier, taking care to avoid all lethal attacks when fighting as he still felt like he had a special connection to the town and the people. Atti swivelled quickly to block an incoming slash from behind, rolling under the soldier's legs and hitting his back with the hilt of his sword. The soldier yelled in pain as a Ranger rushed past him, driving his sword into the chest of the Roman. Atti stood still for a moment, trying to process the scene happening around him. As he was frozen in place Aurelius crashed onto the ground in front of him, dropping his blade.

"Atticus, you're here! Do you have the Gemstone of Moria?"

As the boy was about to answer Lucien leapt towards them both, Atti stepping in front of Aurelius, blocking the attack.

"Atticus! Why do you protect this scum? He has done nothing for you."

"That's where you're wrong Lucien!" Atti exclaimed, knocking the sword out of the Roman general's hand.

"I see your blade work has improved, but your traitorous nature does upset me. Just wait until your father gets here. He will set you right."

"He won't get the chance!" Atti replied, kicking Lucien in the stomach before stepping back, allowing Aurelius to engage Lucien in hand-to-hand conflict.

"Aurelius, we have to leave. If the boy has the gemstone, we have what we came for. We don't want to risk any more casualties," Cassius remarked before swinging at an armoured Roman.

"Yes, we must leave with haste. Men, rally on me!" the Rangers commander bellowed, striking Lucien on the forehead.

Subsequently the Rangers gathered together, narrowly fighting off the waves of oncoming Romans. As soon as they had all assembled in a circular form they began to move toward the nearest street. Creating an opening, the compact group of Rangers including Atti began to run through the town to the wall where their ropes were still in place.

As they neared the wall Atti heard a familiar but aged voice call out from behind.

"Atticus, my son! Do not leave me again!"

For a second Atti turned round to glimpse his father beckoning him from the edge of the palace balcony, his governor's robes torn, black hair messy with bloodshot eyes and an uncontrolled stubble. For once in the longest time, Atti could see through his father's stern and flinty facade and into the worry and care glistening in his eyes. A passing notion. He turned back and focused on reaching the wall.

Once they had arrived, they quickly clambered up the stairs and slid down the other side, rapidly yanking the ropes off of the top of the wall. The many sounds of angry Romans faded as they mounted their horses and began to ride back toward the Castellum Lapideum before the Romans could follow them.

Cassius, who had been chosen to share his horse with Atti, remained unhappy with the boy on the journey, despite Atti repeatedly showing him the alluring gemstone.

For the rest of the night the Rangers rode back in silence, beaten and bruised, mourning the brutal death of their companion. Aurelius especially felt the immense pain after going up against the fearsome Roman general, multiple cuts and bruises plaguing his battered body. As they neared the fortress the early sun rose to meet them, casting a golden light over the wide plains that made the men feel small in comparison to the ample expanse of land that they were travelling upon. By the time they had reached the home of the Rangers the whole acreage was bathed in the blazing sunlight. As they began to dismount their exhausted steeds, Atti silently questioned his actions.

Was it right for me to go back on my friends like that? Was it the right thing? Seeing my father worried, for the first time, it makes you think... Am I on the right side of things?

CHAPTER 14 – The Weapon

Numitor desperately held an outstretched arm extended over the edge of the palace balcony. Streaks of sweat poured down his face like a waterfall, all of his etiquette and formal appearance thrown out of the window in that one moment, when he called, "Atticus, my son! Do not leave me again!"

Thoughts of worry and fear – rare feelings for the governor – rapidly flashed through his mind as he witnessed his only remaining son run away from him with men he considered the enemy. Close behind the troop of Rangers was Lucien and a fresh batch of soldiers pounding their feet against the hard slabs of stone.

The Rangers had started to climb the steps with Atti at the forefront of them. Numitor made an alarmed exclamation as a flaming arrow narrowly missed his son, striking the hard stone wall beside him.

"Watch where you're firing!" he yelled worriedly, desperately trying to come up with a plan.

The governor moved his head from side to side in search of a way to get down when the spy Kaecilius came up behind him. Concerned, he asked, "Governor, what's happening?"

"An ambush, if you could not see already. If you want to be of any use, get over there and bring back my son, now!"

As Kaecilius began to run back toward the outer stairs Numitor called him back.

"What is it, Governor?"

"Do you still hold your cover amongst the militia of Rangers, Kaecilius?"

"I believe so," the spy replied.

"Would it be possible to return to their fortress before that group of soldiers do?" he questioned, pointing toward the commotion of Rangers, a few of which were still clambering up the stairs of the East wall.

"If I had the aid of the fastest steed we have then yes, I could make it."

"Perfect," Numitor stated cheerfully, producing a sealed parchment letter from the inside of his robe and passing it to Kaecilius as well as a copper token with an engraving on it.

"Take that letter and token to the stable and request Aello. If the stable master refuses, present that token to him. I want you to ride to their fortress as fast as possible and leave that letter in whatever room Atticus is staying in, but do this secretly. We cannot jeopardise your position there at any cost, do you understand?"

"Yes, Governor, I will ride at once."

Loud was the clang of the hammer upon the anvil, coming down upon the silver shape with an unmatchable force. The tool struck the iron over and over, the sound ringing throughout the enclosed and smoky forge. When the ash-faced blacksmith was content with his new product, he grabbed the metal piece with his oversized, glove-encased hands and placed it upon a stone-topped workbench. After, he utilised a pair of tongs to fish out a similar steel shape from a lava-filled cauldron which bubbled vigorously as he neared it. The second axe head glowed orange as the blacksmith set it down next to its identical counterpart on the workbench.

Fetching a wooden handle, he joined the pieces together to forge a magnificent, shining silver axe which sparkled in the fiery light of the forge. After this, he hung the axe from a hook to let it cool before returning to work on another weapon, wiping the sweat from his brow.

His black hair was messy and overgrown like an ancient jungle matching his rough, grizzled beard that he sported on his chin. Contrasting his caveman appearance, he had surprisingly soft eyes which hinted at the friendliness he hid inside the tough outer shell. With large, heavy, silver armour on, it was clear the blacksmith had great strength but also a lack of mobility. Just as he picked up another slab of metal to mould, Karvajal and a welcoming party arrived in the constricted forge.

"Vulcan! Drop everything at once, I require your services," Karvajal commanded, his voice echoing throughout the room.

Vulcan cast aside his chunk of metal and greeted his leader at the entrance to his second home, sighing as he knew he would not be able to leave for a while. "What do you need?" the blacksmith asked, bowing his head.

Almost immediately, Karvajal presented the Gemstone of Moria to all around him, its natural sparkle illuminating even the darkest corners of the tenebrous forge. He held the gem with a brown leather glove, advising Vulcan to do the same. Upon him asking why, Karvajal replied, "You do not want to find out."

Rubbing the palm of his left hand as he did so. the blacksmith cupped the gemstone with both hands, admiring its natural effervescence before Karvajal spoke again.

"If you would not mind, Vulcan, I would like you to use this stone to create a tool of great magical power. While it may sound unheard of, I assure you this is the only way for us to vanquish our enemies and become free once again and not fret from pursuit."

Vulcan nodded in response, marvelling at the magnificent source of power he held in his hand. Snapping out of his trance, he looked up and said, "You realise I specialise in metallurgy and not magic."

"I am aware, but I also know you are the finest blacksmith in the country and that you are most definitely capable for this task, and this is not the first time you will have crafted something that is not a weapon," Karvajal said with a stern tone, grimacing at the memory of his love Cecilia and the traitor Numitor.

"Well, now that you mention it, I had made something long ago which might just do the trick."

Vulcan retreated to a back area of the forge, retrieving an intricately carved wooden staff from a shelf above him, bringing it back to his leader. The stave looked as if it could have come from Pax's olive tree, its beauty not dissimilar to that of the gemstone that Vulcan held in his other hand. He set both items of refinement down upon his work bench, grasping his hammer. On the edge of the staff was a spherical mould that looked like it could fit a circular stone inside, which is what made it ideal in the blacksmith's mind.

Using his hammer and chisel, he delicately smoothed the gemstone with exact precision as Karvajal and his guards watched in silent patience; the process taking longer than Karvajal had expected, though he still awaited eagerly like a child waiting for his present.

Each clang of the steel hammer striking the gemstone at different intervals gained a wince from the supposedly indomitable leader, while Vulcan kept a surprisingly calm and tender way about him as he chipped away at the sparkling stone.

After an excruciating amount of time and the course of many deafening crashes of metal striking metal, Vulcan drew a sigh of relief and held up the fully symmetrical sphere in his gloved hand, smiling as he gazed into its glistening, golden glow emitting from the gemstone.

"Is it done?" Karvajal asked curiously but impatiently, taking a step toward the workbench. Vulcan held out a hand to stop him before carefully picking up the staff. With a sense of pride, the blacksmith carefully placed the shimmering stone into the graceful embrace of the wooden staff. As soon as the two connected, it was as if all of time had aligned perfectly to reach this moment. The staff shook vigorously and the Gemstone of Moria shone brighter than ever before.

Karvajal stared upon it greedily, grabbing the staff out of the blacksmith's hands. He admired the mystical weapon fondly, holding it with purpose. Delicately, he waved the staff and the gemstone began to glow accordingly.

As a test, Karvajal cast it forward. The staff shot a thick beam of golden light towards the far wall, a gust of wind emanating from the tip of the staff as it did so, blasting a deep hole in the seemingly impenetrable stone wall.

Guffawing, he said, "Excellent work, Vulcan. This weapon will more than suffice."

The blacksmith felt pleased until a dark thought overcame him. As Karvajal began to leave, he asked, "If you don't mind me asking, I wonder, what is your plan?"

"My plan? Well, of course, to defeat our enemy in Socratis and become free people again!"

"And while I understand that, what shall we do after? As a large community of warriors many of us will not be able to adjust to life without war."

Karvajal turned stern and then smiled before speaking, "Vulcan, I am glad you asked. I have realised that a man's greatest power is ambition. And so, once we defeat that buffoon Numitor, why not capture Socratis? And then, just for fun, we kick them out of their own village and make them the hunted.

Give them a taste of their own medicine, I say. And after that, why stop at one town when we can have more? More power, more land. And maybe, just maybe my dear friend, we can take down Emperor Alexius himself and take the entire empire for ourselves. I mean, with this staff in my hand I feel unstoppable, surely nothing can stop us from taking everything for ourselves?

Let us – the ones in fear – become the ones striking fear into others. We could make a perfect world where people don't need to be scared of anything but falling out of line with our policies. Our oppression can keep people in line, you see? I will be the hero.

With this sort of power that you have provided me, we can do whatever we please. We will be truly free."

The silence after was overwhelming. Vulcan breathed in heavily before replying, "If, if that is how you feel my Leader, I am not one to get in the way of your ambition. Not at all."

Karvajal smiled and left the forge promptly after, chuckling to himself all the while.

Vulcan's heart pounded as he questioned where his loyalties lay. "What have I done?" he said out loud before taking a look around the forge and leaving in search of a friend, someone to confide in.

When Atti entered his room inside of the Castellum Lapideum he took no notice of the mysterious letter sitting upon his bedside table or the scratched piece of copper that lay on top of it. Instead, he collapsed upon his straw-stuffed mattress, groaning as his forehead hit the metal frame supporting his bed before drifting off to a much-needed state of unconsciousness.

By the time he had awoken, it was late afternoon - a result of a light knock at his door. Stirring in his bed, the knock continued and grew slightly more aggressive, prompting Atti to reluctantly get onto his feet, standing up in his bloodied clothes, tainted with dirt, blood, sweat and grime.

Drowsily, Atti grasped the handheld mirror from the bedside table and took a glance at himself, seeing his mucky, messy mop of hair and sullied face, scrapes of mud and sweat across his brow. The bed had a similar story. Disgusted by his own appearance, Atti washed his face vigorously and quickly cleaned himself up before answering the door for the evidently impatient visitor.

Before he even had time to register who that visitor was, Ennia pushed open the door and flung her arms around Atti before shaking her head and stepping back, looking partially displeased.

The second he opened his mouth Ennia countered, exclaiming, "When did you get back? Why didn't you tell me? What was Socratis like? Did you get the gemstone? What the hell happened?"

"Alright, alright. One question at a time, okay? And sorry for not coming to find you, I was kind of exhausted when we got back. A lot happened when we were there."

Atti felt his pocket for the gemstone, but to his initial surprise he found it gone. Then he remembered Aurelius had taken the gemstone just before they had arrived back in the fortress. With his memory coming back to him, Atti recounted the events of the night before, sparing no detail about the retrieval of the gemstone and the magic that had been put in place to prevent any thieves. When he had finished his story Ennia was silent for a few moments before nodding and pointing at the letter on the table.

"What's that?"

Atti squinted in confusion and turned his head to see the sealed piece of parchment, lifting up the copper token to see *Atticus* written in black ink upon the blank side.

"I'm not sure," he replied, picking up the letter and carefully opening it, tossing the token to Ennia.

"It's from my father," Atti stated, and with a prompt from the girl he began to read the letter aloud.

"My dear son Atticus,

I sincerely hope this letter reaches you so that I may deliver some sense into that brain of yours. Now while I do not know of the conditions of your time with these Rangers, I know that for the last five months I have been broken down over and over again in the constant search for you. I hope that I will see you soon and you will reconsider coming back to Socratis, as I know this whole escapade with the Rangers is surely but a phase.

I understand that you are confused and I fully accept this, which is partly the reason I am not performing a colossal invasion on the Rangers just to retrieve you.

You are a smart boy Atticus, and I know you will come to your senses and soon see Octavius the way that I see him, a treacherous, evil, pitiful excuse for a man, for a leader. Align with him now all you want, but it will not change the eventual outcome, I assure you.

On a different note, I had heard about your impressive takedown of Sergeant Titus. A courageous act I must say, and while he was, of course, my ally, I had uncovered his plot to take my place on the throne of Socratis, and so I am thankful for his untimely demise. However, that should not justify the cruel actions of the Rangers and their quite frankly barbaric tactics in warfare.

But still, at least this is proof of your skill. I assume the result of the training you received from Matteo. He wishes you were here; he has a lot more responsibilities now that I am Governor. I know he misses talking with you, Atticus. Just remember that I am always here, in Socratis, and for the time being I am your only family. I may not have been supporting you during the hardest times, but this is exactly the reason why I urge you to come back home, so that we can regain what we have lost! And so, I eagerly await your return..."

Atti stopped reading as he saw the following line which read,

'It is crucial you do not share this next piece of information with anyone but me, especially none of your Ranger acquaintances.'

"That's how it ends," he said, placing the letter on the table.

"Well, it looks like he cares for you and truly wants you back there, but if you are not certain, don't feel compelled to. It's completely your decision and I'll be with you the entire time if you want," Ennia replied while suppressing memories of her own parents.

"Thanks, but I think I need to think this over myself."

"Oh, okay. I'll be in my room if you need me."

Ennia exited the room, hiding a tear from Atti.

Once the door had slipped shut, Atti grasped the letter once more and quietly read the last part to himself.

'Now Atticus, I must confess. I have kept a secret from you for the larger portion of your life, and though this is hardly the way I wanted this to go, I feel I must inform you now.

Shortly after your brother became sick all of those years ago, I put some research into the mysterious disease that had corrupted both Adrian and your mother. None of the scientists of these lands had ever seen the likes of it before. On the night of Adrian's death, which you most likely remember, I had hired two men – known only as 'The Doctors' who had come from a faraway place in the hope that they could cure him. Though, of course, that was not the case.

However, my research did not yield empty results. I discovered that the disease is... passed through the family line. I do not know at this time if you contain the disease or not but this is only even more reason to return to the safety of home where I can help you. I urge...'

Fed up with the letter and not caring about the rest of the text, Atti ripped up the letter aggressively, yelling in anger as he did so, leaving the letter as a pile of shreds on the floor. Enraged, Atti pummelled his fists against his outer wall, before stopping and catching his breath, whispering, "Why tell me now? Why hide the information for all this time? How could this be the best option?"

In a state of distress, Atti slumped back on his bed and silently sobbed to himself, discomforted with the knowledge he had just received. However, after a few minutes and through teary eyes, he angrily leaned forward with the intent of ripping the envelope too, when Atti spotted something poking out of it. Reaching for it, he unfolded the piece of parchment. From the looks of it, it seemed to be a short clipping from a collection of letters, ones much older than the one Numitor had sent him.

Atti struggled to make out the writing at first, but soon he read the whole extract.

'Dear Numitor Caeso,

I am deeply sorry to report that my daughter, your wife Cecilia, has perished due to this unknown illness which our medical assistants here in Syvota could not fix. I am writing to you partly to inform you of her death but also to tell you some pleasant news in an otherwise darkened and deeply upsetting situation, that being the birth of your newborn son who Cecilia had named 'Atticus' as her dying words.

We feel obligated to ask you if you would dearly care for the child as well as little Adrian, although if you feel this is too big of a task, my wife and I would gladly care for the child instead. Please write back to us urgently. Caeso, we await your response.

Garcia Longinus'

Atti stayed gripping the letter for quite some time, his newly created tears sticking to his face or falling onto the aged parchment. He kept his head low, while just outside of his room Ennia waited for several moments before deciding to take a walk through the fortress.

As she moved toward the council room, she overheard two men talking indistinctly round the corner. Edging closer, she recognised one of the voices to be belonging to Aurelius.

"Are you sure about this, Vulcan?"

"Marcus, he said it to my face, in my forge! And now that he has that staff, he really could kill Numitor and do everything else he says he will!"

"But kill Emperor Alexius? That seems like too colossal a task even for our leader *with* this staff you say you built. Even with this gemstone can it really be that powerful?"

"Just wait until you see it, Marcus. Some of my finest work. I just regret giving it to that power-hungry swine."

"I will need to consult Octavius on this, but if what you're saying is true, he really has gone mad…"

Ennia listened in with surprise but eager intent. Once they had finished speaking Ennia turned to return back to her room just as Aurelius spotted her.

"Ennia. What are you doing here in the corridors?"

"Just taking a walk," she replied, hoping the commander would not realise she was eavesdropping on his conversation.

"Well, you best hurry back and clean yourself up, we have the big feast later."

"Of course. I'll see you then."

With that she quickly paced back towards her room, wishing she had not been spotted.

CHAPTER 15 – Heads and Tails

Atti received a light knock at his door at the earliest moment in the morning. The day before, Atti had remained in his room and not spoken to a soul, pondering the letter and its contents. Slightly waking up, his mind tried to guess who it could be before telling him to get up and open it.

Ennia had her hand held up as if to knock again. The door opened. She noticed Atti's wet cheeks and eyes along with the ripped-up pieces of parchment on the table in his room. Thinking better than to question it, she offered to go into her room. Atti agreed and they entered Ennia's room which was significantly messier than his.

Once they had closed the door and made sure no one else was within earshot, Ennia spoke, "I have to tell you something. It's important and I beg that you listen at first and ask questions after, but do not dismiss what I have to say."

"Of course," he replied, sitting down upon her untidy bed.

"Well, you see. Octavius Karvajal is not the man he says he is."

Atti frowned in puzzlement but allowed her to continue.

"Earlier I went for a walk through the fortress and I overheard something. Two people. One of them was

Aurelius but I did not recognise the other. Unfortunately, I was around the corner and could not see the other man, though I know his name to be Vulcan. They were discussing something important. From what I have heard it seems that Karvajal has had the gemstone made into some sort of weapon, and a powerful one at that. Some sort of magic staff I think, but that's not the worst of it...

Vulcan told Aurelius that Karvajal plans to take over Socratis and kill your father! He even said Karvajal wants to kill Emperor Alexius himself and take over the entire Empire! We can't allow this, can we?"

Atti stared for a moment while he processed the information Ennia had provided. After a short moment he stood up purposefully.

"You're lying," he said accusingly, offended that she would even say such things.

"No Atti, why would I lie?"

"I don't know Ennia, but what you're saying just doesn't add up."

"You don't believe me, do you?"

"How can I? Your accusations are wild and you expect me to just accept your word for it and with no physical proof, no evidence?"

"So now you don't trust me? After everything?"

"Of course I trust you, but I also trust Karvajal!"

"You trust the man your father hates? How does that make any sense?"

"My father is a fool! A man unworthy of the title of Governor. Besides, do you question everything I do?

Karvajal and the Rangers have brought us in, fed us, trained us and aided us in every way and now you dare to question his plans?"

"I'm not questioning anything, Atti. I'm simply recounting what I've heard."

"Well maybe you need your ears checked. I'd rather return to my father on a silver platter than believe your word."

"I can't believe this..." she said with a heartbroken but angered tone, grabbing a small bag of things and leaving the room hastily, slamming the door behind her and leaving Atti alone in her room He processed what had just happened and shut down Ennia's claims.

She can't be right, can she?

After a few minutes he left the room but recoiled as a collection of soldiers ran past with full gear on. Atti stopped one Ranger to ask him what was going on, and he replied with, "We're going to war, son. You best get yourself armoured up."

In the midst of the chaos and scuttle of feet, Atti headed toward the armoury in search of Aurelius. He followed the massive crowd of Rangers, assuming they were heading in the desired direction.

Seeing the swarm of soldiers heading to battle around him reminded Atti of the times he had as a small child, admiring the Roman soldiers departing Socratis for a mission, usually led by his father and Lucien. All day he would imagine what adventures and epic fights the soldiers went on until they returned in the late evening. Atti would still be awake despite Matteo's pleading, just so he could question his father as soon as he returned, although Numitor was not much of the talkative type.

Since those days Atti had always wanted to be a soldier which is why he trained nearly every day at every interval he had between his studying and formal dinners with the former Governor Cicero.

How different my life has turned out. I guess I still became a soldier in a way, just on a different side. But is this truly the side I want to be on? I need some answers to be certain.

Soon the bevy reached the armoury where the soldiers dispersed in search of the rest of their gear. Atti asked a Ranger lieutenant where he could find the commander, but to no avail. After what felt like searching for a needle in a haystack amongst the busy population of chattering soldiers, he found Aurelius in a side room containing the commander's armour and personal belongings.

Perfect.

Atti headed into the room with a purposeful stride.
"Commander."
"Atticus!" he exclaimed joyfully, gesturing for him to take a seat in the leather chair next to the planning table

containing a map with many pins placed at different points. He finished fastening on his armour, holding his helmet as he turned back round and asking, "What can I do for you? Looking for some armour?"

"Not quite. I wanted to ask you something... important."

"Well, ask away. I am at your service."

"Does Karvajal plan to kill my father?"

Aurelius' expression turned grave as he studied Atti's question in his mind. He tightened his grip on the helmet and slowly pulled back the chair opposite Atti, the wooden legs scraping against the stone floor with a screech. Aurelius sat down with a sigh, leaning back in his chair while staring into Atti's eyes.

There's no way I am going to escape this conversation, is there?"

"I need to know Commander. This is my father we're talking about."

"I understand, though I wish I didn't. In answer to your question, yes, Octavius plans to take over Socratis and murder your father for his marble throne. If it's any consolation I disagree strongly with this and I wish he would look for a more peaceful solution, but alas I must follow orders."

Atti shook his head in disbelief before replying, "So, I assume that Karvajal also plans to kill Emperor Alexius and control the entire Empire?"

"How do you know of this?" Aurelius said sharply, leaning forward in his chair and landing a fist on the table.

"Never mind that, is it true?"

After a short pause the commander replied, "Yes, and to be completely honest I am glad you know of such a plan. In truth, Octavius has been manipulating you from the start, that was his plan. I sat idly by at first, as I knew it was his full intention to turn you into a weapon to be used against your father as a fail-safe. He believed Caeso would never harm you, allowing you to eventually kill him and fulfil his... prophecy."

"Prophecy? What prophecy?"

"Well...one night Octavius awoke in the early morning and he sought me out, feeling he trusted me. He recounted an all too real dream he had had that night where he was standing on the balcony of the Governor's palace, a benevolent leader to all of the people of Socratis, or at least that's what he told me."

"But that's preposterous! The people would never accept a man like him."

"Maybe so, but ever since Octavius has been obsessed with this 'prophecy' as he calls it, and it's been unfortunately confirmed by this plan he has made. He believes ultimately that if he can become a caring leader of one town, then why stop there? I can only hope he can be helped."

"You could always help me and rebel. I've realised now that I've been fighting on the wrong side, but it's not just me. Karvajal has brainwashed all of these people into thinking he's the benevolent leader he strives to be. We can free these people and then only he has to get hurt!"

"I realise what you are saying is quite valiant Atticus, but I cannot leave with you. Even if I dislike Octavius as much as anyone, he gave me a position here no man would dare to jeopardise. I can't expect you to understand but I know you are a mature enough man by now to make the tough decisions I am unable to make myself. My advice to you now is to leave this place for good, make a life for yourself. You are too young to be caught up in a conflict like this, it is not fair on who you are."

"So, you really won't come with me?"

"I wish I could, Atticus, I really do."

"Then, I guess this is goodbye."

"I'm sure we will see each other again."

"I hope so Aurelius."

With that, Atti departed from the office and escaped through the bustle of soldiers preparing for a fight that deep down they were against.

When he reached the empty corridors, Atti headed for his room to gather his things and prepare to leave this fortress of lies and deception, as he saw it.

Ennia was right, and I shut her down. I wish I could take back everything, but who knows where she went. I really messed up this time, didn't I? I pushed away the only person I can really trust over someone who was using me this whole time. I can't let this bring me down. I will find you, Ennia.

Once he had put on his armour, gathered a bag of belongings and put his sword in its hilt on his back Atti headed toward the entrance to the forest, as that was the place he first met Ennia, the first time she had ran away. There was a scarce amount of people who had aided him, and by the time he reached the cold outside, the sun had started to set. He rushed out into the biting air, yelling Ennia's name over and over.

Running even further into the labyrinth-like forest, Atti desperately called out for his friend until his voice grew hoarse. The night had soon come and Atti fell to the ground in despair, exhaustion and tiredness overcoming him. He started to consider returning to the fortress as a last resort when suddenly the world started to distort and a familiar, deafening screech filled Atti's ears.

The intimidating red eyes returned, more furious than before, burning into his side. Atti screamed out in agonising pain, coming to the realisation that he was in the middle of nowhere with no one to save him.

Down on his hands and knees now, Atti barely survived against the sheer suffering, his back feeling as if on fire. Braving the pain, he jerked up his head to see the malevolent eyes watching him from above. Knowing he had to act, Atti surged forward toward the eyes in an attempt to fight back, but he was only greeted with even more excruciating anguish. Atti collapsed onto the floor hopelessly, accepting that he could not beat the overwhelming agony that befell him.

Just as Atti thought that his life was over and that his downfall was a result of the unknown disease which had destroyed his family, a similar golden light grasped his clenched fist. It then pulled him out of the embrace of the distressing darkness, immediately relieving Atti from the pain. After taking a few seconds to regain his breath, Atti looked up to see Ennia in a worried state, her eyes teary and determined.

"What happened to you?" she breathed, placing a hand on Atti's shoulder to calm him down.

"It was another spasm like before, but even worse. I tried to fight back, but I couldn't. It overpowered me. I felt hopeless."

"But, are you okay now?"

"Yes, thanks to you. I don't know what would have happened if you hadn't saved me. Who knows? I might have even..."

"Stop! Don't say anymore." Ennia pleaded, "The good news is you are alive, and anyway what were you even doing out here?"

"Looking for you," Atti replied, straightening his back and rubbing it, surprised to not find any scorch marks.

"I'm flattered, but why?"

"Because, I realised you were right, and I am so incredibly sorry that I ever doubted you the way I did. I was wrong to trust Karvajal, as I learnt from Aurelius. It turns out the Warmonger has been manipulating me from the start, his plan being to turn me against my own father, and the scary part is that it almost worked. But it's not just me, all of those Rangers admire Karvajal as a benevolent leader but they are blind to his evil intent, it's all an act! His charm, his kindness, his generosity, all of it! And I am ashamed to think I ever supported him in the way that I did. I also learned that Karvajal only plans for this takeover because of some 'prophecy' which he claims to have had in a dream. Surely, he is deluded?"

"Of course, and I accept your apology. I'm just glad we are together again. I feel you are the only one I can trust at the moment, Atti, which is why it was heartbreaking for you to dismiss me like that."

"I understand Ennia, and I feel the same. I don't know who to side with in this oncoming war, but I know I will feel safer with you by my side."

Ennia nodded in agreement and the two embraced warmly, friends reunited in trust. Stepping back, the two looked towards the colourful sunset seeping through the gaps between the trees.

"So, what now?" Ennia questioned in the silence once they had sat down, staying there for the rest of the sunset.

The crickets chirped under the pale moon which hung low in the sky, projecting a pristine twilight onto the landscape below as the pair fell into a deep sleep, accompanying each other once more.

CHAPTER 16 –
The Calm before the Storm

The night was tranquil in Socratis, the moon, a glowing yellowy white, loomed ominously, surrounded by an ethereal haze. Many candles were unlit in the windows of houses, but a warm light emitted from the grandiose palace that stood taller than every other building, its corner spires protruding out into the open air.

The palatial archway opened into the decorated office of the governor of Socratis. Inside sat Numitor with Lucien at his side, and opposite them was Kaecilius clutching a note in his hand.

"Speak, spy," said Numitor, leaning back in his chair, clutching a glass of wine in his hand classily.

Kaecilius began to speak rapidly, and so the governor encouraged him to be calm and say his words slower and with purpose.

"Governor, I have reason to believe that Octavius Karvajal plans to take siege on our town!"

"Now? Why at this time?"

"Because he has created a weapon of great destruction, forged with the item they retrieved from here in Socratis."

Numitor took a minute before saying, "If this is true then we are in grave danger. Do you have any evidence for this matter?"

The spy lifted the parchment in his hand and handed it to Numitor who unravelled and studied it intensely. On the parchment was a rough drawing of the staff created by the Ranger blacksmith containing the Gemstone of Moria. The drawing was scratched and faint, the edges torn and crumpled.

"This is your proof?"

"In all honesty, I have not seen this weapon, but the preparations *are* going ahead and the Rangers are coming here soon."

Lucien then whispered into the ear of his governor, "How can we be certain that the spy is telling the truth?"

"Because he has no reason to lie," Numitor replied with certainty.

Kaecilius raised a finger in a questioning manner.

"Yes?" was the abrupt reply.

"I was wondering if I could stay in Socratis for now and spend time with my family before the Rangers attack. I want to see them as you never know when my last day is on the horizon and with all this time with the Rangers, I have not been spared any time to spend with them, save the time before their ambush. Do you excuse me?"

"Yes, yes I excuse you, spy. Now leave so I can discuss with General Lucien in private," Numitor said, waving a hand.

"Yes of course, thank you also," Kaecilius called as he shut the door into the office on his way out.

Lucien circled around the governor and sat down in front of him in the chair that Kaecilius had been seated in.

Numitor lowered his head as he said despairingly, "No matter how hard I try, or have tried to prevent it, as a soldier, a general, an advisor and now a Governor, war seems to be inevitable. My time as leader has been depressing at most, but I have learnt that peace is but a wishful outcome, a goal that can never come to fruition. And even if you manage to capture some sliver of tranquillity and keep it bottled through violent and undesirable means, the calm and quiet never stays and darkness *always* prevails. Thus is the way of the world, it would seem.

You may ask, Lucien, how does one find happiness in knowing this, and to be truthful there are not many pathways available to reach a state of true happiness. But, if you are willing to push the worries of the world to the back of your mind, I have found that you can find happiness when spending your time with the people you love and care for instead of worrying about an unachievable outcome.

I had experienced this before, my darling wife and I lived in pure joy once, only increased by the arrival of our son, Adrian, and for one limited period of time we were truly happy. Now I have neither of them, my only remaining relative having left me as well, gifting himself into the arms of my enemy just to spite me.

I am Governor of this town, a goal that has come true for me, but as I have said before, my dear friend, I do not feel happy or relieved to gain this position. Rather, it is another burden I must carry on my back as I walk further to the gates of the underworld so that I can become a Di Mane like my ancestors and finally be reunited with my family, the ones I love, so that I can truly be content and rest at last."

"And what of your son?" Lucien asked, staring at the teary-eyed Numitor who held his head in his hands.

"He dissociates with me, hates me. Is that my fault? I pushed him away, and now I shall never have him back on my side. I am fully alone and without my family. What did I do to deserve this?"

The governor wept, then he turned serious, removing his hands from his wet face.

"Atticus has chosen his side. If he wishes to be loyal to that bringer of death then so be it. Karvajal wants me, he has a compulsion to watch me die in my son's arms and that cannot be. I have waited long enough but tonight is that moment. Preparations must be made. Karvajal must be stopped before he causes any more misfortune for me, for my people and for the people of Italia."

"You want to attack the Rangers, Numitor, without the help of the New Guard who we brought in for this exact reason?"

"Do not be fooled, Lucien. This feud between us and the Rangers has always been personal, involving outside forces was a clear mistake by Cicero. He never truly understood our enemy like I do. Besides, I do not trust them, especially now that their leader is dead and the Warlock has disappeared. The New Guard are unpredictable. We cannot put our lives and the lives of my people in their hands."

"So, what do you propose, officially?" Lucien questioned.

Numitor stood up from his chair and moved over to the window overlooking Socratis. He took a sip from the glass of wine he had cupped in his hand before letting it drop to the ground in a crash.

"One week. In one week we attack Karvajal and destroy the Rangers once and for all. Gather all of our soldiers, alert them at once."

"But what if we fail in our venture?"

Numitor paused briefly, "Then Socratis will be doomed under the leadership of a psychotic warmonger for many years to come."

Lucien nodded before standing once again, retrieving his blade and exiting the office. He headed towards the barracks as the luminous moon ascended into the enveloping blanket of blackness, now decorated with miniature specks of brightness like sprinkles on a cake.

The general thought that most of the soldiers would be asleep in their homes at this hour as he opened the gate leading to the barracks. As he ventured further, he started to hear the clang of two blades, the noise ringing throughout the building.

Arriving at the sparring area Lucien was unsurprised to see Gladius and Hortensius fighting with intensity, performing strong blows but being careful not to fatally injure their opponent and friend. Hortensius lunged forward quickly, making it seem like he was going to strike Gladius' leg, but he pulled back while laughing, setting his sword down on the side with Gladius doing the same.

"General. What do you need at this hour?"

"It is official. Numit... our Governor has commissioned preparations for an all-out assault on the fortress of the Rangers in one week. I hope to see you two there with me on the frontlines when we attack. I value you two as some of my best soldiers."

"Then we will be there alongside you, General," said Hortensius, bringing a fist to his chest.

"As will I," Gladius stated, repeating his friend's gesture.

Lucien grinned proudly before saying, "Now leave for your homes and get some rest. I expect to see you here early tomorrow morning for extra training. Understood?"

"Yes General!" both soldiers recited before grabbing their gear and retreating home in the dead of night.

Lucien took a minute to catch his breath and take in the situation, travelling to the town centre to take a seat and let the night air come to him. The night air was stale but contained a slight breeze, passing through the general's hair. He began speaking to himself once he was assured that no one else was about.

"Do I want to do this? Do I want to attack those people, kill them for the Governor? Numitor is a great friend of mine and I would sacrifice myself for him, but sometimes it feels as if he is not in control. As if he is losing his mind. His own son has turned against him. What does that do to a man? If I had a son, I would want to stay by him for every day of his life, or as much as possible like any other, but to be deprived of that person in your life, and for Numitor his sole family, it cannot be healthy.

I will carry out his wishes and battle the enemy, though I will take no pride in killing soldiers who are following a cause, the same as me. Numitor was correct, this fight is personal for him and Karvajal alone, and innocent people are getting caught in the middle. Maybe it is a good thing that this ongoing fight is ending, in one week's time. Too many lives have been lost already. I do not know what I would do if I lost my wife, and many people have lost their sons and daughters also. I guess life is the price of war, although no one seems to acknowledge it..."

As the night wore on Lucien sat on the bench contemplating the ethics of war, while many miles away the Rangers prepared for a fight to come, a fight that would end this personal war between Numitor Caeso and Octavius Karvajal.

Atti awoke to the slightest sliver of sunlight which was peeking over the horizon. The morning air was chilled but refreshing, the only sound being the scarce population of birds nearby, a familiar scene for the two of them. Atti savoured the tranquillity and calmness as he knew it would be brief. He glanced down at Ennia who was still asleep, curled up next to him. Slowly, he got up as he adjusted to the light and replaced his sword into its hilt.

From analysing the weather and pattern of wildlife in the forest Atti guessed it was the start of spring; he had studied the seasons many times with Matteo when he was young. Atti always had a fascination with nature and the way of life, he had just lost the time recently to study the beautiful landscapes he found himself traversing across. The birds above him descended to the tangled ground and greeted him with a cheery chirp. He smiled and watched them for several minutes until his companion awoke with a groan.

"Good morning," he greeted, stretching out a hand to the creature closest to him It tilted its head to the side, hopping forward quickly. As Atti opened out his hand toward the bird, a loud screech from a predatory bird came from above the treetops. Fearful, the small birds dispersed, to his disappointment.

"What was that!" Ennia exclaimed, jumping up from her position and grabbing her bow.

"Just an eagle," Atti replied, chuckling at her everlasting vigilance.

"How long have you been awake?"

"Not long."

She paced up and down before speaking once more, "So, what's our plan Atti?"

"I'm not sure. We need to weigh up our options. For obvious reasons we can't go back to the Rangers, and I don't think going to Socratis is a sensible idea considering I fought many of the legionaries I grew up with."

"So, what then? We can't just hide and bide our time while Karvajal ambushes your father and tries to take over the whole Empire! You know he won't stop."

"Look. I'm still getting used to this 'prophecy' news at the moment, but I agree that we have to do something. The only problem is, we would need an army larger than the Romans of Socratis and the Rangers combined! Your mother couldn't provide an army of that calibre?"

Ennia was shocked at Atti's question, "Atti, my mother has been missing for over a decade! I have not seen her in years. What makes you think she will magically want to be in my life now, huh? You don't know what it's like to have a mother who does not care for you, do you?"

"No, of course not. My mother is dead."

Ennia gasped and covered her mouth, suddenly apologising over and over.

"It's fine, Ennia. You did not know, you couldn't have."

After the girl had felt she had apologised accordingly, the two stood in silence until she spoke once more.

"Are you sure you can't think of anyone who could assist us with an army, Atti? None of your father's old friends?"

"No, I don't think... wait."

"What? What are you thinking?" Ennia eagerly asked repeatedly.

Atti pondered the idea for a moment before voicing his thoughts.

"My father met someone, an old friend now, when he took part in the Trials. Benedict Paulinus. I haven't spoken to him in ages but from what I remember, he held a high position in Rome, one of Emperor Alexius' top legati. I'm sure if we paid him a visit, he would understand our situation and help us decide what to do, and maybe he could ask the emperor to give us that army we are in need of!"

Ennia was flabbergasted at Attis' seemingly preposterous plan.

"So, you mean to go to Rome and ask *the emperor* to help us fight against a small group of warriors led by a magic-wielding maniac?"

"Why not? What other choice do we have?"

CHAPTER 17 – The Capital

After many hours of walking under the now scorching sun, the pair happened upon a long strip of parched dirt next to a river which seemed to be a road of some kind. Spotting a signpost on their left, they read out the places on the scratched placard. It read:

← Rome + Terni – West
Socratis + Matera + Potenza → East

Glad to finally have a direction to head in, Atti and Ennia started their march west toward the capital of their country with the hope of raising an army to cease the everlasting fighting. Although, after just a few more steps, both wanderers collapsed onto the ground with immense exhaustion. For many moments they lay on the course road until they heard the patter of footsteps coming up behind them. Mustering the energy to turn around, they were greeted with the sight of a carriage and horses with a rich couple who had stopped and had started to get out of their vehicle.

"Well, who are these two young-uns who are lying across the road? They look to be in a terrible state!" Atti overheard the woman say.

He pushed himself up onto his feet before helping Ennia stand also. Luckily their Ranger outfits had been ripped and torn enough to be unidentifiable for the wealthy folk.

"W..w...water," he managed to say, leaning against one of the horses and breathing heavily.

"Oh, why of course," the man replied, fetching a bucket from the back of the carriage.

"I am aware it belongs to the horses but it is all I have I'm afraid."

As soon as the bucket was placed upon the ground, both Atti and Ennia dove into it and savoured the cool liquid as they drank it joyously. As they did so, the man turned to his wife and whispered, "Are we sure we want to help these *caenum*, Marisa? They are too filthy for my liking."

"Of course, we have to help them! They are suffering from thirst."

"Fine," the man reluctantly replied, telling the driver of the carriage to wait just a bit longer.

"So, tell me, boy. What are you doing out here in the middle of nowhere?"

Atti took a few deep breaths before replying.

"We are heading to Rome, to visit family."

"Walking to Rome? Alone?" the man questioned, with his wife gasping at the thought of the two of them walking hundreds of miles with no food and drink.

"Oh Marinus, we must help them. We shall take you to Rome, we are headed that way anyway, won't we Mari?"

"Fine. If you insist. What is the name of the family you are visiting anyway?"

Atti struggled to think of a name as his mind had been deteriorating over the past few hours, and so he settled on the first name he thought of.

"Uh, Delphi."

"Hmm, I do not know of a Delphi in Rome. But it is the largest town of all. Hop in, I promise it won't be a long journey."

The pair gratefully clambered into the carriage and sunk into the luxurious, commodious seats and drifted into a much needed sleep as their legs had ached severely from walking so much in the past few months of their adventure. Atti's eyes were open just for a moment as he witnessed the sun lower behind a towering mountain that loomed over the bare landscape.

Long and arduous was the journey but for the tired travellers time passed by effortlessly in their sleep. Atti was relieved to sleep again despite the discomfort he suffered from the wooden bar he rested his head on. As the carriage made its way along the road, it shook when hitting each upturned rock jostling the passengers inside.

Soon the next day passed and darkness arrived again and Atti was sucked into a deeper sleep. He suddenly awoke just in time to see Ennia being thrown out of the carriage. Shaking himself awake, Atti put up his hands as the driver lifted him up and cast him out onto the road.

While Ennia began to wake up, Atti looked to his right at the breathtaking view of the glorious gates of Rome. He grinned at the sight, only ever hearing stories of this magnificent city.

"You two scum should be jailed, I should not have delayed it this much," the rich man snarled, spitting onto the ground. Puzzled, Atti soon understood as he saw two Roman soldiers advancing toward them.

"Ennia, wake up. We need to go!"

"What?" she mumbled indistinctly as they grabbed her. Her instinct kicked in, causing her to strike one soldier in the leg. As she did so, Atti grabbed their weapons from the back of the carriage and ran into the bustling streets of the markets in Rome, trying to lose the soldiers in the discord of events. Separated for a moment, the pair reunited down a small, dingy alley where Atti gifted back the bow to his accomplice, as they caught their breaths and gathered their bearings.

"What is the name of the man we need to find?" Ennia asked, making sure her bow still worked well as she did so.

"Paulinus. Benedict Paulinus. He must live somewhere near the palace and The Colosseum so we should start there."

Confident that they had lost their pursuers, they ventured out into the market and started towards the colossal, golden, pristine colosseum which stood above all of the other buildings, dwarfing even the grand palace which stood next to it. For several moments the pair marvelled at the architecture and intricacies in every building they passed, in awe of the pure creativity and design put into each and every one.

Soon they arrived at the entrance to the great colosseum, hearing the numerous cheers and uproar emanating from inside it. Seeing a guard outside of the impressive structure, Ennia strolled over to ask for the whereabouts of Paulinus. In a suspicious tone, the soldier asked for a reason, to which Atti chimed in, saying he was a 'family friend.'

Grunting, the Roman guard pointed towards a marble house which sat in a row of similar buildings surrounding the palace, no doubt housing other generals, lieutenants and top legati to Alexius.

The house belonging to Paulinus was numbered XII, and the two could see a few candles lit inside. From the outside the house was built with quartz bricks and supported with a rich mahogany wood frame which held up a red canopy which was mirrored in all the other houses. The door was tall, dark and comprehensive like everything else in the city and it had a silver knocker on the door which Atti hesitantly used. After no reply, he felt inclined to knock again, now being greeted by a loud yell.

"ONE SECOND!"

Looking at each other, the pair wondered if they had made the wrong decision as they heard heavy footsteps advancing toward the door. It was flung open rapidly and the bulky, built man who stood in the doorway squinted at the two strangers, scratching his head as he wondered who they were.

"Who are ya?" he asked in an unfamiliar accent, folding his arms, impatiently waiting for an answer.

"Uh, Paulinus. It's Atticus Caeso, Numitor's son. It has been a while I must adm..."

"ATTICUS! Of course!" he yelled gleefully, grabbing the boy in an embrace and lifting him off the ground in a painful hug, with Ennia laughing at Paulinus' antics.

"It has been a long time, ain't it? I mean, I probably seem unrecognisable ay? Because of my voice? I spent a lot of time in Briton, you see. God, they have a beautiful way about them. For an enemy, I mean. Anyway, I'm rambling on. Get inside and tell me how you've been, and who your new lady friend is!"

He started chuckling uncontrollably as Atti and Ennia awkwardly entered Paulinus' home which was as nice on the inside as it was on the outside. The house, despite looking meagre from the outside, was an impressive display of wealth and comfort. Lined with golden silk were each of the armchairs situated around the place, a grandiose candelabra hanging from the ceiling. By the area Atti assumed to be the kitchen was a stack of shelves with an array of various coloured bottles of different alcoholic beverages, something Paulinus seemed to enjoy greatly.

Sitting down upon the cushioned couch in the centre of the luxurious room, they turned to Paulinus who was already pouring out a colourless liquid from a hefty, brown bottle with faded markings on the side.

"Posca, anyone?"

"We're fine, thank you," Atti said anxiously, turning around and addressing Paulinus head on.

"Listen, Paulinus. We came for your help; we have a serious..."

"If it's help you need, my price is non-existent my friend! What do the honourable guests require?"

Ennia jumped in, attempting to break the man's over-optimistic mood.

"Paulinus, we know of an oncoming siege upon the Roman town of Socratis – Atti's hometown – by a man named Octavius Karvajal and his army called the Rangers. We have travelled very far to get here and have risked our lives for this, but we decided we cannot stand idly by and watch this battle unfold, which is why we came here to ask for assistance in any way."

Paulinus kept silent throughout with his eyes opening wider at each sentence, chugging the full glass of posca in his hand. Once empty, he set it down on the table closest to him and held his forehead.

"So, you're telling me, Numitor is going to be attacked by *the* Octavius Karvajal?"

"Yes," said Atti, seeing that Paulinus had finally gained a more serious tone.

"If this group of 'Rangers' plan to destroy a Roman settlement in the holy country, we must act on it, that much is sure. I shall speak with the emperor at once and we shall sort this out, I assure you!"

Atti and Ennia thanked Paulinus who had regained his excitable manner as he gathered his outer garments and his weapons before leaving toward the door, shouting, "Do not thank me, friends. I assure you we shall crush those Rangers until none remain. Stay here until I get back, and help yourself to the drinks!"

He slammed shut the door and the pair glanced at each other in worry. Atti was the first to speak.

"We... We made the right choice, didn't we?"

"Either way, this war will end. Bloodshed is inevitable, you have to believe this."

"But is this the right choice?"

Ennia tossed the question around in her mind while Atti got up from his seat and paced around in thought. After a few minutes Atti felt sleep arising and so he laid down upon the couch. For all he knew, the end would shortly arrive, and he felt unprepared to deal with its dire ramifications.

Only time will tell, he thought, leaning back in the armchair, awaiting Paulinus' return.

CHAPTER 18 – To Battle

'*Magnificent*' Paulinus thought – not for the first time – as he ascended the white marble stairs up to the palatial entrance of the alabaster palace housing the emperor, Alexius himself. Smooth, stone pillars held up the monumental dome which looked as if it had been dropped upon the palace. The burning sunlight reflected upon the shining golden accents that decorated the beautiful building. Creamy white was the exterior, an impressive mahogany door acting as its entrance.

Reaching the top of the stairs, Paulinus crossed the chequered marble patio and headed toward the grand door, nodding to the two guards clad in red before opening it and entering the palace. The main hall was a beautiful piece of work, a circular room with tapestries lining the walls and the dome above. At the centre of the hall was an intricately crafted statue of Alexius in all his glory, with a lack of clothes, modelled out of solid gold. Moving around the figure, the emperor's legatus passed many beggars who had come to ask for money, aid, and the like, signalling to the soldier outside of a restricted room to let him inside.

The small door leading to Alexius' location was unnoticeable amongst the grandeur of the rest of the palace. The trick was that each civilian coming to ask for help was lined up and made to wait until they could speak to Alexius, although only an empty throne sat in the room they were eager to visit. The emperor mainly used the throne for public speeches and executions, but secretly he disliked the riches and grand gestures. His quarters reflected this.

As Paulinus entered, he became accustomed once again to the musty smell and dim lighting of Alexius' room. The young emperor sat upon a feeble stool, staring at his reflection in the silver mirror opposite. He breathed in shakily, carefully moving his hair around with a silver dagger. Unusually, he wore clothes not unlike a peasant's, his emperor's garbs hanging on hooks by his mediocre bed. Any other person would not have recognised this man living in stale conditions to be the emperor of the Roman Empire. Though Paulinus had known the real Alexius for almost all of his life.

"Is that really the best tool for the job?" the legatus joked softly, taking a seat on the decrepit but surprisingly clean bed.

"My father taught me how to cut my hair properly, so that I would look like a true Roman warrior. So that I could scare off any who opposed me," Alexius said chokingly, his voice raspy as if he had been crying recently.

"Why am I not surprised?" Paulinus chuckled, "Your father was a good man, Alexius, but a tonsor, he was not."

A slight chuckle escaped the young emperor's mouth, turning to face the legatus at last.

"Why are you here, Benedict?" he asked, setting the knife down on his desk.

"What? I can't see my fav'rite emperor?"

"You need something. I can tell."

"And that's why you're the emperor!" he laughed some more, reaching at a bottle on Alexius' desk. Taking a swig, he exclaimed annoyedly when no liquid was poured into his mouth, causing him to smash the bottle against the ground. The sound must have alerted the soldier outside as a second later he came rushing in, sword in hand, his eyes darting from the smashed glass and the two men in the room.

"Dramatic, much?" Alexius asked, and suddenly the two burst out laughing. Embarrassed, the soldier returned to his post while the emperor returned to his usual manner.

"So, tell me, what do you need?"

Giving in, Paulinus replied, "Okay, okay. Two teenagers visited me earlier. A boy and a girl. The boy, Atticus, is the son of Numitor Caeso, the governor of Socratis if you recall. The girl... well... I don't really know. Forgot to ask!"

"Get to the point, Benedict."

"Sorry Alexius. The point, yes. Atticus told me about a rebel group named the Rangers that are planning a siege upon Socratis, Numitor's town, at this very moment. As far as I know he was asking for soldiers to help fight them off. It seems like a serious threat."

"Tell me, Benedict. How is it possible that a strong arm of the Empire will fall to a timid partisan group?"

"Atticus mentioned a name I had thought extinct. An enemy of mine and Numitor and a dangerous one at that. What does the name Karvajal mean to you?"

"It sounds familiar, but refresh my memory, Benedict."

"Octavius Karvajal, son of Carrus Karvajal, aristocrat and patrician in Rome.

Octavius took part in the Trials, the same year as myself and Numitor. After Caeso won it and was commended by your father, Albus, Octavius and Numitor fought over a girl, the mother of Atticus. From what I know, Octavius was ashamed of losing to Numitor and he went into exile. I believed him to be halfway to the other side of the world around now, or a dead man, but it seems I was wrong. It seems he has been lurking in Italia all this time."

"So, a powerful man filled with rage is seeking to destroy his enemy in a battle that will barely impact the might of the Empire, and I should feel obliged to assist with this fight because you know the victim of this attack?"

Paulinus groaned and put a hand to his face.

"Listen Alex. This kid, Atticus, lost his mother and brother; Numitor is all he has left. If Octavius takes him too Atticus will be broken inside, leaving him to become another Karvajal, another Warmonger bent on killing and destroying for the rest of his life. But I know him, and his potential. It's not what he deserves. I know you are the big man in charge an' all but, I hope you can share your empathy towards this kid who is in the same position you were only a decade ago."

Alexius sat still and took in Paulinus' words before standing up and retrieving his robe.

"Benedict. I must make a public appearance soon to discuss the Eastern threats, but I think I have an answer for Caeso's proposition. But just know this. I am helping you and them in extension, not for my sympathy, but because we must show that the Empire is omnipotent and that we spare no mercy."

"I thank you for this, Alexius, even though I disagree with your ethics. The old Alex would not discard a young boy's pleas. Sometimes I wonder if the child in you still lives."

"As you know, legatus, I had to sacrifice my childish nature as soon as the crown was placed upon my head. If you cannot accept who I am, you have clearly not understood my situation. I am the emperor of the entire nation and the whole of the Roman Empire. When people in the streets look to their leader, they do not want to see a child on the throne, they desire a strong warrior, and *that* is who I must become. Now alas, I must depart. Oh, but one more thing.... I have one condition for sending out an army to Socratis. Atticus Caeso must compete in next year's Trials. I trust he will agree to this, otherwise, it is their heads that will go. Now, gather a suitable army, I wish you good luck in your endeavours."

He stood, now fully robed and looking almost unrecognisable from before.

As the emperor left the room secretly, Paulinus followed shortly after, leaving via the exit in the back of the palace, leading into the sacred gardens.

Atti awoke from his slumber upon the leather seat as the front door swung open, announcing the arrival of Paulinus.

The boy sat up and looked around for Ennia who was nowhere to be seen.

"Good news!" yelled Paulinus who had pulled Atti up from the couch and grabbed him by the shoulders.

"Alexius agreed to help... on one condition, but that doesn't matter for now! We must gather an army at once and set a course for Socratis! If I go now, shall I expect you and the girl at the front gate?"

Dazed from his sudden awakening, Atti simply nodded, but as the legatus began to leave he called for him to wait.

"What is it, Atticus?"

"When we arrived here, we were almost imprisoned! Can't you help out or something?"

"Well, your clothes *are* horrific under your armour, but there is no time to change. Actually! I shall send with you my finest right-hand man, a gentleman named Aquila. I will tell him to meet you two at the front gate. We shall meet shortly!"

He began to yell as he rushed out of his house with excitement, leaving Atti blinking confusedly. Calling for Ennia, he exited the house to look for his companion. Atti shielded his eyes with his arms to block the blinding sun as he adjusted to the warm air outside.

The street by the palace was more congested than anything he had seen back in Socratis. On one side stood the extensive line of beggars leading into the palace where Alexius resided. On the other, the street extended down a long road crowded with market stalls, the place he and

Ennia had evidently run through, of which they had not had time to see in detail.

With the bustling crowd of people and deafening noises from all around, Atti had no clue where to look for Ennia. Glancing upwards he spotted similar SPQR flags upon the tops of buildings to the ones at home. Red and gold detailing was found on nearly all of the architecture and each building had a personal touch from whatever architect may have designed it. Even as he stood there, Atti could see a man working on a wall in the distance, hammering it with a delicately designed chisel.

Just as he was about to move a short, elderly man pushed past him, nearly knocking him straight over. *Hey!* He thought, regaining his balance. A moment later he began to see men in full Roman armour depart from their houses and head through the market square, presumably toward the front gate.

I should hurry and find Ennia, we need to get to Socratis as fast as...

Interrupting his train of thought was an unusual man wearing a green and white robe, clutching a scroll in his right hand and pushing people out of the way with the other, heading towards Atti. He eventually reached the boy, taking a few breaths before speaking.

"Are you Atticus Caeso?"

Atti raised an eyebrow and crossed his arms sassily, suspicious of the distinguished man.

"Who's asking?" he asked.

"I am a messenger, for the emperor. If you may let me, I shall read out his message."

"Oh," Atti exclaimed, surprised and slightly shameful at his earlier tone, "Yes, please, I apologise for my ill manners."

The messenger simply grunted and cleared his throat before opening the scroll and reading it aloud:

"On behalf of the emperor of the Roman Empire, Emperor Alexius, I read this message to the honourable Atticus Caeso, son of Numitor Caeso. The message reads as follows:

'Atticus. From my limited knowledge of your feats given by my legatus Paulinus, I have deduced that you are a strong and capable warrior like your father and I eagerly await to see that in person next year. I do hope Benedict has mentioned it.

This message is one of hospitality, so do not take it the wrong way. You will be a great leader one day Atticus, and I shall watch your growth into that leader from this day onward with great interest. From what I have heard your journey so far has been a worthy odyssey. Now, to express my forthcomings, I have bestowed to you a gift of my appreciation.

Please accept this proof of my kindness. I await to meet you in person one day. Good luck in your ventures,

Emperor Alexius.'

That is the end of the message."

Atti was stunned that someone of Emperor Alexius' position would compliment him as such. Curiously he asked, "What is the gift I am receiving?"

On cue, the messenger produced a closed wooden box, locked by a padlock on the front. Once the box was in Atti's hands, the messenger held out the key which he took eagerly. Then the messenger left promptly and returned to the palace. Atti stashed the box in his satchel which he had borrowed from Paulinus' house and held the key in his hand.

I'll open this later, he thought, just as he heard a patter of footsteps behind him.

"What are you doing out here?" Ennia asked, startling Atti and causing him to nearly drop the key he was holding. He turned around, clutching the key tightly, saying, "Looking for you."

"Well, you found me. What's that in your hand?"

"A present from the emperor."

"And?"

"I don't know what it is yet, I don't have time to open it. Paulinus is gathering an army right this second. We need to get to the front gate immediately."

Surprised, Ennia took a second to think before replying, "But we were just chased from there?"

"Paulinus has sorted it. We have to meet his friend Aquila and regroup with him later."

"So, this war, it's actually happening?"

Atti looked at her sincerely, taking her hand in his, "Yes, Ennia. And we have to be there, or at least I do. This is my father we're talking about."

"I understand. Now let's go make this the last day for Octavius Karvajal!"

The two then started in the direction of the square, rushing in between the market stalls once again until they neared the front gate, the sun beginning to hide behind the distant mountains as if it knew about the oncoming conflict.

At the front gate were many soldiers gearing up for battle and a lieutenant who leant against the gate. Atti called over to him, asking, "Are you Aquila?"

"Yes, my good man," he replied, "you two must be Atticus and Ennia, right?"

"Yeah, that's us. What's happening at the moment?"

"Well, the soldiers are all getting ready to go fight these 'Rangers' and Paulinus is as giddy as ever. You two sure you're prepared for this? War can be bloody, you know?"

Ennia piped up irritatedly, "Trust me, we've seen way more than you'd believe."

"If you say so," he stated calmly, instructing them to find a horse for them to mount and await Paulinus' return. The pair found a white steed who the soldiers all called Itineribus, or Iter for short. They both climbed upon the horse and soon Paulinus returned, just as the overpowering darkness of night had engulfed Rome.

"Is everyone ready?" Paulinus boomed out into the silence. Multiple replies from the army echoed out and Atti began to shiver. *This is really happening,* he thought, and before he could prolong it any more, the command was made and they were off on the road to Socratis.

CHAPTER 19 – Itineribus

They had been travelling virtually non-stop for six days and the army began to become fatigued. After leaving Rome, Paulinus had decided to take the soldiers through the hills and grasslands instead of the roads in order to get to Socratis quicker. The steeper inclines and rougher ground had made a clear, negative impact on the horses, especially as they started to neigh in obvious pain.

The journey up until that point had been more than arduous and none of the soldiers were happy about it. Exhaustion set in for each and every one of them and the true icing on the cake was the scorching morning sun which had just begun to show its face.

Looking around at all the other horses, Atti guessed there must have been around two-hundred peripatetic soldiers riding with them. Aquila, who was nearby the pair, rode up toward Paulinus who was leading the army.

From what he could see, Aquila had strongly requested that they take a break from the relentless journey, for their sake and their steeds. The legatus agreed and soon the entire army had stopped, finding cover in a valley surrounded by steep, grassy hills.

Dismounting their horse, Itineribus, Atti gladly laid down upon the grass, exhaling deeply as he did so. Ennia soon joined him and after their rest all of the soldiers seemed visibly relaxed.

While stopped, the soldiers unwrapped parcels of rations they had brought with, already packed into their horse's saddle space. When enquiring about his food, Atti was told to check his own horse and to his delight a loaf of olive bread and a flask of water had been placed in the storage for each of them.

At around midday, the army started preparing to set off again, giving Atti a chance to speak to Paulinus, one-on-one just before they left.

"Well Atticus, what can I do for ya?" he asked, optimistically, humming as he packed up his things and mounted his horse, Concordia.

"Before we left Rome, I received a letter from Emperor Alexius."

"Oh, is that right?"

"He gave me a gift which I have not opened yet, but he mentioned something else... something about seeing me next year?"

Paulinus' cheeks suddenly turned red. Laughing it off he said wryly, "Oh yes, that was the condition I mentioned earlier! Alexius only agreed to help if you agreed to take part in the Trials next year. We didn't have much time so I accepted on your be'alf. That's fine, right?"

"Sure..." Atti replied, unimpressed with Paulinus' decision, but he pushed aside the daunting thought of fighting in the Trials for now. Besides, he had bigger things that were more prominent at that moment.

Thanking and saying goodbye to the legatus, Atti returned to Itineribus and Ennia who had finished eating and talking to a young Roman soldier. As the other soldiers began to ride, they mounted Itineribus once more and started on the path toward Socratis which grew closer with every stride.

While on the journey, Atti reached into his satchel and pulled out the intricate wooden box and the golden key, tossing it up into the air and back down.

"Gonna open it?" Ennia asked from behind him, peering over his shoulder. Atti shrugged, feeling each ridge and edge of the box with his finger. Letting curiosity get the better of him, he plugged the key into the keyhole for a perfect fit. Twisting it to the side, Atti lifted up the lid to reveal a sparkling gold dagger which sat on a pure white cushion. The sun above blinded him as it reflected off the dagger's smooth, shiny blade.

"It's beautiful," Ennia proclaimed, and Atti felt inclined to agree. Taking out the dagger from the box, he put the casing back inside his satchel before rubbing his fingers over the edges of the dagger.

It's a true work of art, he thought as he stared at the blade in a mystical trance before slipping it into his belt by his side, covering it with a part of his tunic.

"It is, isn't it?" Atti spoke in return, turning his head to speak to the girl behind him.

After a short while a soldier near the front made a loud exclamation, "I see the town!" and sure enough, ahead of them over the hill was the town of Socratis, looking like it was drawn on a map from their point of view.

Atti wasn't sure, but from his perspective it seemed as if the town was desolate. As the only one having grown up in Socratis out of the group he was most likely to notice something, although they were still quite far from the town itself.

Atti urged Itineribus to follow the rest of the soldiers who had accelerated to alarming speeds down the hill towards Socratis.

As they neared the town it dawned on Atti that he would see his father again, consisting of a proper meeting. As far as he could remember, it had been nearly fifty days since Atti had spoken to his father face to face, and the thought scared him. Dangerous thoughts entered his brain as he started to have immense regret for his recent actions in his adventure, reverting back to the same helpless, desperate child he was all those years ago in the tower, hearing the final screams of his brother on that fateful night. Suddenly he longed for warmth, for love, for comfort.

As if his prayer had been answered, Ennia stretched a hand around him and hugged him, comforting him.

"You were shivering," she said, but Atti just thanked her subconsciously, staring at their oncoming location. As the gates came into view, Atti became confused by the lack of guards standing on the parapets, as well as the absence of soldiers patrolling the perimeter. Glancing at the eastern tower, Atti shook off his negative feeling and rode up to Paulinus' side.

"Something's wrong," he stated, as they became within firing range of the outer wall of Socratis.

"How'd you mean?" Paulinus asked, inspecting every corner of the gate in front.

"There are no guards. There's always guards."

As no man was there to open the gate for the army, a Roman soldier scaled the cobble wall to reach a lever at the top. Once he had pulled it open, the Romans entered the town of Socratis, finding it eerily empty. The barracks were vacant, the main palace deserted. When the soldiers had arrived, Atti understood what had happened.

"They've left already," he said with finality, turning to Paulinus.

"Whenever my father went out on missions the protocol was to keep the gates locked and not let anyone in, and if by any chance people did enter, the aim was for everyone to depart to hidden passages in the caves and tunnels underneath the town."

Paulinus wiped his brow as he replied, "Atticus, as you grew up here you have the best chance to resonate with these civilians. I want you to go down to these tunnels you speak of and ask the people of Socratis for information. We need to know what happened and where Numitor is now."

"Understood."

As Atti dismounted from Itineribus and began to walk through the empty streets, nostalgia overcame him. He recalled when he had escaped Cicero's talk to hide from his father, concealing himself in one of the passages underground. Retracing his steps from the arena, he eventually found the shop where he had hid behind the counter. Finding the trapdoor under a pile of boxes, he opened it up and climbed down the ladder, a sense of deja vu overcoming him.

Once he was down in the caverns he headed over the bridge as he began to hear a lot of voices in an adjacent room. Sidling up to the door, Atti decided to go in quietly and carefully, not wanting to startle the people of Socratis. However, just as he was about to enter, the door was thrust open by a wily man who seemed familiar to Atti. Either way, he knew the boy.

"Dominus Caeso! What are you doing here? We thought it was bandits who had come into Socratis."

"Do I know you?" Atti questioned, puzzled as to who this man was.

"My name is Kaecilius, I work for your father. I probably shouldn't tell you this but he sent me to the Rangers to keep watch over you, although I don't anymore, obviously."

"My father did what?!" Atti shouted, waving his hand around frantically.

"In all fairness, I was tasked with spying on all of the Rangers, but admittedly you became my top priority.

Bewildered, Atti exclaimed, "You're telling me my father sent you to spy on me without me knowing and then he lied to me about it?"

"Yes," Kaecilius replied sheepishly, realising he was not escaping this argument. Pushing the thought out of his mind, Atti turned his attention to the pressing matter at hand.

Next, he asked, "Anyway, where is my father? Or, when did they leave?"

"Oh, right. The governor, General Lucien and every other soldier in Socratis and the whole province left just a few hours ago to besiege the home of the Rangers. I'm sure if your father knew of your return, he would have held out until you had arrived."

"That doesn't matter, spy! We need to catch up with my father immediately. You were a spy in the Rangers, and while that is a horribly disturbing thing to think about right now, we can put it to good use."

"How so?" Kaecilius asked, dumbfounded.

"You know the route to the fortress from here, you can help navigate me and my army toward the Rangers, or else I'll kill you where you stand!"

"Okay! Okay! I'll take you. And by the way you are not as sweet as your father described you."

Groaning, Atti dragged the spy by his tunic toward the ladder leading out of the passages. Once they were back on the surface, Atti returned to Paulinus with Kaecilius before agitatedly and rapidly explaining the situation and what the plan was. Not wanting to waste any more time, Paulinus ordered the soldiers to gear up once again and prepare for their last journey toward the Castellum Lapideum as the Rangers called it.

Kaecilius, taking a ride upon Concordia with Paulinus, had talked constantly on the way there to the overt dismay of Paulinus who had been trying to psych himself into a battling mood. Atti and Ennia had been mostly silent during the final leg toward the fortress, save for the occasional check-in with each other. The rest of the soldiers and their horses were more tired than ever, but Paulinus urged them to press on, repeatedly saying that 'Time is of the essence.'

It was early in the afternoon when the army could spot the mountain in which the Rangers had stationed themselves. Atti could see many Rangers upon the parapets, but what was even more impressive was the sheer number of Socratis soldiers there who stood at the base of the mountain.

As they got closer, Atti spotted his father who sat majestically upon his steed in his governor attire, a bright silver sword wielded in one hand. Suddenly Atti felt faint and the last thing he remembered was the sight of the foreboding, menacing mountain of the Castellum Lapideum looming over him.

CHAPTER 20 –
The Grand Assault

"ATTICUS! ATTICUS! WAKE UP!"

Slowly the light returned to the boy's eyes as he heard an all too familiar voice. The first thing he saw was the dynamic blue skyscape above him, a terrifying hawk dominating the sky, an indomitable force scaring off any birds that dare challenge its authority. Atti's eyes steadily began to focus on the face in front of him, wide, worried eyes peering down at him accompanied by a furrowed brow, a clean-shaven beard sat around his mouth and a crooked nose once broken in battle long ago. Atti knew the only face that could have been.

"Father?"

Numitor's expression became visibly more relieved as he cradled his son's body in his arms.

"Oh, how I've missed you."

Shaking himself awake, Atti got up from the ground and looked around before staring up at the mountain standing before the combined strength of two Roman armies. To his left stood Ennia, Paulinus, Aquila and the rest of the soldiers from Rome. To his right was Lucien, Kaecilius and the soldiers from Socratis. And beside him stood his father, hand clamped on his shoulder.

"There are many things I must talk to you about, Atticus, including the death of Sergeant Titus. Was that really you?" Numitor asked, turning to face his son.

Feeling embarrassed, Atti replied, "It wasn't so much as me as it was Ennia and Aurelius. A strong foe like Decimus Titus was too much for me, at the time anyway. I am much stronger now."

"Ah, alas. It is in the past, and though it caused me some consternation I can look past it. Now who is your female companion, Ennia, is it?"

Surprised, Ennia promptly introduced herself, "Yes, Governor Caeso. Nice to meet you."

"And yourself," Numitor replied, waving a hand by his head to greet her.

Atti then interrupted them, saying, "Now we are all caught up, where is Octavius Karvajal?" Atti was sounding more like a general to his father's surprise.

Lucien stepped over to the two Caeso's, replying, "The Warmonger has not shown his face, which is to our advantage. We still do not know the full capability of that wretched staff."

"I still cannot fathom that the Gemstone of Moria was there, in Socratis, right under our noses all this time," Numitor interjected.

Atti confusedly turned to his father, saying, "Wait, you knew about the Gemstone of Moria?"

"Yes, my son. I had been searching for it for years, to stop it falling into the wrong hands. Who knew it had been inside Gallus' place the whole time."

"Gallus? As in Gallus Caesar?" Paulinus asked in wonder, to which Numitor confirmed.

Atti assumed the two old friends had caught up while he was unconscious.

Atti was also surprised that the Red Azalea had belonged to someone of much importance, that being the former Roman Emperor, Gallus Caesar.

"We are getting off track," Lucien stated, unsheathing his sword and brandishing it powerfully.

"Lucien is right," Numitor agreed, speaking louder so that everyone could hear, "Now is the time to attack."

"Socratis soldiers! You will push up the right side of the mountain, strongest men begin the climb and others shall throw the ropes up. Get the catapults in motion while Rome soldiers will push from the left side. We only get one shot at this, this is our one chance to take down the Rangers and Karvajal, we cannot get this wrong. Now, who's with me?!"

Numitor's stirring speech was met by a chorus of battle cries as each and every soldier began to charge toward the fortress. The Rangers upon the makeshift parapets immediately began to rain fire arrows down onto the Roman soldiers who had started to scale the rocky surface of the mountain. Suddenly, a Roman released a catapult, hurling a boulder into the side of the mountain, making it shake profusely. Paulinus and his soldiers started to charge toward the left side, yelling cries of anger and enjoyment at once.

As the conflict wore on, Ennia gripped onto Atti's hand saying, "Whatever happens, I'll stay by your side at all times. We are in this together."

Atti nodded and they retrieved their weapons from Itineribus before regrouping with Numitor and Lucien who had refrained from joining the fight for the moment.

Many Rangers equipped with melee weapons began to abruptly emerge from a hidden entrance at the base of the mountain, beginning conflict with the Romans on the ground. Lucien, spotting the entrance, alerted the others.

"There, Numitor! If we gather a small troop we can sneak into that entrance and reach the interior to find Octavius before more lives are lost!"

Numitor accepted the plan, and after hand-picking out several strong soldiers from the limited ones who had stayed back, he, Atti, Ennia, Lucien and a few other soldiers including Hortensius and Gladius headed toward the centre of the foot of the mountain, flanking round the main bulk of the offensive in the middle.

The noise of the battle was immense, deafening cries of anguish and anger were called out from both sides, Romans charging forward with blades and shields in each hand. Gradually the ground became painted red with blood, more and more bodies smacking onto the ground.

Paulinus and his companions, including Aquila, had already begun climbing the mountain. Hanging onto the first ledge containing a few archers, Paulinus used his sword to pierce a Ranger's leg, pulling him closer and flipping him over the parapet, leaving him to fall down to the ground, landing upon another Ranger. Hauling himself onto the walkway, he kicked another archer backwards, hitting his head on the hard stone floor. As he did so, another Ranger charged toward him from behind who was suddenly neutralised by Aquila who nodded at his accomplice, signalling him to continue.

Together they fought off the oncoming archers, allowing more Romans to scale the fortress. Just as everything seemed to be going smoothly, a large boulder smashed into the wall underneath their feet, causing the bricks to crumble. Desperately, the two leapt up onto the ledges above as the wall collapsed and slid down onto the ground, crushing a few Rangers who were locked in combat with Roman warriors.

Hanging from the thin ledges of rock, Paulinus and Aquila managed to reach the higher wall by climbing up to it, exhausted as they reached the walkway, painfully greeted by additional archers.

To fend for their life, they made quick but messy work of the Rangers as another catapult shook the mountain.

"We have to find a way inside!" Aquila yelled, stabbing a Ranger in the heart as he did so. Promptly, the pair followed the walkway to a door leading to a spiral staircase. Descending the stairs they reached an armoury containing a couple of soldiers. The one closest to Paulinus took a stab at him unexpectedly, and due to his low reaction time the blade dug into his chest.

Coming to his aid, Aquila threw a dagger at the Ranger, which he had retrieved from a rack behind him, the blade piercing the Ranger's heart.

Breathing heavily and wincing in pain, Paulinus clutched his chest with his left hand and held his sword with the right. Shouting in agony, he pulled the blade out of his chest, chucking it onto the ground as another Ranger charged toward him. He blocked the attack, his hand shaking as he kicked the Ranger's leg, causing him to fall onto his knee. Paulinus took his chance, swinging his blade and decapitating the soldier.

Meanwhile Aquila was dealing with two more Rangers equipped with shortswords who were dealing continuous blows to the worried Roman. Coming to the rescue, Paulinus managed to plunge his blade into the back of one, giving Aquila the perfect opportunity to attack the other, leaving them dead on the floor, the Rangers' blood seeping into the cracks in the stone.

After taking a moment to rest, Aquila assisted Paulinus and covered his stab wound before wrapping his arm around his friend and helping him into the next room. A moment later, a few Romans entered the armoury, battered but able to fight. Relieved, Paulinus ordered Aquila to go further into the fortress without him as he could not bear the pain of his wound anymore. A Roman stayed with him as Aquila went deeper into the home of the Rangers.

Back in the fray of the fighting at the base of the mountain, the Romans appeared to be pushing back the endless waves of Rangers ever so slightly while more boulders were fired into the side of the mountain.

Kaecilius, being the coward that he was, had mounted the closest horse to him and urged it to escape, but to his disappointment the horse would not budge. Deciding that he should do something more worthy with his pitiful life and that he would finally stand up for himself, he dismounted the horse and faced the warzone, retrieving a sword from a dead Roman on the ground.

"I am Julian Kaecilius of the Roman Empire, and I shall fight for my family and for my country!" Yelling, he ran into the battle just as a flaming arrow rapidly descended above him, striking him in the chest and pinning him to the ground, leaving him to bleed out in pain upon the battlefield of the fight that would be remembered for centuries to come. Before the light faded from his eyes, he recalled his wife and his daughter and of his life in Socratis, leaving the mortal world with a vision of happiness and not one of pain.

Edging behind the Rangers who were too busy fighting to notice them, Numitor's group slipped through the hidden door and arrived inside the Castellum Lapideum, where the battle was quieter and less prevalent. The governor lunged at the first Ranger, digging his sword deep into the man's chest as another Ranger swung at Lucien who blocked the attack, countering with a jab to the Ranger's throat.

"We must continue!" Numitor called, heading further into the fortress with the others following.

This is really happening, Atti thought as he heard the faint screaming of battle occur outside the comfort of the fortress. Reaching a broad room which Atti recognised as the entrance hall leading to the various areas of the base, a handful of Rangers stood in the way.

Numitor and Lucien joyfully moved forward having sorely missed the side-by-side combat together, while Ennia pinged arrows at the Rangers by Atti's side. Though so far, he had refused to fight.

"This doesn't seem right," he whispered to himself, stepping back from the fray as his father and the general decapitated a particularly brutish Ranger.

"These people were friends, people who helped me. And now I am helping in their murder..."

Ennia soon noticed Atti's hesitation and backed up to him, keeping her bow poised as the last Ranger was dismembered cleanly.

"Ennia, the Rangers assisted us in times of need... Karvajal is the one deserving of punishment, not these people who have families."

"But they serve Karvajal! Is that not enough?"

Atti shook his head, shouting now, "They are innocent people, manipulated by Karvajal's words!"

Noticing his son's distress, Numitor held off on advancing for the second, pacing over to Atti.

"Listen, my son. These people may not deserve to die, but they believe in their cause, same as we do. And in war people die for their cause, whether they deserve to or not. Octavius must fall, on that we both agree, and unfortunately this is the only way. Now I must ask you, are you going to assist us or not?"

Atti took a minute of hesitation before eventually nodding his head determinedly, gripping his sword.

"Let's find Karvajal and kill him, no matter who stands in our way. Anyone who attempts to stop us is a friend of mine no more."

Together as a group, the warriors headed through the hallway marked 'Throne Room,' striking any Rangers who they came across, turning the walls red. Soon they emerged into a room sitting outside of Karvajal's location. There, standing in front of them was a single Rangers commander wielding a fierce looking broadsword.

"Aurelius," Atti said softly, staring into the man's eyes with sorrow.

"So, this is how we meet again, Atticus."

Numitor turned to Atti, pointing at Aurelius with his sword, saying, "You know this one, yes?"

"He's a good man, father, I swear! Spare his life, if any. I beg of you!"

Grunting, Numitor reluctantly lowering his weapon, allowing Aurelius to leave.

"I thank you for this gesture, Roman, but I am afraid it is not that simple. If Karvajal knew I ran he would not stop looking for me until my death."

"That is why we are here, Aurelius. To stop Karvajal and prevent him from committing more evil," Atti pleaded, desperate for his friend to be free from Karvajal's torment.

"So, you are really letting me leave?"

Numitor begrudgingly nodded.

"Aurelius, wait!" Atti called out as Aurelius turned to depart, stepping forward, "it's not too late."

"How do you mean, Atticus?"

"Just because you served a cruel master, it doesn't mean that's all you are. A true, compassionate warrior like you should feel open to your own opinions and not those of others. Make your *own* decisions, and if you do, I will welcome you back with open arms. Run now and decide later. From this day on you are free from Karvajal's manipulation. Enjoy it."

"Thank you, Atticus. I will see you again."

The Rangers commander fled the room through a side door.

"Well said, son," Numitor complimented, turning to Atti who smiled.

Then, just as Aurelius had left, a door to their right swung open. Out stormed Cassius who wielded a mace, supported by a team of troops including the Ranger, Hadrianus.

"Traitor!" Lucien shouted at the sight of Cassius, and suddenly it made sense to Atti. Cassius had been a Roman defector and had joined the Rangers out of spite against Rome. That is why he had recognised him the first time they met.

"So what, Lucien? I have become stronger here with the Rangers than I ever could have with you! And now, I shall take pride in murdering you!"

The Roman traitor ran at Lucien and engaged him in conflict while Numitor faced the other Rangers.

Hadrianus took a swing at Atti who just barely dodged the attack.

"I never liked you much anyway," the Ranger said, slicing at the air as Atti jumped backwards. Now angry, he fought back, swiping at the legs of Hadrianus. The two duelled fiercely, but Atti began to channel the sparring lessons he had had since a young age and began to search for Hadrianus' pattern and weakness in his fighting style. Sure enough, after avoiding a few more hits with his agility, Atti spotted it.

After every miss, Hadrianus would reset his guard into an offset position, holding the blade by his left hip, and so when he took a swing at the boy once again, Atti rolled underneath the blade and to Hadrianus' right side where he was open and undefended. This meant Atti could plunge his blade deep into the man's chest, causing him to fall onto his knees.

"Fair play, *caenum*," Hadrianus spoke as he bled out onto the ground. Across the room Cassius swung his mace around wildly as Lucien backed away into a corner.

"Do you know how long I have waited to do this?" Cassius asked, a hint of madness in his voice.

"Since you just walked in?" Lucien asked, ducking and grabbing the chain of the mace, headbutting Cassius in his face. Clutching his nose, the traitor dropped his weapon, allowing Lucien to strike him, hitting him in the chest with the hilt of his sword before picking up the mace from the ground.

"Let me show you, Cassius, why no one ever crosses the great Lucien, general of the Romans of Socratis!" and with his declaration, he swung the mace round and into Cassius, sending him back into the ground, leaving his face severely deformed.

The body of Cassius flew into another Ranger who recoiled at the sight of Cassius' face. He then instinctively blocked Numitor's incoming attack, countering with his own strike.

As the governor fought, he kept his son pictured in his mind, and then an image of his wife, Cecilia. Filled with rage, Numitor sliced furiously at the Ranger before providing a flurry of attacks, dismembering the Ranger and leaving him in a deep pool of blood.

"Is that all of them?" Atti questioned as a single tear dropped from Numitor's face. The rest of them looked around, noticing Gladius dead on the floor, a sword sticking out of his chest.

"Damn it, Gladius," Lucien said softly, going down on one knee. Silence filled the room. Atti felt his father's hands who simply stood, staring at the remains of Cassius. He squeezed his son's hands before turning to face the rest of the Romans and Ennia and then the door to the throne room.

"So, this is it then," he said with finality, stabbing his blade into the ground, "There is no one else in our way. It is time we face Karvajal, together."

He turned to his son who embraced him as such, feeding a warm comfort into Numitor, reminding him what he was fighting for.

Ennia joined Atti and soon after so did Lucien and Hortensius. The remaining five looked toward the door leading to the Warmonger, Octavius Karvajal himself, each with the intent of ultimately stopping his reign of terror, no matter the cost.

CHAPTER 21 – United We Stand

He sat peacefully upon the iron seat, a leather cushion providing comfort of which the metal lacked. Gripping the staff in one hand, he rolled it gently with his finger, admiring the amber crystal held in the grasp of the wooden staff. Even in the isolated darkness the gemstone glowed ever so slightly, illuminating the bare room. The walls were made of blackstone creating a malevolent theme inside the throne room, the tall throne being cast as a spiked shadow upon the cut floor.

The Warmonger had heard the commotion outside the door in front of him and so he mentally prepared for combat – something he had been out of practice for. He then relaxed back in his seat and awaited the troupe of warriors who would barge inside at any moment.

Karvajal recalled his dream, his believed prophecy, regarding the day he would become a benevolent leader, struggling to decide whether this path had set him the right way. Casting the pitiful thought aside, he dismissed his inner conflict as the redwood double doors were pushed open suddenly by his old friend turned nemesis, the governor of Socratis.

"Ah, Numitor, what a nice surprise. Care for some wine?"

The five adversaries joined up side by side, staring upon the throne and the cruel man sat upon it.

"I must refuse, Octavius, you have asked twenty years too late."

Sighing, the Warmonger stood up, pointing the staff at Hortenius the Roman soldier, who had set himself into a fighting position.

"Very well," Karvajal responded, and to their horror a blinding flash of light emanated from the staff, striking Hortensius in the chest, causing him to go flying backward, smacking into the wall behind him at an incredible speed, the sound of multiple bones cracking being the only sound you could hear.

"Holy…" Atti started, retreating back a few steps. Ennia soon did the same. However, Numitor and Lucien stood their ground, advancing slowly up to Karvajal.

The Warmonger got up from his seat, saying, "Don't you see, Numi? I have more power than you could ever have imagined, magic! All those years in Salerno being taught about the myths of the world. A strange land with a half-bull half-man abomination, a creature who turned its enemies to stone. All these stories that are brought together by the existence of one myth. Dark Magic. The energy source that I am trying to harness. I guarantee that you all have had experience with this magic before, especially with that hideous creature they call the Warlock, who has escaped both my grasp and that of the Roman Empire.

If you are seeking an evil to distinguish, seek him out as I did once, only to be gravely injured by that malicious beast! But getting to the point, I guess, I am confused as to why you should target me and paint me as the villain? I do not see the fairness in that."

"You tried to manipulate me to turn against my own father!" Atti shouted, stepping forward in frustration.

"Indeed, that was my plan, a plan which I had perfected. I had planned it from the very beginning, in fact and in all honesty, I expected it to work. First, I sent the letter to 'warn' Numitor of my presence, although really, I just wanted to introduce myself to the one who will change everything, as I have no doubts you will, Atticus. After, we set up that pyre, a false distraction so that I could capture dear Atticus and finally speak with him face to face..."

"You murdered Governor Cicero!" Numitor boomed, the sound echoing throughout the room.

"Do not be a fool, Numitor. We had only captured that blubbering idiot. That body was not his, I assure you, a fake dressed up in the governor's clothes. You may ask about the practicality of this, and truthfully it was so that you would become the new governor, my old friend, a gift I thought you would appreciate.

Once I had Atticus in my possession, I knew it would be difficult to keep him in the palm of my hand, but my charm never wavers, as you all know. And from there I am certain you can deduce what other lengths I might have gone to, but the point is that a little, *harmless* manipulation is not grounds for all-out warfare. The Rangers' actions over the past two years have been solely to provide food and service for the starving citizens.

I, at the very least, am trying to aid all of these people who are in dire need of a leader as they are forgotten and discarded by you, by the Empire. All I wanted to do was use this power for good, the good of the people, but now you stand in my way. Now I finally possess a weapon that can achieve my ambitions, and I should warn you, that demonstration was just that! A fraction of this gemstone's power, and you do not want to find out what else it can do.

Whatever this personal feud you have with me is, Numitor, I shall tire of it if it continues any longer, though it is understandable. Besides, I can see why placing a fatal curse upon your family can be... undesirable."

Numitor's eyes widened, his pupils dilating. His heart began to contract faster and faster, more blood being pushed through his vessels, his breathing becoming heavier with each breath. His face became a reddish purple as his body began to tremble immensely.

"YOU DID WHAT?!" he yelled deafeningly, and not wasting a second to let the Warmonger breathe, he charged straight at Karvajal, knocking him backwards. The staff fell to the ground, but Numitor did not notice it. Instead, he started pummelling his fists into Karvajal's face, screaming as he did so. The famed Warmonger could do nothing to prevent his fate as the governor of Socratis released his anger, relentlessly striking at his old enemy, not showing any signs of relenting.

"Father, stop!"

To the sound of his son's voice, Numitor turned his head, leaving a bloodied Karvajal free for a moment.

The governor looked toward Atti with sympathy, his body calming down.

Just at that second, Karvajal had grabbed the staff that sat beside him. In a quick motion, he went to fire it at Numitor, raising it poised in his hand.

"Say hello to Cecilia for me," he said cackling, but instead Numitor heard his voice and, spinning around, he yanked the staff out of the Warmonger's hands before using his knee to break it in two. Then, to finish the fight, Numitor Caeso used the gemstone edge of the staff to stab it into Karvajal's chest, causing him to grunt in pain. To all their surprise, Karvajal just began to laugh maniacally.

"There...you... have...it, Numitor. The truth comes out... as they say," Karvajal sputtered, blood dripping out of his mouth.

Numitor presented no emotion other than infuriation, placing the blood-soaked, broken staff into his belt.

"You know, Octavius, after all these years I debated whether to kill you when we inevitably met again. I questioned if you deserved to die at my hand, or any others for that matter. But now I thank you, as you have finally put the nail in your sarcophagus, you gave me that reason. How does it feel, your downfall I mean?"

"Oh, Numitor... If you... think this is my downfall... you are sorely... mistaken."

The Warmonger coughed before his limbs went limp, his body becoming lifeless.

Atti looked to his hands, expecting to feel something signalling that his curse might be gone, but no such thing arose.

Silence encumbered in the room as each person looked to each other and then to Numitor. Atti was the first to comfort his father, placing an arm round him. Soon Ennia joined in their embrace while Lucien scouted outside the throne room, refusing to speak.

"He's gone now, father. You do not need to worry anymore."

Ennia nodded, and agreeing with Atti she said, "Yes, and now that bastard finally got what he deserved after the *cacas* he put us through."

Unexpectedly, the gemstone encased in the weapon began to shine brighter than ever before from the hip of Numitor.

"What does *that* mean?" Atti exclaimed, and just then Lucien ran straight back into the room.

"Governor, I think we have a problem," he stated seriously, and just as he spoke the entire mountain shook vigorously. It felt as if a colossal lightning bolt had struck the mountain from the heavens.

"What's happening?" Numitor asked urgently, pushing past his son to converse with Lucien.

"I'm not sure, but there's some new threat outside."

"Then let us depart immediately."

As the fortress shook even more, the four of them left the throne room and retraced their steps until they reached the hidden exit they had entered through. But what none of them would have known was that the body of Octavius Karvajal had begun to twitch the second they had left the room.

The squad followed through the dim hallways, Lucien and Numitor heading in front, leaving Ennia to comfort Atti.

"Are you alright?" she asked, putting a hand on his shoulder as they quickly walked through the corridor.

"Yeah, why wouldn't I be?" Atti asked, not turning to face the girl, instead focusing on other things.

"Well, what about the curse? Your father's outbreak? Karvajal's death? You have nothing to say about any of that?"

Annoyedly, Atti replied, "We do not have time to keep our minds on the past, we must deal with the present."

Sensing Atti was not open to speak, though the events had clearly affected him, Ennia was wise to not prod him any further. The only thing Atti was thinking about was the ruckus outside. He had to block the revelations from his mind, despite Karvajal's words echoing inside his brain.

Shaking away Ennia's voice, Atti pressed on, moving close behind his father.

"How are you holding up, Governor?" Lucien asked from beside Numitor, concerned for his old friend.

"Lucien, please, we have been allies for decades. I may be your governor, but in my eyes we are equal."

"I see, *Numitor*. How are you?"

"Well, Lucien, I am tired, angry, annoyed, frustrated and distraught. At this very moment we are heading into the unknown without a clue of what to expect, and my only living son has witnessed me brutally murder a man I used to care for dearly. How do you think I am?"

The general comforted his friend, silently mourning the death of his two best soldiers, Gladius and Hortensius, cursing at Mars all the while.

Soon they had reached the mountain entrance and, pushing the door open, they exited out into a torrential storm, gallons of rain crashing against the ground like a meteor shower.

The ground was littered with inanimate bodies; their blood being washed away by the torrent. However, the storm was not the group's main concern. Both remaining armies of Rangers and Romans had ceased their fighting once the storm had begun, and it was because they had been interrupted by unexpected visitors.

"I don't believe it," Lucien whispered, drowned out by the deafening rain. Lifting a hand onto his brow, he made sure what he saw was authentic, and it was.

"Did you miss me, Numitor?" bellowed the voice of the once dead sergeant of the New Guard, Decimus Titus, who stood upon a golden chariot, the hooded, bird-like creature known as the Warlock standing by his side.

"That's impossible..." Atti mumbled, just as he saw the entirety of the New Guard enforcements slowly advance into view. Titus stood proudly upon his chariot ironclad in steel armour from head to toe, an extravagant helmet protecting his very much alive head. It was as if he had never died in the first place.

With a surprisingly athletic move, the sergeant leapt onto the ground, calling to his troops.

"Soldiers! Tonight, we destroy the Romans of Socratis and then conquer their meagre, little town!"

His cry was met by cheers from the sea of blue-armoured soldiers who raised their respective weapons in the air. Panicking, Atti turned to his father who had the broken staff clutched in his hand.

"What do we do?" he asked, but Numitor did not seem to hear him. Instead, the governor turned to the tired, battered Rangers and Romans left on the battlefield and called to them.

"Listen, Rangers of Karvajal. Your leader is dead at my hand. This conflict has only ever been personal, and divided we stand no chance against this psychopath and his army. So, I beg, I *plead* for your assistance as you are now free from the manacles placed upon you by Karvajal. Join us in this fight and help us vanquish our enemy. If we live, you shall all be welcome as heroes in Socratis and the rest of the Empire. Now, what do you say?"

At first there was silence, until one Ranger raised his blade toward the sky who Atti recognised to be Marcus Aurelius, who had returned to fight, raring to get involved in the battle.

"I shall join you, saviour!"

Then, miraculously, the rest of the Rangers shouted cries of war, joining the Roman forces. Paulinus – who had only just managed to return to the battle – ran up to Numitor, first joyful at the apparent Roman victory and then filled with horror as he gazed upon the massive attacking army opposing them. Breathless, he gasped to Numitor, "My soldiers are fierce, but they are no match for an infantry of that stature. Where is our army?"

"Look around, brother," Numitor replied, as the Romans of Socratis and Rome along with the Rangers encircled the vanquishers of Karvajal, rallying with them against the New Guard.

Paulinus chuckled, ready for the second round. Meanwhile, Atti met up with Aurelius once again.

"You came back!" he said, immensely pleased.

"Yes, I did. What you said stuck with me. I am ready to fight for myself now, and I realised you need my assistance. Let's do this."

Grinning, Atti unsheathed his blade, glancing round at the sea of familiar faces from two factions from his life coming together as one. Ennia accompanied him and his adrenaline then kicked in, Atti feeling the anticipation through his veins.

"How are you alive?" the governor yelled at the sergeant, to which he replied, "There are certain perks to having a magic friend, Roman. Besides, your attempt is futile, Numitor! In my eyes we have already won!"

"How so?" Numitor questioned, pointing his sword toward the army ahead of him.

"With our irrepressible power and my acquaintance's Dark Magic, I plan to destroy your inferior Empire and take the riches for my own nation! Your insignificant gathering here will do nothing but scratch the might of the 'New Guard,' or shall I say, the true Warriors of Athens!"

"Athens?" Atti whispered confusedly, but Ennia had no answer. Though, by the reaction of the men around them, their allies had a dislike for the people of Athens.

"I should have known," Atti heard his father say, "I should have known they were *Greek*. It seems so obvious now."

"What is bad about a Greek? Aurelius is..." he asked, but was cut off by the sergeant.

"That's right, mortal. And Perakles our leader sends his regards. He really would have loved to be here."

"SILENCE, FALSE FRIEND!" Numitor boomed, causing the whole battlefield to fall quiet. Even Titus stirred at the governor's commanding tone. He continued, "In the end, your overconfidence will be your weakness, mark my words."

Decimus Titus, undeterred, signalled to the Warlock to begin preparation.

The magic-user's hands started to glow a familiar green colour which Numitor and Atti had both seen before. Knowing only bad could come from it, they ducked and braced themselves, Ennia copying Atti.

Once again, the Warlock began to speak that unfamiliar language.

Titus then mocked the governor, "Maybe so, Numitor. But then again, maybe not. Now!"

Promptly, the luminescent green energy flew out of the crooked hands of the Warlock. It shot toward each soldier, violently piercing each one's body, entering their unprepared bodies and crushing their hearts in one foul blow. Almost immediately several of the weaker Rangers and Romans collapsed onto the ground, dead instantly.

"What the hell?" Atti said concernedly, although Numitor was already back on his feet. The governor then noticed that the Warlock seemed visibly weaker after the attack. Paulinus gripped his shoulder, making Numitor turn his head.

"Numitor, with power like that we're done for, done for!"

"Not quite Benedict. Now is as good as any to strike, in truth."

Puzzled, the legatus, "Are you going to explain or...?"

"The Warlock is weakened. That attack has left him vulnerable. If we strike now, we can cause some damage before he can regain his power."

"Right!"

Enlightened by the idea, Paulinus leapt onto a nearby rock structure, yelling, "Romans and Rangers, now is the time to attack! Charge!"

In one movement of courage, anger, fear and determination the remaining soldiers charged toward the Warriors of Athens, from enemies to allies. Atti and Ennia dove into the fray, happily slashing at the foreign soldiers. Numitor stayed where he stood, watching Titus, neither warrior moving from their position.

"Numitor, you have to move!" Lucien, the general, said, eager to join the fight but anxious of the many airborne arrows now creating a wave in the sky.

Although Numitor didn't stir until he saw Titus turn to the visibly weaker Warlock.

"What are they saying?" he mumbled, but Lucien became frustrated. The general started tugging on his arm, just as the Warlock stood up and turned, revealing a glowing fireball trapped in between its rotten digits.

"Ah." Numitor spoke as the projectile was sent hurtling toward him.

"Governor, no!" Lucien shouted, shoving Numitor out of the way with his strength, being clipped by the fireball in the chest and being flung onto his back.

Numitor shook his head and got up, heading toward the chariot of Decimus Titus while the battle raged on.

Aurelius and his group of Rangers assisted the fights of Paulinus and his troop of Romans, fighting side by side. Paulinus noticed Aurelius slicing his blade with exact precision.

"Nice blade movement!" he commented as he stuck his sword into the belly of a soldier in front of him, pulling it out and headbutting the man in the face.

"Thank you!" Aurelius returned, "I could say the same to you, Roman!"

The two continued to fight and push back the New Guard forces, although it felt as if the opposing force was unstoppable. Atti had engaged a particularly brutish Greek who stood over a head higher than the boy. Slicing at his legs, Atti rolled under the brute, spinning round and spearing him in the back with his sword. The soldier groaned, slumping to the floor as another New Guard soldier started to lunge at Atti with a spear. He narrowly dodged out of the way and, grasping at an Athenian shield, he blocked the next attack, turning and stabbing the spear-wielding soldier in the liver.

At a distance he could see Ennia raining arrows down upon the soldiers, each one landing in a neck, chest or even an eye. Smiling, Atti was then caught off guard by another strike, the spear just missing his face. Frustrated, Atti swivelled round, knocking the spear out of the man's hands and summoning all of his strength to kick the soldier backwards onto the ground before plunging his sword deep into his chest. He felt exhilarated, his blood rushing straight to his brain.

Daydreaming for just a second, a soldier jumped at him unexpectedly. Atti only noticed him at the last second. For a fleeting moment it felt like the world stood still, the spear edging toward his face ever so slowly. He panicked, not wanting to accept his death when suddenly a sword cut at the neck of his attacker, slicing the man's head clean off. Clutching his chest, Atti turned to see his saviour, Tatius Marcellus, his Ranger friend.

"You, you saved me Tatius!" Atti breathed gratefully.

"Of course. What would I do without you?"

They laughed briefly before more Athenian soldiers arrived. Fending them off, they fought through more guards as a constant stream of arrows rained overhead, the Battle of the Castellum Lapideum raging on.

By this point Numitor had reached the chariot, staring down Titus with his governor's sword in one hand and the broken staff gripped in the other.

"FACE ME!" he yelled, raising his blade to the sky, the gleaming sun beaming off the argent metal, creating a beacon of bright light.

Titus pounded his chest and howled into the air intimidatingly. Not faltering in the way of the stronger warrior, Numitor readied himself, placing the staff in his belt and charging toward Titus with a fierce battle cry. The governor struck first, thrashing his blade against the sergeant's armour, the metal bouncing off it with no impact.

"What?" Numitor questioned in bewilderment, looking from the unharmed blade to the pristine, bulky armour worn by his enemy.

"The power of magic truly is spectacular," Titus mocked, retrieving his broadsword from his back.

"Do you not think that's cheating?" Numitor joked as he lunged forward, grabbing a piece of the armour in an attempt to rip it off, but to no avail.

Pitying the governor briefly, Titus struck him in the chest with his knee, shoving him backwards. Stumbling to the ground, Numitor got up quickly, enraged further at the sergeant who had betrayed him in the end. Roaring, he ran at Titus, pummelling his blade at the armour, blow after blow, although the sergeant felt no pain. After Numitor faltered due to exhaustion for just a second, Titus laughed derisively, slicing his blade at the governor who parried the attack just in time.

"Time out, Athenian?

"Never, Roman."

Titus began to lift his hefty broadsword above his head with both his hands, ready to bring it down upon his opposition. In a swift movement, Numitor lunged forward, dealing an uppercut with his fist to Titus' face who recoiled, dropping the blade onto the ground. With a broken, bleeding nose he cried out as Numitor spotted a flaw.

On the back of the supposedly impenetrable armour was a small niche, a point of weakness the governor desperately needed to exploit.

As the sergeant was keeled over by the floor, his head spinning from the strike, Numitor plunged the blade into the gap in the armour, which began to crack. Seizing his moment, Numitor grasped one edge of the plating of armour as Titus writhed, trying to escape his grip. Triumphantly, Numitor yanked off the armour piece, leaving Titus' back exposed.

However, Titus was now free, leaving him to rush toward Numitor, tackling him to the ground, Titus' helmet falling off of his head as he did so. Caught by surprise, the governor dropped his blade as Titus laid his fists into him, his face becoming bloodier and bloodier as the sergeants' steel gauntlets pounded against it.

Dazed, Numitor peered through blurry eyes as Decimus Titus stood up and took the shimmering silver sword from the ground, raising it over Numitor's chest. Just as the governor thought his life had come to a close and the battle was lost, a loud slash occurred and promptly, Titus' head fell onto Numitor's lap, his body slumping backwards onto the floor.

Wiping the blood and sweat from his face, Numitor glanced up to see his saviour, Lucien, limping and just barely standing, wielding the sergeant's heavy broadsword in his hands, which he let fall to the ground relievedly.

"Lucien!" Numitor exclaimed gratefully, standing and embracing the general who winced in pain.

"What is it? What has happened?" the governor then asked concernedly, gripping Lucien's shoulders. The general removed his hand from his stomach revealing an ugly corruption of magic spreading around his chest.

"No no no no no no no! This is not happening. It can't! I need you, Lucien. I'll find the Warlock and kill him, and that will reverse it. It will work!"

"Numi... Numitor. Forget it. I'm done. I fulfilled my purpose, I fought for you, saved you and vanquished your enemy. Any other good soldier would have done the same."

He coughed, falling to the ground.

"No. Not any other good soldier. You are my top general, I would not rather fight by the side of any other soldier, mark my words. I swear, you are not dying today."

"Numitor, listen to me," Lucien sputtered, blood pouring from his mouth, "My life, it's over. That's how we know it's over. When we have fulfilled our destiny; this was mine. Let me die. Let me become a Di Mane so I may reunite with the ones I lost, and maybe we shall reunite ourselves one day. It is like you told me, you deserve a family, and you can now have that with Atticus. Do not waste it."

The governor of Socratis shed a tear, the clear liquid dripping onto the tainted grass. Shaking his head, he grasped Lucien's pale arm, stating:

"I will not, Lucien, and we will see each other again, even if it is as Di Manes."

Lucien managed a slight nod before the dark corruption reached his head, his pale body falling back onto the grass, Lucien's soul vanishing from his eyes.

On the other side of the battlefield, Atti fought off many more soldiers, although exhaustion began to set in.

"They just keep coming!" he called to Ennia who was close by, releasing arrows one after the other.

"I know! Do you notice their eyes?"

Atti, upon hearing Ennia's question and deflecting a blow from the soldier in front of him, peered into the Athenian's eyes. Sure enough, they glowed an unusual purple, the whites of their eyes replaced by an empty blackness. After dealing with his enemy, Atti retreated to Ennia's vantage point.

"What do you think it is?" she asked as more New Guard soldiers started to ascend the small hill.

"It has to be the Warlock," Atti replied, "It's a kind of magic I've seen before. We find him and maybe we can stop this battle from getting out of hand."

"Great! Where is he?"

Atti gazed upon the chaotic conflict, Aurelius and the Rangers attacking the swarm of the New Guard from the east side with Paulinus and his Romans flanking from the north. In all of the ruckus, Atti spotted the robed, ancient Warlock seemingly recuperating upon the golden chariot near the centre of the battle.

"There!" he shouted, pointing toward the chariot surrounded by the horde of soldiers.

Scoffing at its location, Ennia replied, "There's no way we can get to that chariot in one piece, especially just by ourselves."

"Well..." Atti whispered. After an inquisitive look from Ennia he winked at her before whistling loudly from the top of the hill. Following a few moments of silence, the faint patter of footsteps could be heard amongst the chaos of war.

Itineribus, their new steed galloped up the hill, slowing to a halt next to them.

"You want us to ride through an entire army on Itineribus? It's a death trap!" Ennia exclaimed, terrified of the thought.

"Well, what other option do we have! Trust me, Iter is the best chance we have; he's the best horse capable of the job."

Groaning, Ennia accepted that Atti was right, the two of them hopping onto the back of the horse, taking in a few deep breaths. Whipping the reins, Itineribus propelled forward down the hill gaining increased speed, heading toward the mass of soldiers ahead of them. Unsheathing his blade, Atti attempted to swipe at any Athenian soldiers in their way, swatting them away. Ennia did the same with her bow, releasing arrows with extraordinary speed as the horse charged through the battle.

Ahead was the chariot, the Warlock standing on top, overseeing the battle.

As they neared the cloaked creature Atti suffered an all too familiar migraine, darkness beginning to form all around him. He cried out in pain as the stained nature turned from a green to deep purple, a deafening roar filling inside his mind.

Ennia, who had noticed Atti's immense pain, deduced that it had been the Warlock who Karvajal had hired to place the curse upon Atti's mother, brother and eventually, him.

Close enough in range to the Warlock, she readied her bow, launching an arrow at the magic-user. As it struck him in the arm, the darkness engulfing Atti disappeared instantly and he was thrown back into reality, coming to a stop by the chariot.

"So, you are the hidden devil who has been injecting me with pain. I'm glad I finally get the chance to pay it all back."

Atti smirked as they leapt off the horse, raising their weapons to the Warlock. Rearing its bird-like skull toward them, it cawed and croaked in an unusual and unpleasant language. As it turned towards them, Atti noticed it's piercing red eyes, the ones he had seen in his spasms, and a newfound hatred was fuelled inside his subconscious.

The Warlock slowly stepped down from the chariot, its black robes slightly blowing in the breeze. It seemed almost too calm, standing unmoving with no sign of a weapon or inclination to attack. Eager to fight, Atti lunged at the Warlock quickly, leaping into the air to bring his sword down upon the creature.

At the last second, the Warlock revealed its claws, using a clearly weaker spell to knock Atti backwards. While Atti struggled to return to his feet, Ennia began to rapidly release her arrows which flew through the air. However, instead of dodging, the Warlock whispered something in its strange tongue causing the arrows to freeze in motion and fall lightly to the ground, clattering on the floor.

"He's unstoppable!" Ennia cried, firing her remaining arrows but to no avail. Getting to his feet Atti retrieved his sword, returning to her.

"I know, but we cannot give up. Our allies are depending on us."

They faced the Warlock once again, undeterred by its remarkable power. Just as they were about to retry their attack, a voice called out behind them, urging them to stop. Swivelling round, Atti gazed upon his father, his face soaked in blood, his clothes torn and bloodied, his once silver sword – now a dark shade of crimson – held in one hand, the stave in the other, the sparkling gemstone shining in anger toward the malevolent Warlock.

"Creature of the underworld! Leave my son or you shall face my wrath! Your companion Titus is dead, your army is faltering. You have nowhere to run."

The Warlock hissed in retaliation, taking a step forward, audibly angered.

"To think I ever saw you as an ally," Numitor scoffed, glancing between his two weapons. Atti was ecstatic to see his father seemingly unharmed and without problem. He smiled at the governor who smiled back, alerting him of the gemstone's activity.

Raising the broken staff and pointing the gemstone toward the Warlock seemed to activate it in an unusual way as suddenly it shot out a translucent orange beam which struck the Warlock, engulfing the creature in a golden light.

The magical attack left no physical scar upon the magic-user, although its power had been distinctly weakened. On the other hand, the Gemstone of Moria had suffered irreparable damage, large cracks covering its smooth surface like a spider's web.

"Now's our chance!" Atti yelled, repeating his charge from before. The Warlock this time stepped to the side in a swift movement, turning round and using a hidden dagger to slice at Atti's back. He cried out and fell to the floor while the Warlock revolved back around, turning its attention to an enraged Numitor who had sheathed the broken staff, swiping at the Warlock over and over with his bloody blade, the creature dodging each attack with inhuman speed.

Angered further, Numitor threw his sword like a javelin toward the Warlock who cast it aside with a nimble spell. Reduced to fists, the governor threw his hands at the dark being, coming ever so close to getting a scratch on the creature who managed to move out of the way of each attack. From behind him Ennia rained newly-retrieved arrows, one of which came dangerously close to the Warlock, though he brushed it aside, causing the arrow to fall to the ground.

Taking a chance, Numitor rolled onto the floor, grasping the arrow as he did so. He got back up immediately, attempting to impale the arrow into the Warlock but failing.

With the arrow being split in two by magic, the Warlock fought back by pushing Numitor backwards with a vigorous gust of wind, causing him to fall back and hit his head on a jutting stone, knocking him clean out. Cackling, the Warlock turned to a now worried Ennia who slowly stepped backwards away from the creature as she fired her last arrow. Knowing she had lost, Ennia collapsed to the floor as she began to pray to whatever gods would listen.

At that precise moment a divine strength entered into Atti's body, his veins pumping as he crawled forward, an arm's length away from the Warlock. He glanced down to his belt, Alexius' golden dagger glistening in a godly light.

This is it. This is the moment. For Rome. For my father, for Ennia. For Adrian.
For my mother.

Shouting as he did so, Atti lunged at the Warlock, dagger in hand, spearing it through the creature's chest, its black, inky blood spraying out of its wound. The creature's shriek was ear-splitting and tumultuous, so much so that it was heard for miles around.

Coming to consciousness, Numitor witnessed the Warlock begin to disintegrate before his very eyes, its particles descending into the ground, the creature being reclaimed by the underworld, the Warlock returning to its rightful place in the universe.

CHAPTER 22 – Aftermath

Atti stayed still, the golden dagger in hand, black fluid dripping off it, his body suddenly rejuvenating as if he had broken free from a terrible curse. Breathing heavily, he was unable to move as the New Guard soldiers started to realise what had happened. Promptly, Numitor and Ennia rushed over to him, firstly staring at the pile of black ash that was smoking up from the ground.

"Is it over?" Ennia asked, looking up at Numitor and then around them at the battle which had ceased for the moment, both sides unsure of what to do. From across the battlefield came Aurelius and Paulinus, each having wildly different reactions to the sight of the Warlock's scorched remains. The Roman legatus began to cheer at the sight of their apparent win, whereas Aurelius still seemed sceptical about the Warlock's death.

"Where is Titus?" the Ranger asked Numitor, clasping a hand on Atti's shoulder who had still not moved an inch.

"He is dead, that I am certain of," Numitor replied, recalling Lucien's sacrifice and wincing at the memory.

"What's wrong?" Paulinus asked out of nowhere, ceasing his celebration to question his friend.

"Lucien, he...he was hit by a spell. He knew he was going to die, and yet he saved my life in his final moments. Titus was going to kill me."

"What?" Atti exclaimed, breaking out of his trance and gripping his father by the shoulders.

"Tell me it isn't true! Tell me! Where is Lucien?"

"I am truly sorry Atticus; I cannot bring him back. What's done is done. The only thing we can do is honour his sacrifice, as well as the rest of our fallen soldiers."

"No! There must be a way. What about the gemstone! Its power could bring him back!"

Numitor unsheathed the staff from his belt with uncertainty. Spinning it around in his hand, the damage on the gemstone was clear to see.

"Atticus. Do not fear death," his father uttered, Atti peering up at him with innocent, teary eyes, a look Numitor had not seen for nine years.

"Death is far from the end, and thus we should not treat it that way. Death is but a gateway. A gateway to a better life. A better life that Lucien deserves to live. Like he told me, his purpose had been served, which he interpreted as to protect me so that I may fulfil my purpose of protecting you, so that one day you can become the powerful leader I know you can be.

Today you have shown immense strength, cunning, ingenuity, but best of all, you remain a benevolent warrior, and those are difficult to find in an age of war and bloodshed. Although somehow, I know I am surrounded by true, heartful warriors who I will gladly aid, and I am certain Lucien felt the same way.

Let me reiterate this to you Atticus, and to all who listen; fearing death is needless, as death is natural.

Today has been tough on us all, and the true fact that we all stand here now, alive, is a testament to our strength when combined as one. That is how we should live our lives, together as equals, as only then are we at our peak.

Decimus Titus and his Athenian elitist accomplices may not understand it, but that is why they are the enemy who endanger the lives of innocents, and why we are there to stop them. We are on the right side of history, and this is only the beginning of our story."

"Hear, hear!" Paulinus hollered, raising his sword to the sky. Surrounding Romans and Rangers did the same, and so did a few of the New Guard, although most had fled after the demise of their leader. Joining their respective groups, Aurelius and Paulinus reunited with their own soldiers while Numitor spoke to Atti alone for a moment, with Ennia wandering across the battlefield.

"As the governor of Socratis I have learnt many things, but most of all I have realised that in the absence of you, my son, I have never felt more alone, and that my treatment of you since Adrian's death has been less than adequate, to say the least."

"You could say that," Atti chuckled, sharing a laugh with his father.

"I accept your apology, father, even though it should be me saying sorry. I ran off for months without so much as a word to you, and for that entire time I felt more guilty after every step I took away from home. And while I know it was unacceptable, I believe it made me a better person. I met an incredible friend and a pretty strong general, but also, I believe I found my purpose."

"Oh? And what is that purpose, Atticus?"

"To help people, as you were saying. Although I do not think the leadership role would suit me, it belongs to you more so than anyone else. That speech was as persuasive as ever. Ten times better than Cicero, *that's* for sure."

Numitor laughed, admiring his son through proud eyes, grateful that Lucien had given him the chance to finally watch his son grow into who he is meant to be.

"You know, Atticus. Now that I am governor, I shall have even less time to spend with you than I did before. I know it is undesirable but it is the way of things. I..."

"It's okay, father," Atti said, interrupting Numitor, "I think I have made my decision. All of my travelling these past months have made me realise, I don't want to stay in Socratis any longer. I want to travel, like you did, explore the country and maybe the world. I know my calling is out there somewhere, and that it is definitely not in Socratis."

"The world is a dangerous place, Atticus."

"I know, I know," the boy said sarcastically.

"I'm being serious," Numitor cautioned, "There are many more foes twice as deadly as Titus and 'magic-users' like the Warlock. There is a reason why I have never left Italia in my lifetime."

"That may be true, father, but I want to venture into the unknown. Explore the uncharted. It's what I am meant to do, I just know it."

"Then, if you really believe that, I have no right to get in your way. In fact, I shall support you all the way, as I should have done from the beginning. Thinking about it now, I spent so long mourning your mother and brother that I forgot you were hurting too. I want to make up for lost time now more than ever, though I cannot do that if you run away from me again."

"Then I will stay for a little while, learn what I can about the outside world from the scholars in Socratis and then I'll go. Besides, there's so much I want to show Ennia."

"Ah yes. Ennia. Anything you want to mention about her, Atticus?"

"Uhh..."

"ATTICUS! What sorta celebration is this?" boomed Paulinus from a few metres away.

Atti silently thanked the gods for the opportunity to dodge the previous conversation. Paulinus had bounded over to them after partying with a few of his allies from Rome whereas Aurelius had begun to recruit the few New Guard soldiers that stayed on the battlefield.

Atti turned his attention to the Roman legatus who had firmly gripped each one of them, belligerently saying, "So, Atticus, now I've seen you in proper combat I know for sure you're gonna smash the Trials."

"What?" was the shocked reply that came from Atti's father at the mention of the tournament of challenges Numitor had once competed in, known as the Trials.

"What are you talking about?" Numitor questioned, enjoying the possibility that his son may follow his own footsteps by competing and possibly winning the Trials.

"Well, after I had a chat with Emperor Alexius, he told me he would only agree to help if Atticus competed in the Trials. Though I don't think the lad's too pleased," Paulinus chuckled.

Hearing it out loud, Atti was daunted by the task as well as embarrassed about his father knowing about it. Just as he wanted to say something, Numitor spoke, "So, following in my footsteps Atticus?" Numitor asked half-jokingly, arms folded as if he dared Atti to the challenge.

Feeling chastised, Atti said, "I'm up for it. How hard could it be? I mean, I just beat the Warlock!"

Paulinus scoffed and then laughed, saying, "That may be true, but the Trials are designed to whittle down each candidate to find the one true soldier who represents what this Empire really is. I always thought the idea of a 'Super-Man' was nothing but a myth, until I met your father, of course. He truly is the embodiment of Rome. Let's hope you can also rise to the challenge."

"Yes. Let us." Numitor replied.

"I look forward to it," retorted Paulinus before saying, "I should leave. The emperor will want to hear about this and these soldiers have families to get to. So do I. But I have enjoyed fighting beside you once more, Numitor and making your acquaintance again, Atticus."

Father and son wished him off as he gathered up the surviving Roman soldiers for their departure to Rome. For a minute they stood there, together, gazing over the battlefield, their eyes falling upon the countless bodies of all three factions strewn across the blood-soaked ground.

Atti recognised one Ranger who lay lifeless on the grass, a Roman spear impaled through his chest, Aurelius' advisor Lupus Martialis. Atti thought back to the riddle that Martialis had mentioned to him.

"You can't see it, but you know when it's there.
It lingers in the glances, suspended in the air.
It believes all things, and all things it bears,
And there are those who are its object, who entertain it unaware.
What am I?"

He whispered out loud, "The answer is love."

Numitor replied, peering down at his son. "Where have you heard this riddle before?" he asked, curious at the answer.

"A wise Ranger uttered it to me; it was the last words I heard him say."

"Well, Atticus, that riddle is very famous in these parts of Italia, a riddle supposedly made by Venus herself."

Atti mourned the death of Martialis and all the other fallen soldiers for several minutes. He then bowed down his head, shedding a tear before whispering a question, "Is there usually this much blood?" forcing himself to stare upon each victim.

"Yes," Numitor replied curtly.

"Does it ever get any easier?"

"No."

"Then why do we do it?" Atti asked, looking up at his father who maintained a dead, emotionless stare.

"Because it's the only way we know how. Since the creation of man, arguments have arisen, and history has shown that war is the most effective way. But it never gets easier, seeing the ones you care for die beside you. Their death becomes a burden upon your shoulders, and the ones who have the heaviest shoulders are the ones who hide it the most. I do not want you to become this. I want you to be better, and I know you can be."

"Thank you, father."

The silence around them had engulfed their surroundings until Atti spotted Marcellus from a distance away.

"Atticus! We did it!" Marcellus exclaimed, his joyfulness a surprising contrast to Atti's glumness.

"Yes, we did. We won. But now what?"

Marcellus was eager to answer, "My parents before were cautious of Cicero's rule in Socratis, but after I told them about you and your father, their reluctance subsided and now we are going to live in Socratis!"

"Really? That's great! Although I am thinking of leaving Socratis for a while, I want to carve out my own path."

"Then I will see you when you return, Atticus. Farewell, and enjoy your ventures."

"You too, Tatius. Goodbye, friend."

Marcellus then returned to the Castellum Lapideum, causing Atti to think of all the civilians they had ignored inside the fortress.

Finding Aurelius with some Romans, he asked, "Aurelius, what will happen to the civilians inside the fortress now that Karvajal is gone?"

The commander turned to face him before replying, "I do not know. Many have expressed their dislike of your Empire, though I am sure your father can persuade them. But enough of them for the moment, how are you, Atticus? I only saw from a distance your vanquish of the Warlock."

"I am alright, Aurelius. To be honest, it is all a bit surreal, I can't believe it's over. I have no idea what to do next."

Aurelius smiled and comforted Atti, "You need a rest, Atticus. I am certain another adventure will happen sooner than you would like. That is the life of a true warrior."

"Right. But what about you, what are your plans?"

The commander pondered the question for a minute, turning to face the horizon in the distance.

"I am not sure, although I know whatever the rest of my life has in store for me, it is out there in the world and not here. I must leave to find my destiny."

Atti reverted to a saddened tone, "Then I guess this is goodbye for the second time."

"Yes, Atticus. Although we shall meet again, I'll make sure of it."

The two then parted ways as Atti spotted Ennia sitting on the ground, spinning an arrow in her hand. He sidled up to her and sat down, Ennia smiling as he did so.

"Hey, you alright?" he asked, gazing upon the war-torn battlefield.

"Yeah, I guess. That was some pretty impressive stab by the way. Thanks for saving my life."

"Anytime. I mean, after all, I owed you one."

Ennia chuckled, "Consider that debt paid."

"So, what's next for us, I mean you, unless?" Atti asked, stuttering as he did so.

"Well, I helped you out, smooth-talker, and I probably need help finding my mother, so..."

"Sure! I'll help. It's the least I could do."

"Great, thanks," Ennia said while smiling, giving Atti a lingering hug and a peck on the cheek, which made him blush.

"See you soon, Atti," Ennia whispered as she got up and left.

Atti remained on the ground, everything washing over him. He suddenly felt immense grief for all of the dead Romans and Rangers, deaths he could have prevented, but most of all he would miss Lucien. A childhood friend, someone who had been there when his father wasn't. A great man, someone who didn't deserve to die in the way that he did.

I guess this is what life is. Life is full of death. Like my father said, it's natural. Lucien died for me to live my life with my father. I can't let his death be in vain. Though I doubt my father doesn't have plans to honour his best general already. He is probably even more distraught than me, I just don't understand how he hides it so well. It's what makes him a great leader, I guess.

As Atti sat, the day wore on until the battlefield was scarce, save for his father and a few soldiers focused on aiding the Rangers civilians. As far as he knew, Ennia had departed to

Socratis, and he would soon make his way there, but for the time being, Atti endured the cold, brisk air and the disheartening stench of bodies on the ground. Soon his father signalled to him, and the two continued their conversation.

"Atticus."

"Father. What will happen to the fortress?"

"I'm glad you asked, son. I have decided to renovate it into a remote training camp for the Roman army, in fact I was about to return to Socratis to get the men for the job. When were you planning to leave? I'm certain I could have seen Ennia leaving a few hours earlier?"

"Yeah, I saw, but I wanted to stay. It didn't feel right just moving on after the carnage of what happened here. I know that's what happens in war, but I oppose it."

Numitor smiled with acceptance and put his arm around his son.

"I know, and I'm proud of you for it. You know, Lucien was right."

"How do you mean, father?"

"Well, I remember something he said to me, as a friend a few nights after I found out the 'disease' was hereditary all that time ago. He had supported me through it all, and what I remember most was this. He told me I should be proud of the child I still had, and that the gods had kept you alive for a reason, and that it was fate that you did not succumb to the darkness, his reason being that you were the strongest, most powerful kid he had ever seen, not just physically but mentally too. He said you would do great things, become a great leader, and now I see he was correct in every way. You really are a gift from the gods, Atticus Caeso."

A lone tear rolled down Atti's cheek.

"Thank you, father."

The golden sun had begun to set, the sky on the horizon turned pink with a shade of vermillion, illuminating the atmosphere with hope.

Atti and Numitor, surprised at how long they had been on the battlefield, returned to their home together, both content with the knowledge that after nine years of ignorance and neglect, they had finally shown their love for each other, something both of them had been concealing for too long.

As the sun set over the less peaceful town of Socratis, thanks to the new arrivals, Atti drifted into a heavy, deserved sleep as one less burden was taken away from his shoulders. A tranquillity had overcome the whole of Italy, though this would not last, as Atti would shortly find out...

EPILOGUE

Benedict Paulinus ascended the very same steps he would tread on every morning as a legatus for Emperor Alexius. The pristine, white palace remained as glorious as ever, the enormous mahogany door swinging open for him, giving him access to the hall of the palace. He had missed Rome for the entire fortnight that he had left it, having arrived early that morning. Like the usual routine, Paulinus retreated to the small, lack-lustre bedroom hidden away in the grandness of the palace, housing the emperor of the Roman Empire.

When he entered the room after the Roman guard had thrust open the antique, heavy wooden door, Paulinus found it empty. He carefully sat down upon the minimalist bed and silently waited alone inside the tiny room, from his perspective.

Paulinus took time to inspect the paintings placed around him, one depicting a desolate crop field with a broken farmhouse, the wooden framework had fallen and a pillar of smoke had erupted from it, bellowing up toward the sky. In the field stood a lone figure who looked upon the burning house, clutching a pitchfork in his hand. The farmer's face was not visible, which only added to the mystery of the story behind the painting. Underneath was a caption embroiled on a golden plaque. It read: '*The end of hopes and dreams.'* The legatus knew Emperor Alexius suffered quite unusual dreams, and so he deduced that this had been one of them.

Some elders in the city had hypothesised that Alexius' dreams were so significant that they even hinted at events to come in the near future, though Paulinus had always dismissed their claims. However, after seeing true dark magic with his own eyes, he ruled that nothing was out of the range of the plausible, and that those elders could have a point. Paulinus had begun to inspect another painting that was much brighter in nature when the back door was opened slowly, revealing Alexius, dressed in his pristine white and gold robes.

"Ah, Benedict. You have returned."

"Yes, *my emperor,*" he said half-jokingly, "I see you had an important meeting to attend."

"If important was a synonym for extremely mundane, I would be inclined to agree."

Paulinus chuckled, glimpsing the painting of the farm from above Alexius' head.

"What news do you bring me of Governor Caeso and your battle?" Alexius questioned, carefully stripping out of his elaborate robes, revealing his unpredictably bland clothes underneath.

"A lot of news, actually."

"Do tell, Paulinus."

"The threat of Octavius Karvajal has been neutralised and the Rangers are now allies to the Romans of Socratis..."

266

"This is good news," replied Alexius, "Why do I sense a darkness in your answer?"

Paulinus continued, "Because, Alexius, that was not our only battle. We were attacked by the New Guard, or as we found out, Athenians. And, to add more to this bizarre turn of events, they were led by a certain Decimus Titus, a sergeant who was believed to be dead. He arrived alongside a magic-user who had the power to wield dark magic. Even with our Romans and the Rangers teaming up, it was a challenge to defeat them. Titus was murdered once and for all by Caeso's top general and his kid turned out to be the one to vanquish the magic-user, who I believe they called, the Warlock. Few of our soldiers perished, though there were more casualties than you might expect. The rest of the Athenian soldiers either fled or stayed to serve us, and so I left promptly to inform you of everything."

Alexius looked into Paulinus' eyes with a lifeless certainty. His stare was grave and more alarming than Paulinus had ever seen.

"Benedict. Would you believe me if I knew this would happen?"

After a brief puzzlement, the legatus replied, "I don't understand."

"I believe the elders, Paulinus. I have dreamt of this exact moment happening, although not as precise. I have seen a foreign army led by a walking contradiction, aided by a freak of nature, though like any sane member of society I brushed it aside, but this reveals something to me. I have seen prophecies. Events destined to happen years from now.

I cannot explain it, hell, I don't want this! But I'm afraid it is the only explanation. You can believe that, right?"

Paulinus, who did not know what to believe anymore, simply nodded before taking a tactical standpoint all legati had perfected, causing him to ask, "What was your most recent dream?"

The emperor took a moment to answer as he pondered the question, searching within his mind to recreate the experience in immense detail.

"I cannot remember, Benedict. But I do know that this is not something to take lightly. The limited knowledge of magic that we have is concerning, and in fairness we should explore this phenomenon more. Would you be open to researching this, Benedict?"

"Of course, Alexius," he replied, "I shall leave at first light and not return for a month. And I agree, from what I have seen, magic is more dangerous than one could possibly imagine."

"Indeed," stated Alexius, the emperor bidding Paulinus farewell and returning to his paintings, trying not to worry about what other premonitions may occur in the future.

It had been several months since the battle of the Castellum Lapideum, but the fortress looked the exact same as the day of the destruction. Vast craters populated the sides of the mountain, the man-made structures infested with overgrown vines of ivy. Numerous arrows remained jammed into the ground and mountain; some tainted a reddish-brown with dried blood. Most of the bodies had been left on the ground to decompose, but each had been stripped of their weapons and armour.

It was about midday when Numitor arrived at the scene, not having been there since his victory months before. He peered up at the desolate, abandoned fortress, a lifeless carcass of a once prospering people, led by a raging lunatic. The governor had come to scout the place for his plans for a new barracks, but despite the space, Numitor doubted the rotting location could serve any purpose for them.

Together with his group of soldiers, Numitor advanced to the mountain, attempting to find the hidden entrance they had used to infiltrate the base initially. Because of the lack of attention, the entrance had been masked by a hanging portion of vegetation which the governor took pride in slashing. With the help of Matteo, Numitor's servant who he had brought along, they shoved open the heavy door which creaked as they did so, revealing the dark interior.

Striking a torch, Numitor entered the deserted fortress, with Matteo and the soldiers hesitantly following behind. Having split up, the group explored the empty base, relighting any burned-out torches hung on the wall. Slowly the place became more homely, and the ominous sense of dread was soon lessened off each of them.

Retracing his steps that he and Atti had taken months before, Numitor arrived at the door to the throne room, the very room where he had murdered Octavius Karvajal, a dear friend turned enemy. Mustering up the strength, he pushed open the heavy stone doors and held out his torch, only to drop it promptly in astonishment.

"What is it, Governor?" Matteo worriedly asked, rushing into the room without a thought. Numitor did not reply, instead he frantically darted his head around the room as if looking for something, but from their perspective, the space was completely empty.

"He's... he's gone," the governor whispered, staring at the blank spot by the throne where a dried puddle of blood lay, oozed out in a sporadic pattern.

"Who? Who is gone?"

Numitor turned around to look his servant in the eyes with a half-concerned, deadly serious face before replying, "Octavius Karvajal is alive!"

THE END